L. T. Meade

A Sister of the Red Cross

L. T. Meade

A Sister of the Red Cross

1st Edition | ISBN: 978-3-75244-328-8

Place of Publication: Frankfurt am Main, Germany

Year of Publication: 2020

Outlook Verlag GmbH, Germany.

Reproduction of the original.

A SISTER OF THE RED CROSS

A TALE OF THE SOUTH AFRICAN WAR.

BY MRS. L. T. MEADE

CHAPTER I.
CONSECRATION.

Sister Mollie Hepworth was twenty-five years of age. She had just completed a long and exhaustive training as a nurse. She had served her time in the London Hospital, entering as a probationer, and finally being promoted to the proud position of a ward sister. She had then undergone a period of six months' probation at the Royal Victoria Hospital, Netley, as her dream of all dreams was to nurse our soldiers in their hours of danger and death.

Mollie was a bright-looking, handsome girl. Her eyes were brown and well opened; she had a healthy colour in her cheeks; and she held herself as upright as any soldier in Her Majesty's army. No one had ever seen Sister Mollie perturbed or put out—her self-control was proverbial. She had an admirable temper, too, and never allowed an impatient word to cross her lips. She was reticent, and no gossip. Secrets, even important ones, could be intrusted to her without any fear of their being betrayed. Her eyes looked clearly out at life. Her lips were firm; her whole bearing that of one who has made up her mind, whose career is fixed, whose watchword is duty, and whose desire is to benefit her fellow-creatures.

"Put my luggage on the cab, please, porter; there is not a moment to lose, or I shall miss my train," said the clear voice of the Sister on a certain sunny morning early in September 1899.

The man obeyed. A neat trunk, followed by a hat-box, was deposited on the top of a cab, and a moment later Sister Mollie had left Netley. She was going to spend a fortnight with her sister in London.

"A fortnight of absolute rest," she said to herself; "a whole fourteen days with nothing special to do! No necessity to think of my patients; no obligation to rise at a given hour in the morning. To be out of training for a whole fortnight! I can scarcely believe it. I wonder if I shall enjoy it. I know one thing, at least, that I shall enjoy, and that is seeing Kitty. I have not met my darling for nearly two years!"

As this thought came to Mollie Hepworth, dimples visited her cheeks, and her eyes shone so brightly that some of her fellow-passengers turned to look at her.

She was wearing her nurse's uniform, and it set off her clear complexion and graceful figure to the best possible advantage. Sister Mollie arrived at her destination between five and six o'clock that evening. Her cab conveyed her to a large house in Maida Vale.

The moment she entered, a merry voice shouted her name, and a girl, with complexion and eyes very like her own, rushed downstairs and flung herself into her arms.

"O Mollie, this is like heaven! I have been counting the moments until you came. And how are you? Do let me have a good look. Are you altered? No, I declare, not a bit! Come upstairs; you and I are to share the same bedroom. You will have such a hearty welcome from Aunt Louisa; but she is out now with Gavon."

"Do you know, Kitty," replied Mollie, "that I have never yet seen Gavon Keith?"

"He is at home now," replied the other girl. "You will see plenty of him

3

by-and-by. Oh, how I have missed you, and how delightful it is to have you back again!"

"And I have missed you, my darling little Kitty."

The girls had now reached a large and beautifully-furnished bedroom on the first floor.

"This is our room," said Kitty. "Aunt Louisa did not wish us to share it, at first; she thought you would rather have a room to yourself, but I over-persuaded her. We can have such cosy talks. Oh, I have a lot to tell you! There are some things joyful, and some things—well, just a bit worrying. But there is a whole beautiful fortnight when we can talk and talk to our hearts' content."

"And I am a full-blown Sister, absolutely through all my training," said Mollie.

She took off her nurse's bonnet as she spoke, and let her cloak tumble to the floor.

"You look superb, Mollie, in your Sister's dress; but you must not wear it while you are here. You and I are exactly the same height, and one of my pretty dinner dresses will fit you. I have been saying so much to Gavon about you. O Mollie, I don't like to tell you, and yet I think I must."

Here Kitty broke off abruptly. She toyed with the ribbons at her belt; her eyes sought the ground.

"What is it?" asked Mollie, half guessing at the information which Kitty was so anxious and yet so afraid to bestow.

"It is this," said Kitty restlessly: "I am not *quite* engaged, but I am all but."

"To whom, darling? You know you are very precious to me, and I am much older than you. I shall have to look into this matter."

"Oh, you will like him; you will be more than satisfied with him. You cannot help it," replied Kitty. "It is to Gavon—yes, to dear Gavon. I have loved him for so long. He has not quite absolutely spoken, but he will—I know he will. I think he will say something while you are here. The words often seem to me to be trembling on his lips. O Mollie, this is not like ordinary happiness! it is so deep that it frightens me."

Kitty's face grew very pale. She sank down in a chair, clasping her pretty hands together on her knee. Then she looked full up at her sister.

"This is quite splendid!" replied Mollie. "I shall look on Captain Keith with great interest now. Am I to see him to-night?"

"Of course you are. I told him you were coming. He is certain to be in, if not to dinner, very soon afterwards. Here is his photograph."

Kitty sprang up as she spoke, ran to her chest of drawers, took a photograph encased in a neat leather frame from a pile of others, and brought it up to Mollie.

"Here," she said, "look at his face. Is he not splendid?"

Mollie looked. A puzzled expression came into her eyes. It seemed to her that she had seen that face before, she could not recall where.

"What is the matter with you, Mollie?" asked Kitty.

"Nothing; only the face seems familiar."

"Perhaps you have seen him. You must have seen many soldiers at Netley."

"I cannot remember," said Mollie, returning the photograph to Kitty. "Thank you, Kits. He looks very nice, and, I think, even worthy of you. I am glad, after all, you are marrying a soldier, for I mean to devote all my life to them."

"Oh, how splendid of you, Mollie! But I do hope we are not going to have war. It would be too awful to have Gavon away, and his life in danger; and you also, darling Mollie, for of course if we do fight the Boers you will go to South Africa."

"Time enough to think of that," said Mollie. "Come and sit down. It is good to have a chat with you, Kitty. I may as well say it; I hope my chance to do something great will come before I am much older. I am just pining to be doing, and helping, and saving lives. Oh, mine is a grand mission!"

"I suppose it is," answered Kitty. "But, after all," she added, her eyes sparkling, "it is not half so grand as being engaged to the man you love best in the world. Oh, I do hope Gavon will soon speak, for I love him so very, very much!"

The girls chatted a little longer, and then Kitty ran downstairs to tell Mrs. Keith that Mollie had arrived. A young man, with dark hair, a straight moustache, and an otherwise clean-shaven face, was standing in the hall. He turned as she approached.

"Is that you, Kitty?" he said.

She ran up to him. He held out both his hands, and clasped hers. Her face turned first crimson, then pale.

"What is the matter?" he asked. "Have you heard what I was talking about

5

to the mater?"

"You must not be frightened, Kitty," said Mrs. Keith. "After all, nothing may come of it; but Keith says the news from the Transvaal is anything but reassuring."

"War may be declared at any moment," said Keith.

"But your regiment won't be ordered abroad?" cried Kitty, with a catch in her voice.

"I hope it will!" he replied. "I want to get a bit of real fighting. Some stiff active service would suit me down to the ground."

Kitty's pretty lips trembled. She struggled with her emotion. Then raising her eyes, she said in as bright a tone as she could muster,—

"We must not think of dismal things to-night. Our Red Cross Sister has just arrived. I want you both so badly to see Mollie."

"I shall be delighted to make her acquaintance," replied Keith; "but I am not dining at home to-night. Sorry, little girl, but can't help it. I will be in as early as I can. Why, what's the matter, Kit?" for Kitty's eyes had filled with tears.

"I have been so looking forward to your seeing Mollie," she answered; "I am dying to know what you think of her. But there," she added, brightening up the next moment, "if you will come in soon after dinner, all will be right. And I am not going to be disagreeable," she continued, "for, of course, you cannot help it."

"Tell your sister, Kitty, that I will come up to see her in a few moments," said Mrs. Keith.

The girl nodded, and ran out of the room. In the hall she stood still for a moment, wrestling with her emotion.

"I wonder if he really cares, or if I am only imagining it?" was her thought.

"That is a dear little girl, mother," said Gavon, turning to speak to his mother when Kitty had left the room.

Mrs. Keith looked at her son gravely.

"I am very fond of Kitty," she said then. "I am glad that I adopted her. She is a delightful companion and a dear little soul. But how nervous she is, Gavon! I have noticed it often of late in your presence. I cannot help wondering—"

Mrs. Keith broke off abruptly.

"Wonder at nothing, mother," was his answer. "There is nothing between us—nothing at all. Kitty is a dear little sort of cousin—no more."

"You must remember that she is not really your cousin. Kitty is my adopted niece. Just as good as a real one, but in case by—"

"I know, mother; I know all you would say. I like her very much, but I have never yet met the girl I want to marry. I have never yet been in love, although I am twenty-eight years of age. You don't want to hand me over to the tender mercies of a wife too soon, do you, mater?"

"My dearest, as far as I am concerned, I like you best without a wife. But you must marry some day, Gavon; and if it should so happen that you really liked Kitty, why, why—"

"You would like it too? Well, I will think it all out, mother; but at present I fancy my attention will be turned to other matters. We are going to have fighting, and I am rejoiced to know it."

Mrs. Keith laid her hand on her son's arm. Just for a moment that hand trembled. Then she said in a brave voice,—

"Well, and I am the mother of a soldier. I must take the bitter with the sweet."

She turned away as she spoke. Gavon followed her, put his arm round her waist, bent down and kissed her on her forehead, and then left the house.

Meanwhile the girls upstairs talked as fast as a pair of eager tongues could manage. Each had a great deal to say to the other. Mollie and Kitty were orphans. Mollie was six years Kitty's senior. Their parents had died within one week of each other—when Mollie was seventeen years of age, and Kitty eleven. An aunt had left Kitty twenty thousand pounds, which was to accumulate for her until her majority. Mollie, on the contrary, had only fifty pounds a year of her own. Kitty was adopted by Mrs. Keith, who took a fancy to the pretty girl, and afterwards grew so much attached to her that she could scarcely bear her out of her sight. Mollie, at the age of twenty, took up nursing seriously as a profession. From her earliest years Mollie had shown a great aptitude for this noble work. She had that calmness of nature which denotes strength; she was not easily ruffled; and when she made up her mind she stuck to her resolves.

If there was one person in all the world whom Mollie loved better than another, it was her little sister Kitty. Each girl idolized the other; and although for long years now they had been to a considerable extent separated, their early love was still unchanged. Kitty was almost frantic with delight at the thought of a whole fortnight of her sister's society.

7

"Everything must happen in that time," she kept saying to herself —"everything that is possible and delightful. Gavon shall tell me that he loves me. I know he does—I know it; and he will tell me so while darling Mollie is with us. And auntie will consent, of course. And the wedding shall all be arranged, and Mollie shall advise me as to my trousseau, and Mollie shall see my engagement ring. And Mollie shall talk to Gavon and tell him what a naughty, silly, and yet affectionate little girl he has secured as his future wife. Oh, life is too beautiful, too beautiful! Even though I am in debt, horribly in debt for my clothes, and Aunt Louisa knows nothing about it, the joy of life is almost too much for me!"

Now Kitty poured out a great deal of her heart to Mollie. All her conversation was about Gavon Keith.

"He has not spoken, but I know he will speak," she kept on reiterating; "and I don't mind telling you, Mollie, for I have always told you just everything."

As Mollie listened, she could not help feeling just a little anxious. Suppose by any chance Kitty was mistaken! But then she made up her mind to hope for the best.

"The child would not speak as she does if she were not quite, quite sure. All the same, I wonder she can talk of him as she does until he has told her in so many words that he loves her as she deserves to be loved," was her grave inward comment.

"You shall see him for yourself to-night," said Kitty, at the end of almost every speech. "You shall tell me to-night what you think of him."

Just then a little clock on the mantelpiece struck the hour of seven.

"Who would have supposed it was so late?" said Kitty, starting up suddenly. "Now, Mollie, I will bring in the dress you are to wear. Gavon won't dine, but he is certain to be back about ten o'clock; and even if he keeps us up a little later, it does not matter, does it?"

"Certainly not, dear. I have had a day of perfect rest, and am good for any amount of sitting up to-night."

"You always were a darling! Now, I wonder which of my dresses would best become you?"

"It seems so ridiculous for me to wear anything but this," said Mollie, and she looked at her nurse's uniform with affection.

"Oh, I love you in your nurse's dress!" said Kitty. "You make me quite wish to be ill, in order that you may put me to bed and pet me, and give me my medicines, and tonics, and nice, tempting invalid food. But as I am not ill —as I am, on the contrary, in the most radiant health and strength—I should for the time being like to see my own Mollie in some other guise than that of a Red Cross nurse."

"Well, I would do more than that to please you, Kitty."

"We must be quick, or we shall be late for dinner, and that is just the kind of thing which does disturb Aunt Louisa."

The next half-hour was spent by both girls in getting into their evening finery. When their toilets were complete, they went and stood with their arms round each other in front of a tall mirror which stood in one corner of the room.

"I must say, though I say it who should not," said Kitty, with a laugh, "that we look as presentable as any two girls I have ever come across. Why, Mollie, I did not know until now that you were quite an inch taller than I am. But never mind; your dress looks perfectly sweet, and your feet are so pretty it does not matter whether they are seen or not. And oh, Mollie, what a white neck you have, and such round arms! I do think black lace is the very prettiest evening dress of all. But stay; you must have colour. I will run down to the conservatory and bring up some scarlet geraniums."

Kitty flew away, returning in a few minutes with a bunch of the brilliant flowers. She fastened them into her sister's belt, and stepped back to look at the effect.

"Now you are perfect!" she said. "You are a young lady enjoying one of her first peeps into society. Oh dear, it is too comical! Here am I, almost sick of going out (for Aunt Louisa takes me somewhere nearly every night); and here are you, with just the airs of an *ingénue*. And you are five-and-twenty, are you not, Mollie?"

"Quite old compared with you, Kitty."

"I shall be twenty in a month," said Kitty, "and then in one year my fortune comes in. Oh dear, what a horrible thing money is!"

As she spoke a change came over her face—a wistful, puzzled, distressed expression. Mollie noticed it.

"It is impossible the child can be in money difficulties," she said to herself. "I must speak to her about this later on."

The dinner gong sounded, and the two ran downstairs. Mrs. Keith was in the drawing-room. She gave Mollie a hearty welcome.

"You look very well indeed," she said. "How like Kitty you are, and yet how different!"

This was quite true. Kitty was far and away the prettier sister, and yet no one would look at Kitty when Mollie was present. It was difficult to account for this fact; nevertheless it existed. The very tone of the elder girl's voice was arresting—there was a dignity in everything she said; and yet she never posed, nor had she a trace of affectation in her nature. One secret of her influence may have been that she absolutely, on every possible occasion, forgot herself. Her life was a consecration. To make others happy was the whole aim and object of her existence. When her father and mother died, she had been old enough to feel their deaths intensely. But the greatest sorrow of all had never come into her life; and beautiful and perfect as her character seemed, there were hidden depths yet to be explored, and greater heights to be reached, before Mollie Hepworth would gain the full crown of womanhood. As to love, in the sense in which Kitty loved Gavon Keith, Mollie had never even thought of it. Her feeling, as she sat now at her aunt's luxurious table, was that nothing would induce her to marry.

"A consecrated life shall ever be mine," was her thought.

Nevertheless she was quite healthy enough to fully enjoy the present, and she drew Mrs. Keith out to talk of her son, and asked Kitty many fresh questions with regard to her employments and interests.

CHAPTER II.
MUSIC.

"I wish you would scold Kitty," said Mrs. Keith to Mollie in the course of the evening, "she is so very frivolous."

"O auntie, what a perfect shame!" said Kitty. "I frivolous! If frivolous means being intensely affectionate, I am that, but I don't think I am frivolous in any other sense of the word."

"I am not complaining of you, Kitty—you suit me perfectly; but you are just a dear little gay butterfly flitting about from flower to flower, always sipping the sweets and enjoying life to the utmost."

"Oh, I do enjoy life," said Kitty; "it is perfectly heavenly even to be alive!"

"Whereas Mollie," continued Mrs. Keith, "takes life, this very same life, Kitty, in a totally different way."

"Kitty and I were always different," replied Mollie. "What suits one doesn't suit the other. I should be sick of being a butterfly and just sipping the sweets out of the flowers. Such a life would be absolute misery to me. Therefore I cannot consider myself in any way praiseworthy for adopting another."

Mrs. Keith uttered a quick sigh.

"There are moments when life is serious to us all," she said gravely. "Hark! what are they crying in the street?"

Mrs. Keith raised her hand to listen. Both girls held their breath.

"'Further trouble in the Transvaal: serious disturbance,'" repeated Mrs. Keith, her lips turning white. "I am afraid there is no doubt that we shall have to go to war with the Boers."

"It looks like it," replied Mollie, and her eyes kindled.

"You would love to air your knowledge about nursing soldiers," said Kitty. "How horrid of you!"

"Well, Kitty, can you blame me? What is the good of being a soldier's nurse if I am never to enter on the full duties of my profession?"

"Surely it is not necessary to have war just to give you experience?" said Kitty. She turned very white as she spoke, and her brown eyes filled with sudden tears.

Mrs. Keith glanced at her, and then turned away. But as, a moment later, she passed Kitty's side, she took her hand and gave it an affectionate squeeze. Kitty jumped up impatiently.

"Mollie," she cried, "I am going to sing to you. You shall see at least that I have some accomplishments."

She ran to the piano, opened it, crashed out a noisy waltz, and then burst into a rollicking song. Her voice was powerful and beautifully trained. It lacked a certain power of expression, but was finished and very pleasant to listen to. Mollie was standing by the piano, and turning over the pages of her sister's music, when the door was opened, and Gavon Keith in his dinner dress came in. He was a striking-looking and very handsome man. As the girl raised her eyes to look at him she gave a sudden start. She had seen him before; he was not, after all, a stranger. She had seen him, and in such different circumstances that if she were to disclose all she knew this little party would indeed be electrified. When she recognized him, he also recognized her. The colour left his face; he stood still for a moment; then recovering himself, he went up to his mother.

"Introduce me to Miss Hepworth, won't you?"

Kitty, who had been singing, let her voice drop; her hands came down on the keys with a crash. She saw the change on Gavon's face when he looked at Mollie. Her love for him made her intensely jealous. Was it possible? Oh no, it could not be! She danced up to his side as he came up to Mollie and took her hand.

"We must not be strangers," he said. "We are relations of a sort, are we not?"

"I don't know," replied Mollie. "We are friends at least, I hope."

His eyes seemed to convey a warning as he looked at her. She returned his gaze with a full, frank expression on her face, and he knew at once that he had nothing to fear from her. The magnetic influence which she always carried with her wherever she went affected him strangely, however. He sank down on the nearest chair and began to talk to her. Kitty flitted restlessly about. Gavon did not once glance in her direction. After a time he said,—

"What is the matter with you, Kit? Can't you sit still? I am much interested in what your sister is telling me."

"Tell me too, then, Mollie," said Kitty, and there was a note of sadness and entreaty in her voice.

She slipped into a seat close to Mollie, who put her arm round her waist.

Keith continued to ask eager questions. He was interested in Mollie's experiences as a nurse at the Victoria Hospital, Netley. All of a sudden he seemed to recognize a change in her. Her voice at first had been full of enthusiasm, but when she felt the touch of Kitty's small hand her manner changed—it became formal. She rose after a moment.

"I did not know that I was tired, but I find I am," she said. "Will you excuse me, Aunt Louisa? I should like to go to bed."

"Do, my dear, certainly," replied Mrs. Keith.

"Then, Kit, you must give me another song," said Keith.

His words and request immediately chased away every cloud from her face. She took her seat at the piano, and Mollie went out of the room.

CHAPTER III.
KITTY'S DREAM.

Several months before the events just related, as Mollie Hepworth was returning late to the hospital at Netley, she was arrested by seeing a figure lying by the roadside. Her professional instincts were at once aroused, and she hurried towards it. She bent down, to discover a gentlemanly-looking, well-dressed man. He was breathing heavily, and was evidently quite unconscious.

She gave a hurried exclamation, and fell on her knees by his side. She took one of his limp hands in hers, and bending low, perceived a smell like that of opium on his breath. Had he been drugged by another? What could have happened? Her first instinct was to shield him from any possible disgrace; her second, to restore him to consciousness. She looked to right and left of her. The road was lonely—there was no one in sight. Exercising all her strength, she pulled the man more to one side. She then applied a vinaigrette, which she happened to have about her, to his nostrils, and finding a little stream of water not far off, took some in the palms of both hands, and flung the liquid over his face. He sat up, rubbed his eyes, and looked at her.

"She took one of his limp hands in hers," Page 29.

"She took one of his limp hands in hers."

"Where am I?" he said. "Who are you? What has happened?"

"I am a nurse," said Mollie—"a Sister of the Red Cross. I am a nurse at the Royal Victoria Hospital. I found you lying here: Let me help you home."

"Oh! what can have happened to me?" he exclaimed heavily, and yet with great consternation in his voice. "Give me your hand," he said then. "I am better; I can walk alone if you will help me to rise."

She got him to his feet with some difficulty, but he tottered, and she had to give him her arm.

"Lean on me," she said. "Where shall I take you?"

"I remember everything now," he replied, speaking more to himself than to her. "I have been drugged: I felt the effects, and came for a walk, hoping to walk them off. Before I knew what I was doing I became unconscious. What would have happened to me if you had not been passing by?"

"Some one else would have found you," said Mollie.

"It would have been reported at barracks, and I should have been disgraced."

"You are one of the officers, then?"

"Yes."

"Well, I will take you back."

"I will walk with you a little way, but I am fast getting better. What a mercy you found me!" he kept on repeating at intervals.

He leaned heavily against her. She was strong and tall. They paused at last just outside the barracks, under a lamp. The light fell full on her face. He looked into her eyes, and the colour mounted into his own forehead.

"To whom am I indebted?" he asked.

"To a Sister of the Red Cross," she replied. "But I don't need thanks," she added hastily; "I am only too glad to have been able to help you."

"As far as I can tell, I owe my life to you," he replied.

He looked at her as if he expected her to say more; but she did not ask his name. There was an expression of relief on his face as she turned away.

"Good-night; God bless you!" he said. "I shall thank you for this in my heart to the longest day I live."

She held out her hand, and he grasped it. Never before had he felt so strong, so cool, so firm, so strength-giving a hand.

Mollie went back to the hospital, and in the rush and excitement of her daily life more or less forgot this incident. But to-night, when Captain Keith entered the room, it all came back to her; for the handsome, careless face of Gavon Keith was the very same she had seen, pale and under the influence of opium, a short time ago. She had noticed then the upright figure, the straight features, the shape of the eyes, the well-formed lips, and as she recognized him she saw by a light which suddenly rushed into his eyes that he recognized her.

Mollie sat down and thought over this strange circumstance. She had been tired, really tired, when she left the drawing-room; but she was wide awake now, and not at all inclined to go to bed. It was past midnight when Kitty, her cheeks on fire, her eyes dancing, came into the room.

"What!" said the younger sister; "still up, Mollie? I thought you were so sleepy! Do you know, I stayed downstairs on purpose just to give you a chance to get very sound asleep before I disturbed you."

"I shall have plenty of time for sleep later on," replied Mollie.

"Oh, you made me so jealous, my darling Moll, when you talked to Gavon; but I am all right now. I will just slip off my dress, put on my dressing-gown, and we can renew our delightful conversation while we brush our hair."

"No," said Mollie, rising abruptly. "I find that, after all, I am tired. I want to go to bed."

Kitty looked at her in some surprise.

"But what does this mean?" she said. "I have so much to say to you. I cannot rest until you have told me what you think of him."

"Think of whom, Kate?"

"How stiff of you to call me Kate! No one does unless they are displeased. Are you displeased with me, my own Mollie—are you?"

"You must not talk nonsense, Kitty," said Mollie, in a grave voice. "I am tired, and am really determined to go to bed. I shall not utter another word to keep you from your own rest."

Kitty pouted, but Mollie was resolute. She was not a nurse for nothing. She knew that Kitty was already so excited that she might not sleep for some time. The sooner she got to bed, however, the better.

With a discontented pout on her rosy lips Kitty watched her elder sister undress. The little girl was happy, however; the last hour with Gavon had chased all uncomfortable feelings away. He did love her—he must love her. Was there not love in his eyes and tenderness in his voice? The moment, therefore, she laid her head on her pillow she fell asleep, to dream of him.

Not so Mollie. She felt uncomfortable and alarmed. She dreaded she knew not what. An intuition had already taken possession of her that Kitty's love affair was not to end happily. She doubted very much whether Keith really cared for her little sister. If so, what was to become of Kitty's passion? Keith had looked at Mollie as if he wished to confide in her. Would he allude to that circumstance in both their lives which had taken place a few months ago?

It was towards morning when the tired girl sank into slumber, and in consequence it was late before she arose. When she opened her eyes, Kitty was standing over her.

"Gavon has gone out long ago," she said, "and Aunt Louisa too; and it is nearly ten o'clock, and we have all breakfasted. And you, you lazy girl, are to have breakfast all by yourself in the morning-room. Or would you prefer it here?"

"Oh no; I am ashamed of myself," said Mollie. "I will get up at once and join you downstairs within half an hour."

"You are privileged, you know, Mollie dear," said Kitty. "Aunt Louisa says the carriage is to return for us both at eleven o'clock. I want to do some shopping, and I thought perhaps you would come with me."

"With pleasure, dear," replied Mollie.

The moment her sister left the room she rose, dressed in her nurse's uniform, and went downstairs. When she entered the morning-room Kitty was seated at the tea tray, looking as radiant and free from care as girl could look.

"Gavon was in a great state of excitement when he went off this morning," she said to her sister. "He is persuaded there will be war."

"Well, and if there is war," said Mollie, "it will do us a great deal of good. Oh, I know you think me heartless, but our army wants active service again. We need to test our strength."

"You talk just as though you belonged to the army yourself," said Kitty.

"And so I do. If there is fighting, I shall be in the thick of it."

"You don't think of me," cried Kitty, turning pale. "Please remember that if there is fighting Gavon is certain to be sent to the front. You will go as nurse, and he will go as soldier. What is to become of poor Kitty?"

"Kitty will be brave, and help us all she can at home," replied Mollie.

"That is all very fine," said Kitty, "but I must tell you frankly I don't like the rôle."

Mollie looked up as Kitty spoke.

"You are changed," she said slowly. "In some ways I should not know you."

"What do you mean?"

"You have been too much in the world, Kitty. My little Kitty, did I do wrong to leave you? When mother died she left you in my charge. Did I do wrong to let Mrs. Keith adopt you? It seems to me—I scarcely like to say it—that you—"

"Oh, do say it, please—do say it," remarked Kitty.

"You are less unselfish than you used to be, and more—oh, I hate myself even for thinking it—more worldly."

"No, no, I am not; but I am anxious," replied the younger girl. "There are many things to make me—yes, anxious just now. But I hope I shall be the happiest girl on earth soon."

"Kitty, suppose—"

"Suppose what?" asked Kitty. "Oh, what awful thing are you going to say now, Mollie?"

"Nothing. I won't say it," replied Mollie suddenly. "I have finished breakfast. I can go out with you whenever you like."

Kitty gazed in a frightened way at her sister.

"It is nothing, dear," said Mollie tenderly. "I have given you my little lecture, and I will say nothing further at present."

"And I am not all bad, and I love you, and I hope to be the happiest girl on earth before long," was Kitty's rejoinder. And then she flew upstairs to put on her hat and jacket.

The girls drove first to Madame Dupuys, a fashionable dressmaker in Bond Street. Madame received them both in her large showroom. Her face was rather grave.

"I had hoped to have a letter from you before now, Miss Hepworth," she said, in a significant tone, to Kitty.

"It is all right," replied Kitty. "You may expect to hear from me any day."

"Very well, miss."

"And I want to order a dress at once. I am going on Monday evening to the fancy ball at the Countess of Marsden's house on the Thames. I cannot possibly wear any of my old dresses."

"What will you have?" asked the dressmaker.

"Something very, very pretty, and absolutely out of the common. Madame, I should like to introduce my sister to you; she is a Red Cross nurse."

19

Madame bowed gravely in Mollie's direction. She was a very handsome woman, beautifully dressed.

"We are all interested in the Red Cross Sisters," she said, after a moment's pause. "Have you heard the latest news, miss? They say war will be declared within the week!"

Kitty turned white.

"I am determined not to think of disagreeable things before they occur," she said; "and I want my dress to be white, with silver over it. Now, do show me some designs."

"I will fetch some fashion-books," said madame, "and we can discuss the style."

"Kitty," said Mollie, the moment they were alone, "surely you are not in debt for any of your beautiful clothes?"

Kitty's face looked troubled.

"I am just a wee bit harassed," she said slowly, "but it will be all right by-and-by. Don't worry, Mollie."

"It seems so wrong," replied Mollie.

"You know nothing about it," answered Kitty, tapping her small foot impatiently on the floor. "I go out a great deal, and I have to look my best, because—" she stopped. "You would act as I do if you had the same reasons," she continued. "And you must remember that in about another year I shall have plenty of money."

"Well, it is wrong to go in debt," replied Mollie. "If you are in money difficulties, it would be far better to speak to Mrs. Keith."

"To Aunt Louisa? Never! she would tell Gavon. Ah, here comes madame. —Madame, my sister has been reading me such a lecture," and Kitty smiled her incorrigible smile.

Madame Dupuys made no remark. She opened the fashion-book, and soon Miss Hepworth and the dressmaker were deep in consultation over the material and style of the new dress.

"Don't you think it will be exquisite, Mollie?" said Kitty, as they left the showroom.

"Very pretty indeed, dear," replied Mollie.

They came home to lunch, where Captain Keith awaited them.

"My mother has left you a message," he said. "She is going to see a friend, and will not be back until dinner time. Now, I happen to have a whole afternoon at my own disposal. If I place it at yours, can you make any use of me?"

"O Gavon, how quite too heavenly!" said Kitty. "You shall take us somewhere. This dear Mollie does not know her London a bit. Her education must be attended to, and without any loss of time. And, Gavon, I have been ordering a dress for the Countess of Marsden's dance on Monday."

"Another dress!" said Keith, shrugging his shoulders. "What an extravagant girl!"

"Don't you like me to wear pretty dresses? I thought you did."

"Of course I do; and you look charming in everything you put on, but I did not know you wanted a new dress. You had something soft and furry, like the breast of a rabbit, the last time you went to a dance with me. I remember it quite well, although I cannot describe it; for the fur was always touching my shoulder, and it came off a little. I found the white hairs on my coat the next morning."

Kitty blushed.

"I am glad you liked that dress," she said; "but you will like what I am going to appear in on Monday even better. I want to be a vision—a dream."

Keith looked at her; a thoughtful expression came into his eyes. He noted the colour which came and went on her checks, the brightness of her brown eyes, the love light, too, which was all too visible, as those well-opened eyes fixed themselves on his face.

"Poor little girl!" he said to himself. Then he glanced at Mollie, and his heart beat quickly. "If only those two could exchange places!" he thought; "it would be easy then to—"

He checked the unfinished thought with a sigh which was scarcely perceptible.

"Where shall we go?" he said. He took out his watch. "Although it is out of the season, there is a passable concert at St. James's Hall, and you are so fond of music, Kit. What does Sister Mollie say?"

"Oh, please call me Mollie," said the elder girl.

"What would you like, Mollie?" he asked.

"The concert, by all means."

"We can take tickets at the door. We will go there, and afterwards have tea at my club."

21

"Delicious!" said Kitty. "You don't know, Mollie, what tea at Gavon's club is like. Only I do wish—"

"What, dear?"

"That you would not wear your uniform. I didn't think nurses thought it necessary when they were taking holidays."

"I won't, if you dislike it," said Mollie. "I have brought a dress which I can wear. It is not very fashionable, but I don't suppose that matters."

"Would you not rather, Gavon, that Mollie did not come in her uniform?" asked Kitty, in an eager voice.

"Mollie must do exactly what she pleases," was the reply.

"I see you would both rather not have attention drawn to me," said Mollie. "That is quite enough. I will dress as an ordinary lady."

"And lose a good deal," said Gavon. "But perhaps you are right. There is so much disturbance in the air, that anything even savouring of the military draws attention at the present moment."

"Come upstairs at once, Mollie, and I will help to turn you into a fashionable lady," said Kitty, with a laugh.

CHAPTER IV.
THE CONCERT.

But this was more easily said than done. Mollie had a certain style about her —the style which accompanies a perfectly-made body and a well-ordered mind. But she had none of that peculiar appearance which constitutes fashion. Her hair was simply knotted at the back of her head, and was without fringe or wave. The only dress she had at her disposal had been made two years ago. The sleeves were too large for the prevailing mode, and the bodice was by no means smart. Mollie, however, put on her unfashionable garment with the best faith in the world, and tripped up to Kitty when her toilet was complete.

"How do you like me?" she said.

Kitty turned to her, and her brown eyes flashed fire.

"Oh, you must not go out looking like that," she was about to say. But she suddenly stopped.

She herself was the very perfection of dainty neatness, of fashionable, yet not too fashionable, attire. Her hair was picturesquely arranged. Her hat was stylish; the very veil which hid and yet revealed the roses on her cheeks and the brightness of her eyes was what the world would call *the mode*. Beside this dainty and perfectly-arrayed little personage Mollie looked almost dowdy.

"And I could change all that in a minute," thought Kitty. "It is just to lend her my brown hat with its plume of feathers, and the jacket which came home last week, and the deed is done. But shall I do it? Gavon already admires her too much. Now is the time for him to see the difference between us. She shall go as she is. I dare not run the risk of losing him; and he likes her—oh, I know he likes her. This day, perhaps, will settle matters; and Mollie, my darling Mollie, for my sake you must not look your best."

Aloud, Kitty said in a careless tone,—

"Very nice, indeed, Mollie. And how do I look? What do you think of your little sister?"

"How pretty your face is," replied Mollie, "and how neat your figure! Do you remember how I used to scold you long ago for not walking upright? You are very upright now."

But as Mollie spoke Kitty perceived that she had never glanced at the fashionable dress. She only saw the soul in the bright eyes and the happy smile round the lips. Gavon's voice calling them was heard from below. They ran downstairs.

When they appeared, Captain Keith glanced from one sister to the other. He was dimly conscious that a change, and that not exactly for the better, had come over Mollie, and that Kitty looked, as she always did, the perfection of charm. Nevertheless, the expression in Mollie's eyes and the tone of her voice continued to arouse that strange, delicious foreign feeling in his breast. He found that he liked to touch her hand, and that he also liked to look into her brown eyes. He was not yet aware of his own sensations. He only thought,—

"I am but tracing the extraordinary likeness and the extraordinary difference between these two girls. Of course I know Kitty's dear little phiz, and Mollie's is almost the same, feature for feature, and yet there never were any two girls who have less in common."

The three arrived at St. James's Hall in good time. Gavon secured seats for his party, and they soon found themselves listening to a fine concert. Mollie had a passion for music, and as she sat now and allowed it to fill both heart and soul, her eyes kindled, and the colour came rich and deep into her cheeks. Gavon continued to watch her almost stealthily. Kitty chatted whenever she could find a moment to give her gay little voice a chance of being heard. Gavon sat between the two; he answered Kitty, and talked with her, scolding her now and then, and desiring her on many occasions to "hush," "not to make so much noise," to "behave herself," and much more to the same effect. As long as he spoke to her at all, poor Kitty was in the seventh heaven of bliss. From her present position she could not see how often he glanced at Mollie, and fancied that her little stratagem to make her sister not look quite at her best was bringing the most satisfactory results.

24

The first half of the concert was over, when a man pushed his way along the line of people and dropped into a seat by Kitty's side. She uttered an exclamation, half of annoyance and half of pleasure.

"How do you do, Miss Hepworth?" he said. "I have not seen you for a very long time.—Ah, Keith, how are you?"

"I did not know you were in London, Major Strause," answered the girl.

"London is practically empty; but, all the same, this war news is bringing many of us up," he replied.

Mollie looked round to see what the newcomer was like. She noticed a somewhat thick-set man, with reddish hair and a very long moustache. His eyes were of a light blue. His face was considerably freckled. Mollie voted him at once commonplace and uninteresting, and would not have bestowed any further thought upon him had she not observed a curious change in Keith's appearance. His face turned first white, then stern and sombre. He ceased to talk to Kitty, who was devoting herself now, with all that propensity for flirting which was part of her nature, to Major Strause.

"Do you know him well?" asked Mollie suddenly, in a low tone.

Keith gave a start when she addressed him. He turned and looked full at her.

"You already hold a secret of mine," he said, "and I am about to make you a present of another. The man who drugged me that night six months ago is Major Strause."

Mollie had too much self-control to show the surprise which filled her.

"I have something I want to tell you," continued Keith. "Can I see you somewhere alone?"

"Gavon, the music is going to begin again; do stop talking," cried Kitty, in a restless voice.

A girl who made her name at that concert came to the front of the stage, and her magnificent organ-like notes filled the building. Mollie, however, much as she loved music, scarcely listened. It was not only the tone in Gavon Keith's voice, but the words which he had uttered, which filled her mind. Something was undoubtedly wrong.

The song came to an end, and in the *furore* which followed Keith seized the opportunity to bend again towards Mollie.

"I shall be in the front drawing-room to-night at seven," he said. "Can you come down a few moments before the rest of the party?"

25

"I ought not," was Mollie's response.

"I ask it as a favour—a great personal favour. Will you refuse me?"

Mollie did not reply for an instant.

"I will come," she said then.

Major Strause did his utmost to make himself agreeable to Kitty, who, after the first moment of excitement, paid him but scant attention. Keith, having received Mollie's promise, was now quite ready to devote himself to the little girl, and his gay remarks and her smart repartees caused considerable laughter on the part of all the young people.

When the concert was over, Major Strause invited the entire party to have tea with him at his club. Mollie looked at Keith, expecting him to reply in the negative; but to her surprise he accepted the invitation with apparent cordiality. They all went to the Carlton, where the major entertained them; and as if thoroughly satisfied with his conversation with Kitty, he now turned his attention to Mollie. She told him she was a Sister of the Red Cross; whereupon he looked her all over, and said, bowing as he spoke,—

"Then we may have the pleasure of meeting again, and under different circumstances."

"What do you mean?" she asked.

"Why, my dear Miss Hepworth, need you ask? I mean that war is inevitable: my regiment, and that also of my friend Captain Keith, will be among the first ordered to the front. If you are a Sister of the Red Cross—"

"I shall go to South Africa," replied Mollie. She spoke in a low tone, and there was a thrill of enthusiasm in her voice.

"Then we are quite certain to meet again," he said, and he turned from her to Kitty to address a remark on a totally different matter.

It was past six o'clock when the girls got home. Kitty was inclined to dawdle downstairs; but Mollie, remembering her promise to Keith, hurried off to her room. Kitty stayed behind for a moment. She suddenly stretched out her hand to Keith, who took it in some astonishment.

"Well, little girl, what now?" he asked.

"Tell me what you think of her," said Kitty.

"Think of whom?"

"My sister—my Mollie."

"I admire her very much; she reminds me of you."

26

"Oh, does she?" answered Kitty. She dimpled and smiled. "Is that really why you are so much interested in her, Gavon?"

"It is one of the reasons," he replied, after a pause. "She reminds me most wonderfully of you. But at the same time there is a great gulf between you. Your sister has been trained in one of the finest professions a woman can possibly take up. She has therefore a force of character, an individuality which—"

"Which I lack. Oh, you need not apologize," said Kitty, looking half amused, half sorrowful. "Mollie always, always had just what I lack. But I thought—"

"Let your thoughts run in the old groove, Kitty," replied the young man. "You are the most charming friend a man could possibly possess. But I hear my mother's voice. We shall meet again at dinner."

Kitty mounted the stairs slowly.

"I wonder what Gavon really thinks about me, and about her," she said to herself. "It was to me he spoke whenever he had a chance this afternoon, but it was at her he looked. Did he wonder at her dowdy dress? Darling Mollie was not at her best; and I felt such a wretch, for I could have made her lovely. When once I am engaged to Gavon, my Mollie shall want fornothing."

Kitty hummed a gay air as she entered the large bedroom which the two girls shared. Mollie was arranging her hair before the glass, and the lace evening dress which she had worn on the previous night lay on her bed.

"What a hurry you are in!" cried Kitty. "We have oceans of time. We need not begin to dress until seven o'clock."

"But I must dress at once," replied Mollie.

"Why?"

Mollie did not answer immediately.

"Why?" repeated Kitty, whose nerves were so strained that she could brook no suspense of any sort.

Mollie thought quickly; then she turned and looked at her sister.

"I will tell you," she said. "Captain Keith wants to see me for a minute or two. It is in connection with a matter which I happened to hear about when I was at Netley—a matter of which you know nothing. Dear little girl, if you are worth your salt you will not be jealous."

Kitty's face turned very white.

"But I am jealous," she said then, slowly. "I suppose I am not worth my salt. I am jealous—horribly so. O Mollie, don't go to him; don't, Mollie! Mollie, do stay here, for my sake."

"I am sorry, Kitty. I have promised Captain Keith to give him a few moments, and I cannot break my word. You must trust me, and not be a goose."

Kitty crossed the room slowly. Her very steps trembled. She reached her bed and flung herself on it. When she raised her face after a moment or two, the tears were streaming down her cheeks.

"This is intolerable," thought Mollie. "I never could have guessed that my little sister would be so silly. The best thing I can do is to take no notice." So she checked the impulse to go up to Kitty, take her in her arms, and fuss over her and pet her, and went on with her own toilet.

As the clock was on the stroke of seven she turned to leave the room. She had just reached the door when Kitty gave a cry.

"Mollie," she said.

Mollie went up to her at once.

"Dress yourself like a good child and come down when you are ready," was her remark. "And let me say one thing: *Don't be a little goose.*" Mollie closed the door behind her, and Kitty covered her face with her hands. She shivered.

"Is it true?" she murmured. "Is it possible that after all these months and years, and all these hopes and all these dreams, I am doomed to see him love another, and that other my own sister? Oh, it is too cruel! It will kill me—it will drive me mad!" She clenched her hands till the nails penetrated the tender flesh. Then she opened them wide, and looked at them with self-pity.

"It is too cruel," she said to herself. "Even now he is talking to her, telling her secrets. He never told me a secret in all his life. He has always just been the very dearest of the dear, but he has never yet told me even one secret. He has not known her twenty-four hours, and already he is confiding in her. I won't stand it. I wonder what they are talking about. Why should I not know? I have a right to know—every right. I am all but engaged to him. All my friends think that I shall marry Gavon. His own mother thinks it—I know she does. And Gavon—oh, he must, he must know what I feel for him! He must return my love! Life would be intolerable without him. If he has a grain of honour, he will engage himself to me, and soon, very soon. It is not right, therefore, that he, an almost engaged man, should tell secrets to another woman. Those secrets belong to me. Oh, how I have loved Mollie! but just now I hate her. Mollie darling, it is true—I hate you! I hate that calm face of yours, and that gentle smile, and those cool, comforting hands. And I hate your manner and the way you talk. I hate your very walk, which is so dignified and so full of confidence. You have all that I never had, and in addition you have got my pretty features, my eyes, my lips, my teeth, the same coloured hair, the same colour in your cheeks. It isn't fair, Mollie darling, it isn't fair. Life is too hard on Kitty if you take from her just the one only man she could ever love. I know what I'll do. I'll dress in a jiffy, and I'll go into the back drawing-room. I know how I can slip in—just by that door that is so seldom opened. I will stay there, and I'll hear everything. They won't look for me; but even if they do it doesn't matter, for there is that in me which—oh dear, am I mad?"

Kitty sprang from the bed. She rushed to her washstand, poured out some hot water, laved her face and hands, and then arranging her hair with one or two quick touches she put on her black net evening dress. She was too excited to think of her usual ornaments. Her little round throat had not even a solitary string of pearls encircling it. Her arms were destitute of bracelets. She opened her door softly, and put out her head to listen. There was not a sound. The thickly carpeted passages and the stairs were empty. The first dressing gong had sounded, and there was yet quite a quarter of an hour before dinner. Catching up her skirts to prevent even the rustle of the silk as she flew downstairs, Kitty reached the drawing-room floor. She opened a door which was seldom opened; it led into the small back drawing-room, a room which in its turn opened into the conservatory. The back drawing-room was seldom lighted, except when Mrs. Keith expected company. It was quite dark now, and Kitty, agile and watchful, flung herself on a sofa in a corner, where she knew she could not be seen. She bent a little forward and listened with all her might.

"I have told you all that I can tell you, and you understand?" said Keith.

These were the first words that fell on her ears. Keith's voice sounded a great way off, and Kitty perceived to her consternation that her sister and Captain Keith were standing at the other end of the long drawing-room. In order not to miss a word, she was obliged to leave her first hiding-place and steal more towards the light. The couple, however, were too absorbed to notice her.

"I have told you," repeated Keith; "you know all that is necessary now."

"Yes," answered Mollie. Then she said, "But a half-confidence is worse than none."

"I have good reasons for withholding the rest," was Keith's answer. "I have resolved to keep it a secret."

"On account of—Kitty?" was Mollie's remark.

It was received with a puzzled stare by Captain Keith. He stepped a little away from her, and then said emphatically,—

"Yes, for Kitty's sake, and for my mother's sake. What is the matter? Why do you look at me like that?"

"I don't believe in keeping these sort of things secret," said Mollie. "It would be very much better to make a clean breast of the whole affair. It is never wrong to tell the truth. I have always acted on that motto myself."

"It is easy for a woman to act on it," replied Keith; "with a man things are different."

"They ought not to be," said Mollie, with passion. "It is, I firmly believe, the right and the only right thing to do. Now you to-day—"

"Ah, I understand; you must have thought me inconsistent. I was, doubtless, in your opinion too—cordial."

"You certainly were."

"I could not have done otherwise. Kitty would have been amazed. Whatever one's inclinations, one has to think of the feelings of others."

Before Mollie could reply to this Mrs. Keith entered the room.

"Why has not John lit the lamp in the small drawing-room?" was her first remark.

At these words Kitty softly opened the seldom-used door and fled. She rushed to her room.

"Now I know; now I know!" she panted. "Yes, I know everything. Mollie thought him too cordial, and he said that he did not wish to hurt my feelings, whatever his own inclinations might be. Oh, can it be possible that Mollie is false to me? But there! hearing is believing."

The dinner gong sounded, and Kitty was forced to go downstairs. Her cheeks were bright, and she looked remarkably pretty; but her head ached badly. She sat in her accustomed place, close to Captain Keith. He began to talk to her in the light, bantering, and yet affectionate style he generally adopted when in her presence. She gave him a quick glance and shrugged her shoulders.

"I have a headache," she said abruptly; "I would rather not speak."

"My dear child," exclaimed Mrs. Keith, "I hope you are not going to have influenza!"

"And I trust I am," replied Kitty, in a defiant voice. Then seeing by the astonished pause that she had said something even more *outré* than usual, she looked round the company and gave a ghastly smile. "I mean it," she said; "it would be such a good opportunity for Molly to nurse me."

"But you can have the horrid thing half a dozen times," said Keith. "Come, Kit, do be pleasant. It won't do you any harm, even if you have a headache, to laugh at my jokes."

"You are like all men—horridly selfish," retorted Kitty. And then she added, as if to put the final cap on her rudeness, "And your jokes are never worth laughing at. You descend to puns; could any human being sink lower? Oh, talk to Mollie, if you must talk to any one. I mean what I say—I would rather be silent."

Keith shrugged his shoulders. He was fond of Kitty, and was sorry to see her put out.

"What can be the matter?" he said to himself. He knew her well enough not to place much faith in the headache.

The rest of the dinner was a dismal failure, and when it was over Kitty retired to the back drawing-room. Nothing mattered, she said to herself; Gavon, after all, did not care for her. He was polite, civil, even affectionate, because he did not want to hurt her feelings.

Meanwhile Mrs. Keith, in the other room, was talking to Mollie.

"Gavon tells me that there is not a doubt that war will be declared immediately," she said. "There are moments when all mothers have to crush their feelings; but when it is the case of an only son it is terribly difficult. It is hard to see him go away into danger, and to feel that he may never return!"

"And yet you would be the very last woman on earth to keep him back," replied Mollie.

"That is true," answered Mrs. Keith. "I would not restrain all that is noble and good in him for the world." She looked around her. "Kitty!" she cried. There was no response. "Where can the child be?" she said suddenly; "she seemed ill at dinner."

"She ought to go to bed if she has a headache," said Mollie. "I will go and speak to her. Ah, I see her in the back drawing-room. She is reading something."

"Then don't disturb her," said Mrs. Keith. "Sit near me, Mollie; I like to talk to you. Ah, here comes Gavon.—Gavon, go and have a chat with poor little Kitty; for some reason or other, she is very much put out."

Keith crossed the room and sat down by Kitty.

"How is the head now—any better?" he asked.

His tone was always sympathetic; at this moment it was dangerously so.

Kitty swallowed her tears and looked full up at him.

"It is not my head," she said.

"I thought not," he replied with a laugh, which, in spite of himself, was uneasy. "Something has ruffled the small temper. Is not that so? What is the matter, my dear little coz?"

"Don't call me that."

"Why not? You are my cousin after a fashion."

"I am not, and I don't want to be."

Captain Keith coloured.

"Come," he said, "this is serious. I did not think—I mean when you were —yes, cross at dinner, I did not suppose that it would last. But you use words which it is difficult to understand. What have I done to offend you, Katherine? Have we not always been good friends?"

"What have you done?" she answered. She trembled all over, and in her agitation blurted out words which she had thought never to utter. "You are false, and I thought you true," she said. "Why did you lead me to believe—"

"Hush!" he said sternly. He laid his hand for a moment on hers. "Little girl, you will say something which you will regret all your life. Don't talk to me while you are angry. Recover your self-control; then I will listen as long as ever you please."

"Oh yes, my pain is nothing to you!"

"I beseech you to exercise self-control. Do be silent for the present, I beg, I implore of you."

"What do you mean?" she said. "Your manner frightens me."

He dropped his voice.

"Kitty," he said, "I want you to be courageous and strong, and to help my mother. An hour of sore trial is close to her, and I have not told her yet. I do not want her to hear until the morning. Kit, little Kit, my regiment is under orders to sail for South Africa on Saturday week—just ten days from now. I have just ten more days in the old country, and during these ten days, Kitty —"

"O Gavon!" she cried, "if you go—"

"What?"

"Take me, oh, take me with you!"

"Kitty!" His tone was a shocked exclamation. He stood up also and backed away from her.

"I know what you feel," she said recklessly. "You have shown it all too plainly. I will speak now if I have to be silent all the rest of my life. Were you blind, Gavon, not to see that I—that my heart is breaking?"

"Poor little girl! But the mother would not go to South Africa, and you could not go without her."

"Oh, don't you, *won't* you understand?" she repeated.

He shrugged his shoulders, looked at her as she gazed up at him with all her burning passion shining in her eyes, and then sat down to face the inevitable.

"I cannot pretend to misunderstand you, Kitty," he said then; "I do know what you mean. You ought not to have spoken. No girl should put a man in such a position."

"A man thinks nothing of putting a girl in such a position," she retorted, with spirit.

"I have not done so." He longed to say something more, but checked himself. "Yes, you have made a mistake," he said. Then, endeavouring to calm his voice, "And a man cannot take his wife into the battlefield. War is inevitable. This is no time to think of—"

"You don't love me—that is what you mean," said Kitty.

He hated to give her pain. Perhaps he was weak enough to have said words just then which he might have regretted all his days, but just at that moment a vision of Mollie, as she had looked when he spoke to her before dinner, returned to him.

"It is true that I do not love you in that sort of fashion, Kitty," he said then. "I am fond of you, my dear; but you must know, you must guess, that there is a difference."

"Oh, so wide!" she cried. She stretched out both her arms. "There is a love which fills the heart, which covers the horizon, which colours every single thing one does; and there is also what people call an ordinary friendship or attachment. How dare people speak of the two in the same breath? You, Gavon, give me an ordinary friendship. In return for my pretty speeches, and my songs, and my gaiety, and my fun, you give me an ordinary friendship. And I give you—oh, just everything!" Kitty spread her arms wide. Her face was pale, the tears had partly dried on her cheeks, and her eyes looked larger and more full of soul than he had ever seen them before.

"I am not worthy of it, Kitty," said the young man, and he bowed his head.

She looked at him as he did so, and then one of her queer impulses came over her. He was shocked and yet touched by her words; she would undo everything by her next confession.

"Before dinner," she said, "I was mad with jealousy. You wanted to see Molly—Molly whom you have not known twenty-four hours. I felt that I could not bear it. I came in here, and I overheard—"

"What, what?" he asked. He sprang to his feet and seized her arm.

"I didn't hear everything," she continued, backing away from him. "But you told her a secret. You alluded to something which had happened to you long ago. And she accused you of being too cordial—too— Oh, I know what she meant. What you said to her and what she said to you gave me my headache. But it was not really headache; it was heartache. I won't talk to you any longer now. Good-night."

He caught her hand as she was leaving the room.

"In spite of these painful words on both sides," he said, "may not our old friendship continue?" He looked full at her. She did not speak for a moment; then she said,—

"When do you sail?"

"Saturday week."

She began to count the days on her fingers; then with a broken-hearted smile she left the room.

CHAPTER V.
A LEGACY.

A year and a half before this story opens Gavon Keith had got his captaincy in the North Essex Light Infantry, and just about the same time he found himself in a serious scrape. In a moment of weakness he had put himself absolutely in the power of Major Strause. Major Strause was his senior officer. There was a young subaltern in the regiment, of the name of Aylmer. Percy Aylmer had conceived a most chivalrous and passionate attachment for Keith. Keith had been good to him when he first joined, had put him up to the ropes, had been on every occasion his warm friend, and the young fellow in consequence gave the deepest devotion of his heart to Keith.

Now Percy Aylmer was second cousin to Major Strause. Both his parents were dead, and he was possessed of large private means. He had no near relations, and often boasted that he could do exactly what he liked with the thousands which belonged to him. Major Strause was always more or less in money difficulties. He was a man who both gambled and drank. His character in the regiment was by no means without reproach. It was whispered that he was quite capable of doing shady actions, and although nothing absolutely to his discredit was known, he inspired little trust, and had few friends. From the moment that Aylmer had joined the North Essex Light Infantry it had been Major Strause's intention to make use of him. His young cousin's money would help him out of his many difficulties. He intended to make use of it, and probably would have done so but for the influence of Gavon Keith. Keith, upright himself, scrupulously honourable, straight as a die in all his words and actions, read through the major, and in his own way counteracted the influence which he tried to exert over Percy Aylmer. Without saying much, Keith contrived that Aylmer should look at Strause somewhat with his own eyes. And the consequence was that on many occasions Strause's endeavours to get large sums of money from his kinsman were foiled.

There came a day when Aylmer hastily appeared in Keith's quarters, flung himself into a chair, and said,—

"Now what's to be done? Strause is evidently up a tree. He wants me to lend him five thousand pounds. I have all but promised, but as you have always been my best friend, I thought I would let you know."

Keith looked annoyed.

"Where is the use of talking?" he said. "You are aware of my opinion. Strause is a confirmed gambler. Whatever you let him have he will lose either on the turf or the Stock Exchange."

Keith had never said as much before, and he bit his lips with annoyance when the words had passed them.

"Do you really think as badly of him as that?" asked Aylmer, in an anxious tone.

"Yes," said Keith stoutly. "As I have spoken, I hold to it; I cannot mince matters. Strause is not an honourable man, and the less you, my dear boy, have to do with him the better. By-the-way, Aylmer, how old are you?"

"I shall be two-and-twenty in a month," was Aylmer's reply.

"And on my next birthday I shall be twenty-nine. You must see what a gulf of experience lies between us. Now, Aylmer, I like you."

"You are the best friend a young fellow ever had," was Aylmer's reply.

"And I don't want to see you going straight to the devil."

Aylmer fidgeted.

"You may or may not be right with regard to Strause," he said, after a pause, "but one doesn't care to see one's kinsman in distress. Strause says he will be obliged to leave the regiment if I don't help him."

"To the extent of five thousand pounds?" remarked Keith.

Aylmer was silent.

"I tell you what it is," remarked the older man suddenly. "You leave me to see Strause over this matter."

"But he hates you, Keith," was Aylmer's naïve reply.

"All the same, I think I'll tackle him," said Keith. "Don't lend him money, Aylmer. For any sake, be firm with him. Strause can be the very devil if he once has a hold over a fellow."

Keith had cause to remember his own words later on, but at the time he thought only of Aylmer and how best he could save him.

That evening Keith called upon Major Strause, and had, as he expressed it, a straight talk with him. What one said to the other was never known, but when Keith left his brother officer's quarters he was under the impression that Aylmer was saved. This appeared to be the case. Strause was still quite friendly to both men, and Aylmer soon afterwards informed his friend that the loan of five thousand was no longer required.

Some weeks went by, and one evening Aylmer casually mentioned that he was making a fresh will.

"I made one soon after I joined," he said, "about three months after, just when you prevented me from making an ass of myself at mess. Do you remember?"

Keith smiled.

"Yes," he said. "I thought you one of the nicest boys I had ever seen afterwards."

"Well, I made a will then, and—Keith, you must not be angry—I put you into it."

"I wish you would make another, and leave me out," said Keith bluntly.

"That is just what Strause wants me to do."

"Oh," said Keith, altering his manner, "has Strause anything to do with this?"

"A great deal. I went up to town yesterday to consult his lawyer."

"Why? have you not your own business man?"

"I have; but Strause thinks a great deal of Mr. Gust."

"And have you made a will and signed it?"

"There is a will being drawn up. I cannot tell you its contents; it would not be fair, as you are one of those who will profit by it."

Keith sprang to his feet.

"Look here, Aylmer, old man," he said, "I have as much money as I need. Don't put me in your will; strike that part out. I don't want a man to leave his money away from his relatives."

"Well, then, Strause gets about everything. I am an only son of an only son, and my mother had neither brothers nor sisters."

"You talk as though you were dropping into the grave," said Keith. "All in good time you will marry and have children of your own. Don't sign that will, if you take my advice. Strause is playing his cards for his own ends. And now I will say no more."

A week after this Aylmer quite unexpectedly fell ill. At first it was reported that he had taken a bad chill when out hunting, and would be all right again in a few days. Then the doctor began to look grave, and said something about sudden developments and possible danger. Keith heard the news in the mess-room, and went straight to Aylmer's quarters. He found the poor fellow tossing about, flushed and miserable, with Strause in close attendance.

"Keith!" he cried, the moment Gavon Keith entered the room. "Oh, I am glad to see you! So you have come at last!"

"At last!" cried Keith; "I only heard of your illness an hour ago."

"But I have been sending you note after note," said the poor young fellow. "I wanted you so badly last night—yes, and the night before too."

"I'll sit up with you to-night, Aylmer," said Strause.

"Oh, it was dreadful last night!" moaned the boy. "I was alone, and I got so giddy, and thought for a moment that I was dying."

"Why has he not a proper nurse?" said Keith, turning sharply round and facing Strause.

"He doesn't wish for a nurse, nor does the doctor think it necessary. I am prepared to give up all my time to him."

"O Keith, do sit down; don't go quite yet," said Aylmer. His voice was low and his breathing rapid.

Keith did sit down by the bedside. He perceived at a glance that Aylmer's blue eyes were full of suppressed trouble, and resolved, if possible, to see him when Strause was absent. Presently Aylmer gave Keith a glance full of meaning, and the next moment looked in his cousin's direction. Keith bit his lips with annoyance. Strause had evidently no intention of leaving the room.

To Keith's relief, however, a moment later an orderly arrived with a message desiring Strause to go to see the colonel immediately. Strause was obliged to comply. The moment he did so Aylmer clutched Keith by the hand.

"Don't leave me alone with him," he said; "he frightens me. If I want a nurse, he says he knows a woman who will come, and I shall be more in his power than ever. Do you know, I have not signed the will. I would rather the old will stood—I think I have remembered every one in it—all the old servants, I mean. I made the sort of will when I first joined that my father and mother would have liked had they been alive. Keith, I am afraid of Strause. He is mad about this will. He is never alone with me that he does not talk of it. It has arrived, and I have only to sign it, and he will easily get witnesses. And he will *make me do it*. I feel he will if he is alone with me. When you are ill you get nervous in the middle of the night. Don't you understand, Keith?"

"Yes, I understand," replied Keith, in that sympathetic voice which was one of his greatest charms.

"O Keith," continued the boy, "I did not think I could be such an arrant coward!"

"You are ill, and are therefore not responsible," replied Keith. "Now listen, Aylmer. I mean to look after you to-night. I am off duty, and if I cannot get Strause out of the room I will stay here too; so you need not worry about that will, for you cannot sign it while I am here to prevent you."

"No, that's right. What a relief it will be! God bless you, old chap!"

"Cheer up then, now, and go to sleep."

"You don't know how bad I feel, and what awful attacks of pain I get. I have to be more or less under an opiate all the time. What is the hour? Oh, I ought to have my medicine—not the opiate, but the other. You will find two bottles on that table, Keith. Do you mind giving me a dose of the one which is marked 'To be taken every two hours'?"

Keith crossed the room to a little table where some bottles were neatly arranged. One was a little larger than the other. On one were the simple directions that the medicine within was to be taken, two tablespoonfuls at a time, every two hours. The other medicine was to be taken only at the rate of a teaspoonful when the pain was very bad.

"I wish I might have a dose of the other medicine too," said Aylmer, in his weak voice; "it dulls the pain and makes me drowsy. I hate this stuff."

"The pain is not intolerable now, is it?" asked Keith.

"No; I feel much better—more confident, I mean—now that you have come to me."

"I am going to see you through this bout, Aylmer," said Keith; "so rest comfortable, old man. I won't desert you."

"The sound of your voice makes me feel ever so much better."

Keith arranged the sick boy's pillows. He then put the bottles back on the table, and noticed that two doses had been taken from the larger bottle, and that there was enough of the smaller one to last until the next day.

"I wish the doctor would come," said Aylmer, after a pause. "I know by my feelings that I am going to have another paroxysm of that awful pain."

He had scarcely said the words before the doctor softly opened the room door and entered. He was a clever young man, with all sorts of up-to-date knowledge, he made a careful examination of the patient, and the expression on his face was grave.

"He ought to have a trained nurse," he said.

"You must have one to-morrow, Aylmer," here interrupted Keith. —"Perhaps, Dr. Armstrong, you will choose a nurse and send her in."

"You ought to have a nurse to-night, Aylmer."

"Oh no, no; Keith has promised to look after me to-night."

"Yes, that I have," replied Keith; "and I know something of nursing, too," he added.

"Don't go back on your word, Keith," said Aylmer again. "You will do me more good than fifty nurses."

"I will certainly keep my promise," said Keith.—"But I should like to have a word with you, Armstrong, in the other room."

The doctor and Keith went into the anteroom.

"It is a serious case," said Dr. Armstrong: "there is a good deal of inflammation, and it is just possible that there may be a sudden termination; but he has youth on his side. I am glad you are going to stay with him for a bit. His nerves are very much out of order. I believe there is something worrying him more than this illness."

"I give a guess to what it is," said Keith; "and I don't think at a time like the present anything ought to be hidden from the doctor. Now, Dr. Armstrong, without explaining matters too fully, I want you to give me authority to forbid Major Strause to come to his cousin's rooms. The fact is, Strause worries him —it is a money matter. I dare not say any more. Aylmer ought not to be worried."

"I understood that young Aylmer was very rich," said Armstrong.

"So he is; but Strause is poor. Can you not take a hint?"

The doctor smiled.

"I'll have a talk with Strause," he said. "What you tell me explains much. He must not come near his cousin's rooms until the morning."

"Have I your authority to keep him out?"

"You certainly have."

The doctor went away, and Keith returned to his charge. He was a very tender-hearted, sympathetic fellow, and had much common-sense. He made the sick-room as tidy as any woman would have done, and gave his patient food and medicine at the prescribed intervals. The doctor called again late in the evening, and said that Aylmer was going on quite as well as could be expected. He had scarcely gone before Strause appeared. Keith went to the door of the outer room and spoke to him.

"You are not to come in," he said. "Aylmer must not be worried."

"Worried! I am his cousin," said Strause.

"I have the doctor's authority. I am in charge of the case under Armstrong until the morning."

Strause's dull eyes flashed an ominous fire.

"I won't stay if I'm not wished for," he said, after a pause. He raised his voice on purpose. "But I want just to say a word to Aylmer. I shan't be two minutes." As he spoke, with a sudden movement he pushed Keith aside and entered the anteroom. The next instant he was in the sick-room. "I want to say something to my cousin alone," he repeated. "I shan't worry him, and I shan't be long."

"Anything is better than making a fuss," thought Keith, and he went and stood by the window of the sitting-room, trying to stay the impatience which had possession of him. "I must turn Strause out if he stays too long," thought the young man; "but anything would be better than kicking up a row inside Aylmer's sick-room." He noticed, however, that all was quiet in the room. He could not even hear the sound of voices. Strause seemed to be moving about on tiptoe.

After a moment or two he came out.

"Aylmer is asleep," he said. "I didn't disturb him. What I have to say must keep. You need not have been so chuff in your manner just now, Keith. I am glad to hand over the case to you for to-night. You are good-natured, and Aylmer is fond of you. I hope the poor boy will pull through. What does the doctor say?"

"Armstrong says it is a critical case."

Strause's face looked grave.

"He is right," he replied, after a pause. "None of Aylmer's family are sound. The father and mother died young. Well, poor chap, he has an abundance of this world's pelf: it will be a pity if he does not live to enjoy it. I will look round in the morning. Bye-bye for the present."

Strause's manner was friendly, and Keith reproached himself for the marked dislike he felt towards him. Presently he softly entered the sickroom, and sat down. Aylmer was sleeping. He awoke presently, and said in a drowsy tone,—

"My eyes hurt me; can you do without a candle in the room?"

"Certainly," replied Keith. "I will have a light in your sitting-room, and the door between the two rooms can be open."

"I am better, I think," said Aylmer, after a pause. "Is it time for my medicine?"

"Not for half an hour," replied Keith. "Go to sleep; I won't wake you if you happen to be asleep. The doctor says it is not necessary."

Aylmer closed his eyes and lay still. In a few minutes he moved fretfully, and said in a voice full of pain,—

"That horrible torture is beginning again. You must give me some of the opiate."

Keith rose immediately, took the smaller bottle of medicine, went into the anteroom, and poured out very carefully a teaspoonful, which he brought to Aylmer. Aylmer took it and lay still. In about a quarter of an hour he called out,—

"Keith, are you there?"

"Yes; what's up?"

"The pain is no better. It grows intolerable—I cannot endure it. I must have a second dose at once. Make it a little larger—do, like a good fellow—a dessertspoonful."

"I can't possibly do it, Aylmer. The doctor said that you were not to have this special medicine oftener than once an hour, and it is not a quarter of an hour since you had the last dose. You shall have a second after an hour is up. Now stay quite still, and then perhaps the pain will go off!"

Aylmer lay as still as he could, but the dew on his forehead and the pallor of his drawn face showed the agony through which he was living. His restless hands began plucking at the bed-clothes. Keith suddenly took one, and imprisoned it in both his own.

"My mother used to say that I had the hand or a mesmerist," he said. "Let me mesmerize you now. I will that pain goes."

Aylmer smiled. His blue eyes grew full of gratitude.

"There never was any one like you, Keith, old man," he said. "Whatever happens, I'd like you to know—I'd like you to know what I feel—I mean my gratitude to you. Keith, I believe I'd have gone to the dogs but for you, old fellow. But now—"

"Don't talk, Aylmer; you have to live a long life and prove your words."

"Oh, this agony!" cried the poor boy. "Keith, I don't believe I'll ever get better. Will you send for the doctor again? I know I am much worse."

"I will give you your opiate again at the end of an hour," said Keith, "and then, if you are not better, I will send for Armstrong. But, remember, he expected these paroxysms at intervals. He thought you going on nicely when he saw you at nine o'clock."

"I am worse now—much worse."

Keith suddenly rose.

"Why, it is time for your other medicine," he said; "perhaps you will feel easier after you have taken it."

Keith now crossed the room to the little table, took up the larger bottle, and went into the anteroom. He poured out a full dose of two tablespoonfuls, and brought the medicine in a glass to Aylmer. Aylmer drank it off, uttering a sigh as he did so.

"It doesn't taste quite the same," he said, "but—" His voice dropped away into a drowsy monotone. "You were quite right," he remarked in a minute: "the pain is dulled—I am beautifully sleepy. Don't disturb me, please."

"Certainly not. Go to sleep now; I am close to you."

Keith sat for some time motionless by the sick man's side. He knew by the gentle breathing that Aylmer had dropped into profound slumber. Presently he moved into an arm-chair, stretched himself out, and closed his eyes. Without

43

intending it, he dropped off himself into sleep. During that sleep he had terrified dreams that Aylmer was calling him, and that Strause was preventing his going to him. At last he started up, his heart beating very fast.

"Did you call, Aylmer?" he said in a low voice, and yet loud enough to be heard in case the sick man was awake.

There was no reply. Startled by the stillness, Keith rose to his feet and went to the bedside.

"He is sleeping very quietly indeed," thought Keith; "I cannot even hear him breathe."

Then his own heart began to beat in an irregular, nervous fashion; a cold fear took possession of him. He went into the anteroom, struck a match, lit a candle, and brought it to the bedside. One glance showed him that Aylmer was dead.

Such a sudden termination to a young life caused a good deal of excitement in the regiment, and Keith was so knocked up that he was unable to attend to his duties for a day or two. The doctor expressed no surprise, however, at the sudden ending of the disease. A death certificate was duly given, and a few days afterwards Major Strause followed his young relative to his grave. The other officers of the regiment also followed Aylmer to his last resting-place; but Keith was still suffering from a queer, nervous seizure, which had come to him when he had found his charge dead.

"I can never forgive myself for falling asleep as I did," was his thought. "Perhaps if I had been wide awake and on the alert I might have been able to give the poor fellow a stimulant, and so have saved his life."

After his death Aylmer's will was read, and it was found that he had left Gavon Keith ten thousand pounds. The rest of his money went to different charities, with the exception of a few legacies to old servants of his father's. Major Strause's name was not mentioned at all. This was the will made by Aylmer when he had been three months in the regiment. A few of his brother officers expressed surprise when they heard that Keith had got so large a legacy. He was congratulated on all sides, however, for he was a prime favourite.

A fortnight went past, and one afternoon Major Strause went to see Keith. Keith was better, although he still looked pulled down, and his face was white.

"Well," said Strause, "glad to see you looking more like yourself."

"Yes; I am pulling round at last," replied Keith. "I cannot think why I gave way in this beastly fashion."

"It was a shock. No wonder," said Strause. "You know, of course, what a lucky chap you are? Ten thousand pounds to the good! It is worth having a small shock in such a cause."

Keith did not reply.

"Are you dumb, man?" said Strause, in some annoyance. "You have heard of the legacy?"

"I have. I wish in all conscience that he had not done it."

"Gammon!" was Strause's rude remark.

Keith flushed, and walked to the window. He wished that Strause would leave him. Strause, however, had no intention of doing so.

"There's something I want to say to you," he remarked now, pulling a chair forward, dropping into it, and lowering his voice. "I did not like to tell you before. At present the fact is known only to myself. Whether it goes further remains with you."

"What do you mean?"

"I will explain. Keith, an ugly thing happened in connection with Percy Aylmer's death."

Keith drew himself up very stiffly. He looked full at the major.

"I don't understand you," he said.

"You will soon, if you listen. Of course it was an accident, and a deplorable one, but you, Keith, gave that poor lad the wrong medicine."

"Oh, horror!" cried Keith. He sprang to his feet. A terrible weakness seized him; his head seemed to go round; he clutched a chair to keep himself from falling. "What do you mean?" he added.

"What I say," answered Strause, who read these signs of agitation with pleasure. "It happens that I am in a position to prove my words. You know I was nursing Aylmer all day until you arrived and interfered. Your interference was unwarrantable; but I say nothing of that. I had been giving Aylmer his medicines, and happened to know exactly the amount in each bottle. The alterative medicine, as it is called, had just been renewed, but the bottle containing the opiate was more than half full. The opiate was in the smaller bottle, as you know. The alterative medicine was to be given in tablespoonfuls —two tablespoonfuls to a dose. At the time I gave up my charge of Aylmer to you there were in the larger bottle five doses, but the bottle which contained the opiate was a little less than half full. Do you follow me?"

45

"I hear you, but I cannot imagine what you are driving at."

"You will soon know. On the morning of the death you were terribly agitated. I rushed off to the poor lad's quarters when I heard the news, and found that you had left, saying that you would be round again presently. I went to the table where the medicines stood, and casually took up the bottle which contained the opiate. The moment I saw it I opened my eyes. The bottle was very nearly empty! Even allowing for your giving him a teaspoonful at a time, it was absolutely impossible that he could have taken anything like the amount which was now gone. I then looked at the other bottle, and found that only one teaspoonful had been taken from it since you had charge of the case. You follow me, don't you? In the bottle which contained the alterative medicine there were still *four doses*; in the bottle which contained the opiate there was not more than a *teaspoonful* left. Beyond doubt what happened was this: you gave Aylmer, quite by mistake, two tablespoonfuls of the opiate—a dose which of course caused his death."

"You lie!" said Keith. "How dare you come to this room with that trumped-up story? I did not make a mistake with regard to the medicines. I was most careful, and I am prepared to swear in any court that I took two tablespoonfuls of the alterative medicine, which was in the larger bottle, and brought it to Aylmer between nine and ten o'clock that night."

"Swear it, then," said Strause, in a contemptuous voice, with a sneer on his lips, and a malicious light in his eyes which caused Keith to recoil from him as though he were a serpent—"swear it, and go right through with the whole thing. I have the bottles in my possession, and although there are no witnesses on either side, believe me it will be at best a nasty case for you. You were alone with the sick man—you gave him a fatal dose of the wrong medicine—you were remembered in the poor fellow's will to the somewhat unusual tune of ten thousand pounds. My fine fellow, you are in my power. Even supposing the murder is never brought home to you, your career as an officer in the North Essex Light Infantry is over."

As Strause said the last words he left the room, swaggering out with his usual gait.

Keith sank into a chair and pressed both his hands to his throbbing temples. Was this true?

CHAPTER VI.

46

A TRYING POSITION.

When he had first got over his start of dismay, Gavon Keith's impulse was to defy Strause. He fully believed that the story was invented by Strause for his own purpose, and that poor Aylmer had not been given the wrong medicine. For what ends Strause should bring such a horrible accusation against him Keith could not at that moment guess. He thought matters over, however, with all the common-sense of which he was capable; and that evening, although he still felt weak and giddy, he went to see Major Strause at his quarters, and found that officer within.

"Ah," said Strause, "I thought you might call round. Well, what do you intend to do?"

"Nothing," replied Keith.

"You sit down under the accusation?"

Keith turned first red, then white.

"I do nothing of the sort," he said. "I deny your charge absolutely. I did not give the wrong medicine. I was particularly careful with regard to the medicines. It is true that poor Aylmer disliked the light—I therefore kept his sick-room in comparative darkness; but on the two occasions when I gave him medicines on that fatal night I took the bottles into the sitting-room. Between ten and eleven o'clock, as he was in considerable pain, I gave him a teaspoonful of the opiate. I distinctly recall the bottle and the words, 'One teaspoonful per dose.' He took it, and said it did him no good. He wanted me to give him a larger dose. This I refused. Soon afterwards the hour arrived when he was to take the other medicine. I took that bottle also into the sitting-room, and by the light from a gas jet poured out two tablespoonfuls—no more and no less. I brought the medicine back with me, and he drank it off. He seemed to find relief as he did so, and dropped off asleep immediately. What are you sneering at?"

"You give yourself away so splendidly," said Strause. "Aylmer would naturally feel relief from such a powerful opiate as you administered."

"I did not administer the opiate. I gave him two tablespoonfuls from the other bottle. It is, I suppose, within the region of possibility that the medicines may have been shifted into wrong bottles. For that I am not responsible. You will recollect, perhaps, the fact that you visited Aylmer in his room soon after nine o'clock that evening. You were there for a couple of minutes, and came out afterwards, telling me that he was asleep. I noted that you were quite two minutes in the room, by the little clock on the mantelpiece. I also observed that you walked about softly while there. If you bring this charge against me, I can but repeat what happened."

"And who will believe your word? you have no witnesses."

"Nor have you."

"I hold the bottles," said Strause, with another sneer.

Keith was silent for a minute or two.

"I see nothing for it," he said, "but to try and get an order to have the body exhumed, and thus have the case properly sifted."

Strause uttered an uneasy laugh. He walked to the window and looked out. Then he returned to Keith.

"You do not know, perhaps," he said, "that the effects of opium are very short-lived, and that long before now all traces of opium would have left the poor fellow's body."

"Let the case be brought openly to trial," was Keith's next remark.

"What! you would have yourself ruined, if not worse?"

"I would rather risk anything than put myself in your power."

As Keith spoke he rose and left the room without even saying good-bye to Strause. All that night he kept to his resolve to sift the matter thoroughly, and then repeated to himself,—

"Anything would be better than getting myself into Strause's power."

But the following morning he received letters from home which caused him to look upon the affair from a fresh point of view. His mother had been seriously ill; his cousin, as he always called Kitty Hepworth, wrote to him to say how nervous she had become. She also said that Mrs. Keith was troubled about money matters, having lately lost a large sum through the failure of an Australian bank. If there was any one on earth whom Keith worshipped, it was his widowed mother. Without a moment's delay he wrote to her to tell her of his unexpected legacy, and to ask her to put at least two thousand pounds of the money to her own credit. He further resolved not to give her anxiety by allowing the case of poor Aylmer's death to be investigated. In short, he deliberately, and without at all realizing what he was doing, put himself in the major's power.

For the first few weeks his enemy lay low, as the expression is. But soon he began to use the dangerous weapon which Keith had supplied him with. The poor fellow was blackmailed, and to a considerable extent. Strause now informed him that his delay in having the case investigated made it black against him.

"Had you acted when you first heard my suspicions, a jury might have been inclined to look leniently at the matter; but your reticence, and the very fact that you have used some of your legacy, would tell terribly against you."

Keith believed him, and that evening handed him five hundred pounds. From that moment his fate was sealed.

His face lost its youthfulness; he became haggard and worn. He hated himself for what he termed his cowardice. He was convinced in his own mind that if there was foul play in the matter Strause was at the bottom of it.

Meanwhile Strause was dropping hints in the regiment which bore fruit in a coldness towards Keith. Strause hinted that Keith held a secret, and that this secret had something to do with his lucky windfall, as it was termed. No one believed much what Strause said, but the evidence of their senses caused his brother officers to gaze at Keith in some surprise. Aylmer's name, mentioned on purpose, caused the man to start and change colour. The mention of the legacy was like touching a raw place. It was known that Aylmer had died very suddenly, that Keith had been with him at the last, and that there was no nurse. It was also known that Keith's legacy was an unexpectedly big one.

There came an evening when Strause and Keith dined together, and Strause, who wanted a very large sum of money from Keith, introduced a peculiar drug into his wine. This drug had a curious effect on the mind—stimulating it at first into unnatural activity, but weakening the judgment, and altogether causing the moral senses to remain in abeyance. It was an Indian drug, which Major Strause had learned the secret of from a native some time before. Its later effect was very much that of ordinary opium.

Keith was asked to dine with his brother officer in his own quarters. Two other men were present. Wine was handed round, and they all made merry. The other men were, however, on duty at an early hour that evening. Strause knew this, but Keith did not. Strause and Keith found themselves alone, and Strause produced the bottle which had been previously prepared. Keith took a couple of glasses—quite enough for Strause's purpose. Soon the effect which the drug always produced became manifest. Keith lost his self-control without knowing the fact. Strause brought the full power of a clever mind to bear on his victim. In the end he got Keith to sign a cheque for three thousand pounds in his favour.

Strause had now, by large sums and small, secured nearly half the legacy. The present three thousand would stave off immediate difficulties, and he resolved, for a time at least, to leave the young man alone.

Keith went out to return to his own quarters; but the excitement of the drug was still on him, and he resolved to take a walk. He had by this time forgotten that he had signed the cheque; but his mind kept dwelling on Aylmer, and it seemed to him that at every turn of the road he saw the dead lad, who came to reproach him for being the cause of his early death.

"If this sort of thing goes on," he said to himself, "I shall end by believing that I really did change the medicines."

Suddenly, as is always the case, the effect of the drug which he had imbibed changed. He became sleepy and stupid. His head reeled, and he staggered as though he were drunk. Presently, unable to go another step, he fell down by the roadside. There Mollie Hepworth found him.

By the next morning he was himself again, and he then remembered all that had occurred. He was convinced that he had been drugged the night before. His suspicions with regard to Strause became intensified, and he felt that if this sort of thing continued much longer there was nothing for him but to leave the army, a ruined, and, in the eyes of many, a disgraced man. For he was quite aware of the fact that Strause dropped hints by no means in his favour. In no other way could he account for the coldness that had arisen amongst his old friends. He was thoroughly miserable, and but for his mother, would have left England for ever.

A few days after this Strause met him with the information that he had exchanged into another regiment.

"I am heartily glad to hear it," was Keith's rejoinder.

Strause looked him full in the eyes.

"All the same, we shall meet again," he said; "I have not done with you, my fine fellow."

Keith had a good deal of recuperative power, and after Strause went he began once again to recover. Hope returned to him; the brightness came back to his eyes, and the vigour to his frame. He never ceased to regret that he had not insisted on Strause's ugly suspicions being brought into the light of day; but being relieved from the man's society, he once more began to enjoy existence. He resolved not to let Major Strause ruin his life.

He sincerely hoped that he and his enemy might not meet again. The loss of five thousand pounds of his legacy mattered but little if he had really got rid of Strause. He became once more popular and beloved, and at the time when this story opens he had, to a great extent, got over the shock which Aylmer's death and its subsequent events had caused him.

Several months had passed since that fatal time when Mollie Hepworth had found him, drugged and insensible, by the roadside. He had tried to forget all the incidents of that dreadful night, except one. Over and over, often when he was dropping asleep, often in his busiest and most active moments, the face of Mollie, so kind, so calm, with an indefinable likeness to another face which he knew, and in a great measure loved, came back to him. He felt that Mollie was his guardian angel, and he wondered if he should ever meet her again. When she arrived at his mother's house, and he found that the girl who had helped him in the lowest moment of his life was really Kitty's sister, his surprise and delight were almost indescribable. Before twenty-four hours had gone the inevitable thing had taken place: he had lost his heart to Mollie Hepworth.

He loved her with all a young man's first passion. He had liked girls before, but he had never loved any one till now. Yes, he loved Mollie, and he did not see that there was any obstacle to his winning her. When he stood by her side in the front drawing-room in his mother's house before dinner, when once or twice his hand touched hers, and when many times his eyes looked into hers, he thought of a moment when he might draw her close to him and tell her everything. He had not told her everything yet. All he had told her was that he knew for a fact that Major Strause had drugged him; that he was in the major's power, and did not see any way out. He had told her nothing about Aylmer. He felt that the story, if it were to be kept a secret, ought not to be known even by one so trustworthy as Mollie. And as he talked to her and listened to her grave, sensible replies, he felt that he loved her more and more each moment. How glad he was now that he had never gone too far with pretty, gay, dear little Kitty! His mother had hinted more than once that Kitty would be a desirable wife for him. He had been wise not to listen to his mother's words. He had always been fond of Kitty, but he had never, he felt, said one word to her which she could justly misinterpret. Yes, he was free— free to woo Mollie, and to win her if he could. He knew that he would woo earnestly and with passion. He had a sudden sense, too, of belief in his own ultimate success. She loved her profession, but there was that in her which would make her love him even better.

He sat down to dinner in the best of spirits, and his eyes often followed the girl who was now occupying all his thoughts. After dinner he was destined to see the other side of the picture; for Kitty, in her despair, had shown him so much of her heart that he could not for an instant mistake her feelings. He was shocked, distressed. Once again he blamed himself.

"I am doomed to be unlucky," he muttered, as he tossed from side to side on his pillow. "Is it possible that Aylmer came by his death by foul means? O my God, I cannot even think on that topic! Is it also possible that at any time I gave poor little Kitty reason to believe that I cared for her other than as a brother? Honestly, I don't think I have done so. Poor little girl! I don't love her in the way she wants me to love her. She would make a dear little sister, but a wife—no. Kitty, I don't love you as a wife ought to be loved, and I do love your sister Mollie. What a position for a man to be in!"

CHAPTER VII.
CONFIDENCES.

When Mollie went to bed that night, she found her sister seated by the fire. Her cheeks were deeply flushed, and traces of tears were plainly visible round her pretty eyes. When she saw Mollie, she turned her head petulantly aside. Mollie, in some astonishment, went up to her.

"Why are you not in bed, Kit?" she asked.

Mollie's matter-of-fact, almost indifferent words were as the proverbial last straw to the excited girl. She sprang to her feet, flung her arms to her sides, and confronted her sister, her brown eyes flashing, her cheeks on fire.

"You ask me that!" she said—"you! Why did you ever come back? If you meant to devote your life to nursing, why did you not stay with your patients? Why did you come back now of all times to—to destroy my hopes? Oh, I am the most wretched girl in the world!"

"What do you mean, Kitty?" said Mollie, in astonishment. "I do not understand you. Have you lost your senses?"

"My heart is broken," answered Kitty; and now all her fortitude gave way, and she sobbed as though she would weep away her life.

Mollie was very much startled. She thought she knew Kitty, but she did not understand this strange mood. She went on her knees, put her arms round the younger girl, and tried, at first in vain, to comfort her.

"You must save me!" cried Kitty presently, and her voice rose to a high hysterical note. "I shall die if you don't."

"But what am I to save you from, Kitty? And die, my darling! What extraordinary, intemperate words!"

"Oh, what do I care for my words? I am too wretched, too miserable! Don't you know what is going to happen?"

"No; what? Do speak."

"Gavon is going away, perhaps to be killed. He—is going to South Africa on Saturday week."

"Then, Kitty," replied Mollie, "are all these tears—is all this awful misery —on account of Gavon?"

Kitty struggled out of her sister's embrace.

"And why shouldn't it be?" she asked. "Have I not loved him for years? Oh, I don't mind saying it. Did I ever care for any other man? I could have married long ago, but I would not. I never cared for any one but Gavon all my days. All my hopes were centred on him, and he—O Mollie, yes, it is true— he did like me until you came."

Mollie felt a crimson flood rush to her face; she also felt a choking sensation round her heart. So this was the secret of Kitty's misery! She was silent for a moment, too absolutely astonished to speak. Then she said in a voice which was stern for her,—

"Dry your tears. Sit down, please. We must talk this matter out."

But Kitty's only response was a fresh burst of weeping.

"She is hysterical; I can do nothing with her until she gets over this attack," thought Mollie. She pushed her sister towards a chair, and said gravely, "If you will not listen to me now, we will defer our conversation. I am going to bed."

She went to the other side of the room, and began immediately to undress. For a time Kitty kept on sobbing, her face buried in her arms, which she had flung across the back of the chair. But presently, seeing that Mollie took not the slightest notice of her, she said in a semi-whisper,—

"I will be good, Mollie. I know I am horribly naughty, but I will be good now. I will listen to you."

"I am glad you are getting back your senses," replied Mollie; "but, Kitty, you must prepare for a scolding."

"Oh, I will be very good," answered Kitty again. "Scold me if you like. Do anything except keep silence; do anything except look so awfully, awfully indifferent."

"Indifferent!" cried Mollie; "how very little you know! But, Kate, my dear, I am ashamed of you. Your want of self-control distresses me. I don't know much about love and lovers, but I do know that, in our mother's day at least, no girl would talk as you have done to-night; no girl would wear her heart on her sleeve; no girl in the old days would declare her love for a man who had not spoken to her of his."

"And what do I care for the old-fashioned girl?" said Kitty. "I am modern, and I have modern ways. I do love Gavon, and I don't mind saying so. And, Mollie, I swear that he did love me before you came."

"Is this true?" said Mollie, in an altered voice. "Tell me everything."

"Yes, it is true. The moment he saw you there came a change over him." Here Kitty looked full up at her sister. "And you love him too, I believe," she said suddenly.

"No, Kitty," answered Mollie; "that is a remark I cannot permit you to make. If Gavon is your lover, he can be less than nothing to me. Now, please, do not conceal anything from me."

Thus adjured, Kitty spoke.

"I am terribly unhappy in every way," she said. "It is not only that for a long time I have hoped to become Gavon's wife, but I have got—yes, it is true, Mollie—I have got desperately and hopelessly into debt. I owe Madame Dupuys a large sum of money. Madame Dupuys knows that when I am of age I shall have quite a nice little fortune of my own, and until lately she seemed quite willing to wait to be paid when it was convenient to me; but of late she has pressed and pressed me. I have not been really frightened, for I thought the very moment Gavon asked me to marry him Aunt Louisa would be so pleased that she would help me to satisfy madame's requirements. But if Gavon doesn't ask me—and now, oh, now I begin to think that he never, never will!—I shall not know what to do. I shall be not only a miserable, forsaken girl, but I shall be disgraced."

"Nonsense, Kitty. It is very wrong indeed to go into debt, and for my part I do not understand any girl going into debt for mere finery."

"Oh, you are so grand and above us all," interrupted Kitty. "You don't understand the failings, the weaknesses, the longings of poor girls like myself."

"In some ways I am glad I don't," answered Mollie. "But there, we need not discuss my feelings in the matter. The thing is to know how to get you out of your present scrape. As to your sensations with regard to Captain Keith I have nothing to say, for I cannot understand your want of reticence in the matter. But the other thing ought to be attended to. You must allow me to tell Aunt Louisa, if you are afraid to do so."

"No, no, Mollie—no, no," answered Kitty; "that would quite destroy my last hope. Auntie has a perfect horror of girls who go into debt, and so has Gavon; I have heard him say so. I heard him say once that even if he loved a girl, and he found that she was frivolous, and extravagant, and ran into debt, he would never, never marry her. And that made me finally make up my mind that under no circumstances was he to know. You must not tell Aunt Louisa. I will get out of it some way, somehow, but you must not tell her."

"It is a very puzzling story. I scarcely know what to do," answered Mollie.

Kitty's eyes had now grown bright. She had ceased to weep so bitterly.

"After all," she said, "if you will only help me, things may come right. I shan't go into debt after this week, and I will try to make some kind of arrangement with madame. I have great hopes that on Monday night Gavon may ask me to marry him."

"Why on Monday night, Kitty?"

"Oh, I am going to Lady Marsden's fancy ball at Goring, and Gavon is to be there; and the beautiful dress I ordered from Madame Dupuys is to be worn on that occasion. I am to go as the Silver Queen. I think Gavon will like me in that dress, and—anyhow it is my last chance. If he proposes to me, all will be well. I shall be engaged—as happy as the day is long; and I don't mind Aunt Louisa knowing then—I don't mind anything then. And there's one way in which it can be done, and one way only."

"What is that?" asked Mollie.

"You, Mollie, my darling, must go away. You must not see Gavon. O Mollie, won't you, won't you help me? I want you to keep right away. I want you to go somewhere just until after Monday. Give me Monday night for my last chance."

"Suppose it fails?" said Mollie, almost in a whisper.

"Then," answered Kitty, with a shiver, "I will try hard to be good. I will take up my poor, broken failure of a life and make the best of it. But please, please give me my last chance. If he says nothing on Monday night, I shall have no hope. Please go away, Mollie, for the next three days."

"I could do so," answered Mollie. "I wonder if it is right. This is Thursday evening. I have a great friend, Nurse Garston, who is also a Red Cross Sister. She has often asked me to visit her in her home in the north of London."

"Then go, Mollie; do, Mollie darling, go!"

"I would do so if it were really the best thing for you."

"It is the only thing."

"But would you marry Gavon, Kitty, if you knew that he did not love you?"

"But he does."

"If you knew that he did not love you just in the extreme way in which a man ought to love the woman he is about to make his wife?"

"I don't care—yes, I would marry him. I would *make* him love me utterly, completely, if only I were his wife."

Once again Kitty flung herself into her sister's arms, and once again her tears flowed. Mollie was silent for a moment, standing very upright, allowing the young, slight figure to rest against her with all its weight. An imperceptible shudder went through her frame—she was seeing a picture. She saw in Gavon Keith's eyes an expression which no woman ever yet saw and mistook. A secret was whispered in her ear; her heart gave one throb of inexpressible joy, and then went down, down, as though it were sinking out of sight. The next instant her brave young arms were flung around Kitty.

"Come, Kitty," she said, "you are giving way to nonsense, and are hysterical. I will put you to bed. and you must fall asleep."

CHAPTER VIII.
THE PURSE MARK K. H.

Kitty did sleep, but Mollie remained awake. All her healthy nature was disturbed; the daily routine of her useful life was passionately interrupted. She had now come face to face with tragedy, and this tragedy surrounded her own young and dearly-loved sister. Katherine, reckless, undignified, destitute of self-control, had given her heart to Gavon Keith. His heart had not responded to hers. Kitty was driven to despair, and was not strong-minded enough to conceal her feelings.

"He does not care for her," thought Mollie; and as the thought came to her she shivered, and put her hand before her eyes and tried to shut out a picture. It was a picture which fascinated her, and which she had often, often seen since it had first revealed itself to her as a reality. She saw a man lying by the roadside, and a girl bent over him. The girl saw his dark eyes open, and a look of bewilderment, then of gratitude, fill them, and she knew that from that moment she was never to forget those special eyes or that special man. She had never forgotten, and when she saw him in Mrs. Keith's house, and knew that he was, after a fashion, her cousin, and knew also that he was the supposed lover of her sister, the weight on her heart had never lifted. For she knew also that he might have been the one man in all the world to her. She might have given him a woman's first great, tender love. For Mollie, whose deepest affections were hard to touch, when once won, would have been won for ever; and Gavon Keith might have won her. Yes, she knew it; she was too honest to disguise her own feelings. He was in trouble too, and this very night he had taken her into his confidence. Such a confidence was dangerous. She knew that she was on the edge of a precipice; and although there was that within her which was strong enough to resist temptation, yet the temptation was keen, bitter, dreadful. She was in danger of loving the man whom Kitty loved. The predicament was a terrible one. Keith's half-confidence, too, had puzzled her. She felt uneasy about him. In what possible way had he put himself into Major Strause's power?

Towards morning she fell asleep; and in her sleep her dreams were of Keith. She fancied herself alone with him in a country far from England—alone, and in circumstances of exceptional difficulty. He and she were both tried in quite an unexpected manner, but in the trial their hearts drew nearer together; and as Mollie opened her eyes that morning she found herself murmuring his name.

"This will never do," she thought. "I must go away immediately. I will not see him again until he is engaged to Kitty. Oh, he must marry her—he must return her love!"

Mollie rose and dressed quickly. Kitty was still sound asleep. Mollie wrote a little note, and left it on the dressing table. It ran:—

"DEAREST KITTY,—I have one or two old friends to visit in the north of London. One of these friends will in all probability offer me a bed. If so, I shall stay away for two or three days—until after Monday. Please tell Aunt Louisa not to expect me for a few days. MOLLIE."

It was not yet eight o'clock when Mollie ran downstairs. She asked for breakfast, and waited for it in the breakfast-room. She ate hurriedly, being afraid that Keith might come downstairs.

It was close on nine o'clock before Kitty awoke. She could not at first make out why there was such a weight at her heart; then it returned to her—Gavon did not love her. Gavon beyond doubt loved her sister.

"I cannot bear it," thought the petulant and angry girl—"I cannot bear it. Why should Mollie come and take him away from me? Have I not loved him for years?"

She rose, and the first thing she saw was Mollie's little note on her dressing table. She opened and read it, and a look of relief crossed her face. She dressed slowly, putting on her most becoming and stylish garments. Her tears of the previous evening had but added pathos to her beauty. Her face was pale, and her wide-open eyes looked large. She ran downstairs in time to meet Mrs. Keith and her son.

"Where is Mollie?" asked the good lady as Kitty entered the room.

"She left a note. She has gone to visit some friends in North London," said

Kitty. "Mollie won't be back for a day or two," she added. As she spoke she flashed a glance at Gavon, who was seated at the table. He rose, and went to the sideboard.

"Shall I cut some ham for you, Katherine?" he asked.

"Thank you. Yes, please, a little," she replied. Her lips quivered; she wondered if she could swallow anything.

The meal was about half through when a servant entered, bringing a note. The note was addressed to "Miss Katherine Hepworth." Kitty tore it open. Its contents caused her face at first to turn rosy red, and then very white.

"Say there is no answer," she said to the servant, who left the room.

"What is it, dear—anything that troubles you?" asked Mrs. Keith.

"Only a letter from Madame Dupuys," said Kitty, speaking as carelessly as she could. "She wants to see me. I hope nothing is wrong with my dress."

"You extravagant girl," said Keith, "are you getting a new dress for Monday evening?"

"Yes—a new dress for you, Gavon," replied the girl, and she looked sadly in his face.

There was something in her expression which gave him a pang of remorse.

"I like you in anything you wear, Kitty," he said, with a sort of assumed carelessness. And then, as he went out of the room he laid his hand for an instant on her shoulder. Light as the touch was, it thrilled her. The clouds vanished from her speaking face like magic, and she turned brightly to Mrs. Keith.

"When must you go to Madame Dupuys'?" asked that lady.

"Early—almost immediately. I will take a hansom and drive over."

"You need not do that; I am going out, and can drop you at madame's, and call for you afterwards."

"Oh, thank you, auntie; that will be lovely."

"I am going out immediately," said Mrs. Keith.

"Then I will run upstairs and put on my hat and jacket," said the girl.

She danced up to her room. She still felt that light, very light, caressing touch of Keith's on her shoulder. It tingled through her being. She dressed herself quickly, and ran downstairs. Soon the elderly lady and the young were driving away together in the direction of Madame Dupuys'. Mrs. Keith's face looked troubled. Kitty glanced at it, and then looked away.

"She is thinking about Gavon, and no wonder," thought the girl.

An impulse of affection, a fellow-feeling in a mutual sorrow, caused her to place her little hand inside Mrs. Keith's. Suddenly the young pair of eyes and the old met.

"*How* are we to bear it?" said Kitty to his mother.

Mrs. Keith squeezed the slight hand.

"We must prove ourselves Englishwomen, Kitty," she said then. "A brave woman will always willingly give up the man she loves to the cause of his queen and his country."

"Some women are not brave," said Kitty, in a smothered voice.

They arrived at the dressmaker's, and Kitty went upstairs. She was shown into a large showroom. She wandered about restlessly. The next instant a girl appeared, and asked her if she would step into madame's private sitting-room. Fear—an unreasoning fear—now caused Kitty's heart to sink very low. She followed the girl. She was shown into a small, prettily-furnished room. Madame Dupuys was waiting for her.

"I am very much obliged to you, Miss Hepworth," she said, "for calling to see me so early."

"But what is the matter?" said Kitty. "Why did you send me such an alarming note? What can be wrong?"

"I am more sorry than I can say, Miss Hepworth; but even at the risk of losing your custom, it is absolutely necessary that you should pay me at least half of my bill by to-night."

"I cannot possibly do it," said the girl. "What is the matter? You told me you would give me a little time."

"I am sorry, but I am obliged to change my mind. I am pressed myself to pay a large sum—pressed unexpectedly. I cannot let you have the dress for the fancy ball unless you pay me half my account."

"Oh, how terribly cruel of you! You will ruin me if you act so."

"Miss Hepworth," said the dressmaker, "I have to speak plain words; it is best to be straightforward. You have owed me a large sum of money for over two years. Mrs. Keith imagines that you do not owe me anything. If I go to her, the account will be paid at once. You owe me three hundred pounds. I shall be satisfied for the present with a cheque for half. Can you let me have a cheque for one hundred and fifty pounds to-day?"

"I cannot do it," said Kitty, in a low, terrified whisper—"I cannot do it; and I must have the dress. Give me until Tuesday morning, and you shall have a cheque for three hundred. Yes, I vow it. I must have the dress; nothing else will effect my purpose. Can you not understand that there are occasions when a girl's whole future—all her future—may depend on one dress, worn on one special evening? Can you not understand?"

"I can partly guess to what you are alluding. Are you likely to have a proposal, Miss Hepworth? Are you likely to make a brilliant match? Do you want to fascinate some one on Monday evening? For if that is the case, and if the man is—"

"Oh, think anything you like—I cannot explain. You know that in a year I shall be comparatively rich; and I will pay you in full—I promise it—on Tuesday. Can you not wait until then? and won't you let me have my dress?"

Madame Dupuys looked at the young girl, She was sorry for her. She possessed a sufficient amount of the vanities of nature to understand that the pretty face and charming figure would look all the more taking and bewitching set out as she could set them out. Kitty's was not that simple order of beauty which needs no adornment. She looked best when she was richly apparelled, and Madame Dupuys had an artist's soul, and longed to see her own work displayed to the best advantage. Nevertheless, she was really pressed just now for just that hundred and fifty pounds which Kitty ought to have given her; and there was an American heiress who would look quite lovely in the dress she was making for Kitty, and would pay her down bank notes on the spot. Why should she wait interminably? for she did not at all believe in Kitty's promise for Tuesday night, and she absolutely wanted her money.

"I am sorry," she said at last. "I should like to oblige you, Miss Hepworth; but there is only one alternative. If you cannot let me have a cheque immediately, or at least by to-night, for one hundred and fifty pounds, I cannot let you have the new dress."

"Then you are unkind, and I hate you!" said the girl.

Madame Dupuys was not at all affected by these angry words of Kitty's.

"I think you will find the money," she said, with a smile.

And Katherine Hepworth, with despair written on her face, ran downstairs.

"I have no chance if I do not get the dress," she said to herself. "I wonder if Mollie would help me. What is to be done?"

She was too impatient and perturbed to wait for Mrs. Keith. She went out into the street. A hansom was slowly passing. She raised her *en-tout-cas* to stop the driver. The man drew up to the pavement. The girl got into the hansom. As she did so her foot kicked against something hard. She gave the man the direction of a gay shop in Sloane Street. She intended to buy gloves and a fresh ribbon for her fan there. The man whipped up his horse, and she stooped to see what the hard object was. It was a purse made of Russian leather. She opened it, and saw, to her wonder and delight, that it contained bank notes and gold. Tremblingly she laid it on the seat by her side. But it seemed to sting her as it lay so close and yet so far. She could not get away from the fascination of it. There were a great terror and a great sense of relief all over her.

"What does this mean?" she said to herself. "Oh, of course I ought to give it to the driver, and tell him that somebody has left it here. But why should I? I wonder how much is in it?"

She took it up, and saw further, to her astonishment, that there were letters printed in silver on the outside. The letters might have stood for her own name—"K.H."

"More and more marvellous!" thought the girl.

She opened the purse now, and tumbled the contents into her lap. Altogether there was over a hundred pounds within—about twenty-nine pounds in gold, the rest in notes. Notes are dangerous things to deal with when one wants to be a thief. But Kitty did not think of anything so dreadful as the word "thief" just now. With a hundred pounds she could appease Madame Dupuys; she could get her dress in time for the ball—she could see a way out of her difficulties. Not yet did her conscience prick her; not for an instant did she feel remorse. She would do it. Was it Providence that had put this purse in her way, or was it— She did not wait even to think out the remainder of the sentence. She poked her parasol through the roof of the hansom.

"I want you to go back to 340 Bond Street," she said to the man.

He turned his hansom at once. When they reached the house, Kitty got out, rang the bell, and asked to see Madame Dupuys. The girl who opened the door to her brought her upstairs at once, and in two minutes' time she was in madame's presence.

"Here," said the girl, panting as she spoke, "if I give you a hundred pounds now, will you give me a week or ten days longer to pay the remainder?"

"I will give you six weeks exactly, Miss Hepworth," replied the dressmaker.

"Six weeks!" gasped Kitty. It seemed like a lifetime. She might be married by then. Who knew what might take place long before six weeks were out? "Yes, yes, that is all right," she said.

She took the little purse out of her pocket; it bore her own initials. Madame was not for a single moment surprised at seeing it. Kitty tumbled the contents on the table.

"There," she said again. "There are one hundred pounds. Count them."

The dressmaker bent over the notes and gold. She counted hastily.

"One hundred pounds and five shillings," she said.

She pushed the five shillings back to Kitty.

"No; keep it as a present," said the girl restlessly.

"Certainly not, miss," replied madame, with dignity.

She made out a receipt for Kitty and handed it to her. Kitty picked up the empty purse and left the room.

When she was gone, madame was about to put the notes and gold into a safe place in her writing table, when she was attracted by a little piece of paper which had fallen on the floor. She took it up, and opened it without having any special reason for doing so. The piece of paper contained nothing but an address: "Katherine Hunt, 24 Child's Gardens, Bayswater."

"Miss Hunt!" thought madame. "How queer! Why, she is one of my customers." For a moment she thought she would tear up the little piece of paper, but on second thoughts she put it into her drawer with the notes and gold. "The next time Miss Hunt comes I must ask her if she knows Miss

Hepworth," thought the good woman. "Well, I am glad Miss Hepworth has paid me even that much. And of course, poor little lady, she shall have her dress, and made as nicely as I can make it."

CHAPTER IX.
KATHERINE HUNT.

In the course of that same morning a bright-looking, dark-eyed girl appeared in Madame Dupuys' showrooms. She asked to see madame herself. Madame came out. She gave a start when she saw that the girl who wished to see her was Miss Hunt.

"I have come to order a dress," said Miss Hunt. "I want it to be pretty—as pretty as possible. I have, just at the eleventh hour, had an invitation to go to the great fancy ball at Goring. I am determined to go; the ball is *the* event of the season, and I would not miss it for the world. I have been all morning going from place to place, and have just time to visit you. What can you give me? Money no object. I shall require the very prettiest dress you can conceive and execute, that is all."

Miss Hunt dropped into a seat as she spoke. She had a taking way and a bright manner. She was one of madame's very best customers. Not only was she extravagant, but she was open-handed. She was a very rich girl—the daughter of a millionaire. She always paid ready cash for her clothes. Had Kitty come to demand a dress on such short notice, madame would have negatived the possibility immediately; but with Miss Hunt it was different. If madame could not supply Miss Hunt with a dress, the latter had it in her power to visit one of the most expensive shops in Bond Street, and get what she required at double the money. Money was little or no object to Miss Hunt. She tapped the floor lightly now with her parasol, and looked with expectant eyes at madame.

"Something *recherché*," she said, "and at the same time a little *outré*— something that will attract attention."

"I wonder what she is thinking of?" thought madame. "And does she know yet that she has lost her purse, and that that purse contained one hundred pounds? But why should I think she has lost it? Surely Miss Hepworth would not pay me with another person's money! The mere coincidence of Miss Hunt's address being in the purse means nothing—nothing at all."

"You ask me rather a difficult question, Miss Hunt," she said then. "This is Thursday; the ball is on Monday. I am at my wits' end, as it is, to supply a dress to Miss Katherine Hepworth. Do you know Miss Hepworth, Miss Hunt?"

"No—never heard of her," said Katherine Hunt, yawning as she spoke. "Now, my dear, good creature," she continued, rising, "will you give me a dress? Yes, or no."

"I shall do my utmost to accommodate you, Miss Hunt; but it is only at the risk of offending other customers."

"I will pay you anything in reason," said the girl. "I am so delighted to get this invitation that I shall not rest unless I am one of the stars of the evening. Understand that money is no matter. And now, what can you do for me?"

Madame left the room, returning again with fashion-books and yards of brocade, velvet, and other rich materials. Katherine Hunt became absorbed in the vital question of what she was to wear. She was a girl with a great deal of directness of manner; she always knew her own mind, and on this occasion was not long in making her selection. As the ball was to be a fancy one, she would appear as Anne Boleyn. Madame applauded the idea, saying that the dress would suit the stately figure and bold, bright eyes of the young lady.

"It must be done absolutely correctly," said the girl. "I wish you would send round to Fortescue's now for a book of costumes of the time of Henry the Eighth. I know he happens to have them. I will wait until it comes. We must decide all the particulars immediately."

Madame rang her bell, and an attendant entered the room.

"Will you pay for the book?" she said, turning to the girl.

"Oh yes, certainly." And then Miss Hunt dived her hand into her pocket to fetch out her purse.

Madame looked at her with intense curiosity. The pupils of her own eyes dilated when Katherine Hunt took out a pocket-handkerchief, shook it, and then gazed up at madame with an expression of despair.

"My purse is gone!" she said. "Some one must have stolen it! I went to the bank only this morning, and got a hundred pounds in gold and notes. There were several things I wanted to buy—in especial a wedding present for a friend of mine. The purse is gone! What can be the matter?"

Madame sympathized, but held her own counsel. Miss Hunt looked worried. Rich as she was, the loss of a hundred pounds was rather serious.

"Who can be the thief?" she said. "I remember now: I was in a hansom driving to Bond Street. I took out my purse and handkerchief. I must have left the purse on the seat, or perhaps it tumbled to the floor. Yes, I remember the number of the hansom. I took the number. It is funny that I should have done so, but I did. I can repeat it to you—22,461. If the man found the purse, he will, of course, take it to Scotland Yard."

"Of course, Miss Hunt," replied madame. "But, on the other hand, a dishonest person may have got into the hansom and taken the purse."

"Oh, not likely, not at all likely," said Miss Hunt, in a careless tone. Then she said, turning to the messenger, "Will you pay for the book, please? I will wait until it comes back.—Dishonest people don't often ride in those nice sort of hansoms," she continued. "It had rubber tyres, I remember quite well. Yes, and the number was 22,461. I will drive from here to Scotland Yard. I do hope I shall get back my purse. I was so fond of it too."

"Had your purse silver initials on the outside?" asked madame suddenly.

"Yes, my own initials, 'K.H.' Why do you ask?"

"And was it a Russian leather one?"

"It was; and oh, such a darling purse! It was given to me by one of my cousins a week ago. But have you seen it? How strange!"

"I must have seen it with you," said madame, "when last you called."

"That is impossible. I have not been here for three weeks, and my darling new purse has been one of my pet toys for only a week."

"Then I must have dreamt about it," said madame carelessly. "It is well, Miss Hunt, that you are a rich young lady: you can afford to lose even a hundred pounds."

"Indeed I can't; no one can. And daddy will be so angry. If he is a millionaire, he works hard for his wealth. He will hate to think that I was so careless. But now let us talk about the dress. When shall I be able to have it?"

The conversation became quite dressmakery. The messenger soon returned with the book of costumes, and madame and the girl bent over the pages, criticising, suggesting alterations, and finally making up their minds. The dress was ordered, and Miss Hunt, with a laugh, said that she would desire her hansom-driver to take her to Scotland Yard at once.

"If I get back my pretty purse with my initials, I will let you know," she said, with a nod. And then she went out of the room.

After she was gone madame stood for some time and thought. She was not a hard-hearted woman, and she was sorry for Katherine Hepworth.

"There is not the slightest doubt what has happened," thought madame. "That poor little lady was sorely tempted; she yielded to temptation. The hundred pounds in notes and gold which I have locked away in my writing-table is stolen money. What is to be done? I cannot for a moment allow this thing to go on. I must see Mrs. Keith. I am sorry for Miss Hepworth; but if I passed over a matter of this kind, I should consider myself terribly to blame."

Busy as she was, madame, soon after lunch that day, went out. She took a hansom and drove to the house in Maida Vale. When the servant opened the door, she asked for Mrs. Keith. The woman told her that Mrs. Keith was out, and would not be back until the evening. Madame uttered a sigh of disappointment, and had scarcely done so before a tall, well-set-up young man crossed the hall. Madame had often heard of Captain Keith, and guessed that it was he. He might do as well as his mother, and save her having a second journey—a waste of time which she could ill afford.

"Perhaps Captain Keith is in," she said suddenly.

The young man paused at the sound of his name and turned round.

"I am Captain Keith," he said, coming forward courteously. "Can I do anything to help you?"

"You certainly can help me, sir, if you will," replied madame.

"Then come into the library," said Keith. He ushered the dressmaker in and closed the door behind them.

"I am Madame Dupuys," she said at once. "Perhaps you have heard my name, sir? I am a well-known dressmaker; I live in Bond Street."

"You make dresses for Miss Hepworth," he said, with a smile. "She was telling me only this morning that she was going to see you. She was anxious about a dress she is to wear on Monday night."

"Miss Hepworth is going to the fancy ball at Goring as the Silver Queen," said madame.

Keith was silent for a moment; then he said,—

"Well, and what can I do for you?"

Madame looked full at him. Should she tell him, or should she be silent? Just for a moment she thought that she would reserve her information for the young man's mother; but on second thoughts the memory of her wasted time and the sorry trick which she considered Miss Hepworth had played upon her aroused her indignation. She spoke impulsively.

"I wished to see your mother, Captain Keith, on a matter of great privacy."

"Indeed! Then I cannot help you?"

"Yes, and no, sir. I am very much troubled about a matter which occurred to-day."

"If it is a worry, I would rather you did not tell my mother now."

"Why so, sir?"

"Because she has other things to trouble her: my regiment is ordered south next week."

"I am sorry and yet glad, sir, to know that you are going to help to protect your country." Madame half rose, then sat down again. "I ought to tell some one," she said, as if questioning herself.

"Perhaps I shall do," replied Keith, smiling, and trying to control his impatience.

"What I have to say, Captain Keith, is in absolute confidence."

"I understand."

"It has to do with Miss Hepworth."

"Miss Hepworth!" cried Keith. He coloured, and an uneasy sensation visited him. "Then perhaps I had best not hear it," he said.

69

"Either you or your mother must hear it, sir; and as you are willing to listen to my confidence, I will give it to you. The fact is, I have been placed in a most awkward position. I asked Miss Hepworth to call on me this morning. She came. She owes me money."

Keith made no remark, but waited for madame to proceed. He did not suppose that Kitty had large private funds at present, and a sum of ten pounds or so owed to a dressmaker did not seem to him a heinous offence.

"Perhaps I can accommodate you with a cheque," he said. After all, the woman's story was scarcely worth taking up his time with.

"It is possible that you can do so, Captain Keith; but the matter I have to speak about means more than a mere cheque. Miss Hepworth has owed me money for a long time, and to-day I asked her for a cheque. She said it was out of her power to give it to me. I asked for a cheque for a large sum. When she refused to accommodate me, I told her that I could not let her have the dress she had ordered for the ball."

Keith did not reply. A vision rose before his eyes of the pretty face of his cousin—her sparkling eyes, her tender mouth. She always dressed well, and she would look, as she herself expressed it, like a vision on this occasion.

"I should not like Miss Hepworth to be disappointed," he said slowly.

"The thing is graver than just a mere disappointment, sir. Miss Hepworth could not accommodate me, and I was firm; she left my house very angry and troubled. She returned within an hour, and said she would pay me then a hundred pounds in cash."

"A hundred pounds!" cried Keith, thoroughly roused at last. "You don't mean to tell me that Miss Hepworth owes you more than that?"

"Considerably more, sir. She said she had it in her power to pay me there and then a hundred pounds; and although I had asked for a hundred and fifty, I promised to be satisfied with what she gave me, and I gave her six weeks' grace for the remainder. I also said she should have the new dress. She took a purse out of her pocket—a Russian leather purse, marked with initials in silver, 'K.H.' She opened it, and took from it a hundred pounds in notes and gold. I gave her a receipt, and she left the house. I was about to put the money into my writing-table drawer until I could take it to the bank, when I observed a piece of paper which had fallen on the floor. I took it up, opened it, and read the address of a lady who is also a customer of mine. The lady's name was Miss Katherine Hunt, and her address, 24 Child's Gardens, Bayswater. I thought this a little strange, and instead of tearing up the paper, put it with the notes and gold in my drawer. In less than an hour Miss Hunt arrived. She was also going to the fancy ball, and she wished for a fancy dress immediately. She is a very rich young lady. Her father is a millionaire. He is the well-known David Hunt, who has made his fortune with the new sort of free wheel.

"Miss Hunt always pays me in cash for everything she gets. You will naturally understand, sir, that a hard-worked woman would be glad to oblige such a customer. She proceeded to order her dress, and finally put her hand into her pocket to pay for a book of costumes which she required. She could not find her purse. She then explained to me that she had gone to her bank that morning and had drawn a hundred pounds in notes and gold. She concluded that she must have left her purse in a hansom. Strange to say, she remembered the number of the hansom, and when she left me, went to Scotland Yard to report on her loss, and if the purse had not been returned there, to get the authorities to look up the driver. I got Miss Hunt to describe her purse, and it tallied in every particular with the purse which Miss Hepworth held in her hand when she gave me the hundred pounds. Now, sir, that is the story. I leave you to draw your own conclusions. I do not wish to be the recipient of stolen goods, and I cannot allow the driver whose number was 22,461 to get into trouble on account of the matter."

Keith's face had turned very white. After a time he crossed the room. He and his mother always used the same library for writing in. He took his keys from his pocket, unlocked an inlaid secretaire, and produced a cheque book. He filled in a cheque for a hundred pounds and gave it to madame.

"Will you take this in lieu of the other?" he said. "And will you let me have the notes and gold? I trust your suspicions are wrong. In any case, I am obliged to you for not making the matter public."

"Will you tell Mrs. Keith, sir?"

"I have not yet decided what I will do. Try to forget the circumstance. You are not likely to have anything further to do with it. This is my affair."

"Certainly, sir. I am sure Miss Hepworth ought to be very much obliged."

Keith thought for a moment.

"What is the exact amount she owes you?" he asked.

"Three hundred pounds, sir."

"I will give you another cheque for two hundred pounds; I do not wish Miss Hepworth to be any longer in your debt. And will you kindly, when you send her dress home, let me have the bill. You will not be surprised at my acting in this prompt manner when I tell you that Miss Hepworth is about to become my wife."

"Oh, indeed, sir!" Madame Dupuys dimpled all over her face. She had not expected to get her troublesome debt cleared so nicely. "I hope, sir," she said, "that you will not be hard upon the dear young lady. I regret very much that I should have subjected her to such a temptation."

"Here are your cheques," said Keith, by way of response. "You will kindly give me a receipt in full."

CHAPTER X.
YOU TALK IN RIDDLES.

Madame did give a receipt in full, and soon afterwards left the house. Before doing so, she had promised Keith that the hundred pounds in gold and notes should be forwarded to him by special messenger within an hour.

Keith had not intended to remain in to lunch, but he did not go out. Neither, however, did he appear in the dining-room.

Kitty, restless, with fear now dogging her footsteps, came in. Mrs. Keith was out, and was not expected to return for the day. She inquired of the servant if Captain Keith were within.

"Yes, miss," replied the girl; "the captain is in his study."

"Will you tell him that lunch is ready?" said Kitty.

The maid withdrew to give the necessary information. She came back in a moment or two to say that Captain Keith did not require lunch.

Kitty pouted. She sat down with but a sorry appetite. She ate very little. When her slight meal was concluded, she ran across the passage and tapped with her knuckles at the door of the study.

"It's me, Gavon," she called out. "May I come in?"

"Not now, Katherine," he replied, without opening the door. "I am particularly engaged."

She pouted once more and walked across the hall. She went slowly, very slowly, upstairs to her own room.

"Such an opportunity, and to miss it!" she thought. "I should have had him all to myself; no troublesome Mollie to distract his thoughts, and no Aunt Louisa to watch us both, as I have always seen her do lately. Why did he not lunch with me, and why did he refuse me admittance to his study? I suppose it is all too patent a fact that he does not care for me. I am one of those miserable girls who give their heart unsought, who give their love unasked for. I have read about such girls, and oh, how I have scorned them, little thinking that I should be one of them! The question now is this—Is the case hopeless? Will the fancy ball at Goring open Gavon's eyes? Will he see then that I, his cousin Kitty, possess a heart all on fire with love to him? If he sees me as I shall look that night, will he still prefer the cold, statuesque beauty of Mollie to my living, loving human heart? O Gavon, you cannot do so! When a girl gives up everything for you, you cannot reject her! O Gavon, if you do, my heart will break. I cannot live without you, my darling."

Struggling with her emotion, thinking hardly at all of the grave sin which she had committed, Kitty sat down by her open window.

"He is going away so soon," she thought. "He may never return. I cannot live without him. If he goes I will go too. Yes, I must. I will follow him somehow, in some fashion. How sorry I am now that I did not take up the profession which makes it possible for Mollie to be near him in his hour of danger!"

The large room which Kitty and Mollie occupied was situated in the front of the house, and just then Kitty heard a slight noise below. She ran to the window, opened it, and put out her head. She saw Captain Keith run down the steps of the house and walk rapidly up the street. There was purpose in his walk, and there was also a slight droop of his head, as though something perplexed and troubled him.

Kitty, whose love made her able to read his every emotion, noticed this look, and felt a fresh tightening of her heart.

"Something worries him," thought the girl; "something worries him. Oh, can anything in all the world put wrong right now? If you only knew, Gavon —if you only knew what I did for you to-day! I stole a purse of gold and notes, and all for you. I stole it because I wanted a pretty dress—something to make me look attractive in your eyes. You cannot guess that your Kitty is a thief—you cannot guess that I have risked the most hideous danger for you; for God only knows whether the purse will be missed, and whether the owner will make a fuss, and whether the officers of the law will not discover what I have done. Nevertheless I do not fear. I fear nothing now but the possibility that I shall not win that which I madly crave—your love and devotion."

Meanwhile Gavon Keith quickly reached the end of the long street, turned to his left, and held up his umbrella to a hansom-driver. The man pulled up at the pavement, and Gavon got in. He held a small parcel in his hand. The parcel was tied and sealed. He gave a direction in Bayswater. The man whipped up his horse, and in about twenty minutes drew up at the door of the house where the Hunts lived.

It was nearly five in the afternoon, and the rays of the setting sun were gilding some of the windows of the great house. Gavon rang the bell, and a liveried and powdered footman attended to his summons.

"Is Miss Katherine Hunt within?" was his first inquiry.

"My mistress is at home, sir," replied the man, after a pause, "but I am not sure whether she receives this afternoon."

Gavon was prepared for this reply. He scribbled a few words on his visiting card, and asked the servant to take it to the young lady.

"I will not come in," he said; "I will wait here."

The man went upstairs. Katherine Hunt was lounging in an arm-chair, idly turning the pages of a fashion magazine, thinking of the dress she was to wear on Monday night, and yawning now and then with downright *ennui*.

When the footman appeared, he presented the card on a salver. Miss Hunt took it up and glanced at it.

"Captain Keith, North Essex Light Infantry." Then in a corner were words scribbled in pencil: "I have called to see you on behalf of Madame Dupuys."

"What can this mean?" thought the girl. She sat up, and her *ennui* vanished. "Show Captain Keith up," she said to the servant; and a moment later he entered the room. He came quickly towards her, and she stood up as he advanced, and bowed in return to his greeting.

"Will you sit down?" she said. Then she added, speaking somewhat conventionally, "What can I do for you?"

"I must apologize for forcing myself into your presence in this way, Miss Hunt," replied Keith. "I have a very painful business to transact, and I want to do it as quickly as possible. I want, to a certain extent, also to throw myself on your mercy."

"I will do anything I can for you," said the girl.

She saw that Keith was agitated. His face was white, and although his words were bold enough, she observed that his hand slightly trembled. She pushed a chair towards him; but he did not take it, although he laid his hand on the rail.

Miss Hunt sat down on a sofa which stood near. She looked up with expectancy on her face. Keith thought for a brief moment, and then plunged into the ugly task which he had set himself.

"She looked up with expectancy on her face."

Page 135

"She looked up with expectancy on her face."

"You took a drive this morning," he said, "in a hansom, number 22,461."

"I did," said the girl, in some astonishment.

"You left your purse in the hansom, and that purse contained one hundred pounds in gold and notes."

"It did. It also contained five shillings. Have you heard anything about it? I shall be so thankful to get it back. I went to Scotland Yard, but could get no

76

information. I was just regarding the whole affair as hopeless, although, of course, the police will do what they can. I was wondering how I could break the news to my father. Although he is rich, he hates what he calls wilful waste. Won't you sit down, Captain Keith? I wish you would."

Keith did now drop into the nearest chair.

"My father will naturally accuse me of carelessness for leaving my purse in a hansom," continued the young lady.

"I wish to goodness you had not done so, Miss Hunt!"

"How strangely you speak! Is it possible you know something about it?"

"I do; and because I don't wish the hansom-driver to get into trouble, and because it is right that you should have your money back, I have brought you —this." As the captain spoke he took a small packet and laid it on the table near Miss Hunt.

"Does this contain my purse?"

"It contains the hundred pounds which were in your purse."

"But not my pretty purse itself?"

"No."

Miss Hunt eagerly broke the seals, untied the string, and opened the parcel. The gold was wrapped in tissue paper; the notes were in a neat roll.

"Count the money, please," said Keith.

She did so, and in a very business-like way.

"The sum is quite correct," she said. And now she raised her bright, dark eyes, and looked full at the young man. "What is the meaning of all this?" she inquired. "Why should you give me back my hundred pounds?"

"You are at liberty to draw any conclusions which occur to you," said Keith. He spoke deliberately, and with pauses between his words. "I trust to what I am sure is your kindly nature not to make things too—difficult."

It was with an effort that he could bring out the words; they stung him as they passed his lips.

"I cannot give you back your purse, I regret to say," he continued, "but the money at least is yours again. Will you kindly let the superintendent at Scotland Yard know, in order that the driver may not get into trouble?"

"I will do so; and thank you very much. Then you can really give me no particulars about my purse?"

"I regret I cannot."

"This is strange!"

"It must appear so to you." Keith looked full at her. "Do you intend to make this story public?" he asked.

She laughed, and her laugh was almost harsh.

"It would make a good story," she said then; "and we do pine for that sort of thing in society, girl—a rich girl—loses her purse. An officer in one of Her Majesty's regiments brings her back the money, not the purse."

"You can make your story exceedingly funny," said Keith, but as he spoke he did not smile.

"I will never make it funny," she replied, and she rose and drew herself up. "I am not ungenerous, and if I fail to read between the lines, or to see what you mean me to see, or to understand whether you are acting with chivalry and the desire to screen another, or because yours is merely a tardy repentance for something you yourself have done, you cannot blame me. I shall never know which motive actuates you. I shall be satisfied to go without knowing. The money is returned to me, and the affair goes no further."

"Thank you," replied Keith. Then he added, and the words came out with a visible effort, "Put the chivalrous theory quite out of your head. I thank you most sincerely. Good-afternoon."

He left her, and never was a girl more astonished than she as she stood, her hand resting on the table, with the gold and notes close to her. She was interrupted in her meditations by the entrance of a stout, very red-faced man.

"Hallo, Kate!" he said. "I am glad you are home. I have just requested Jameson to bring up tea. Why, what a lot of money you have lying loose about the place!"

"Only a hundred pounds, dad. I got it from the bank this morning."

"A very careless way to keep it," said Mr. Hunt—"very careless indeed! Money is hard to win and easy to lose. You are never aware of that fact. I wish you were not quite so careless."

"I have been made painfully aware of that fact to-day," thought Katherine, but she did not speak her thoughts aloud. She sat down and gazed straight before her. "The money is right enough; don't fret, dad." Then she added, after a pause: "What is the news from the Transvaal?"

"Have you not heard? We are sending out troops, doubtless as a precautionary measure, immediately."

"Do you happen to know who are going?"

Hunt mentioned two or three regiments.

"Is the North Essex Light Infantry going?" asked the girl suddenly.

"The North Essex Light Infantry!" repeated Hunt, in a tone of surprise. "Why, yes; a contingent of that regiment is ordered south. But why? Do you know any one belonging to it?"

"One man. I shall be sorry if he gets killed," she said, with apparent carelessness.

"You always were a very droll girl, Katherine. How long have you known this man?"

"I only met him to-day. I have taken a fancy to him."

"Why so, child?"

"Because he is one of those rare products of modern times, a man who puts a woman's honour before his own."

"Now you talk in riddles."

"Doubtless, father; and you are not to hear anything more. Only I respect him."

"Take up your money, and don't leave it lying about any longer, Katherine."

She took her money. She put the gold back into the tissue paper and rolled up the notes, and went slowly out of the room up to her own. She had a little cabinet built into the wall, where she kept her most valuable diamonds and trinkets. She unlocked the little cabinet, pressed a spring revealing a secret drawer, and put the notes and gold into it.

"As a souvenir of quite a wonderful adventure," she said to herself. And then she locked the cabinet and went back into the room where Hunt the millionaire was enjoying his tea.

"I have been making a new pile this morning," he said, turning to his daughter. "An investment turned up trumps. Do you want some more money put to your private account, little girl?"

"You might let me have a hundred pounds," she answered.

"What an extravagant piece it is! But I can let you have more than that."

"A hundred will do, father." And Hunt drew her a cheque on the spot.

CHAPTER XI.
THE FANCY BALL.

It was the night of Lady Marsden's fancy ball, and the crowd outside the beautiful grounds of Kenmuir House at Goring grew greater each moment. Policemen were stationed near, in order to keep a free passage for the stream of carriages which came up continually.

Within the noble house all that art and beauty could do to make the scene as like fairyland as possible had been done. Exotics of the rarest beauty and sweetest perfume were placed wherever flowers could appear; the lights were softened by shades of golden silk; the great marble staircase—a feature of the house—was thronged with guests in every imaginable costume. Motley, truly, was the animated scene, for people of all nationalities appeared to be present —Turks, Mohammedans, Armenians, Greeks. Men who seemed to have stepped down from ancient history; men who might have been pictured in the canvases of Vandyck and Romney; men of low degree, and men of high degree; savages with tomahawks; graceful and scented cavaliers of the time of Charles the First; men who came to look foolish, men who came to look beautiful or wise, as the case might be—but all more or less disguised, more or less carried out of themselves by the auspicious occasion—thronged the passages and pressed up the stairs.

The garbs in which the women appeared were even more humorous and striking than those worn by the men, for at a fancy ball imagination can have its full sway. Any daring thought that comes to you you may execute, being assured of at least a measure of success. Provided you have funds, or provided you do not mind running into debt, you can at least look *outré* or *blasé*; you can get, for the time being, out of your true personality, which doubtless is the main fascination of all incognitos. The desire at any cost to get away from *ego*; the desire to be somebody else for at least a few hours—somebody else who carries your heart within him, who hopes with your hopes, who fears with your fears, who carries your anxieties or your joys, your curses or your blessings, as the case may be, and yet who is not wholly you—is worth struggling for. In its way there is no charm like this; you see yourself from a novel standpoint. Sometimes you learn fresh and great truths with regard to yourself.

The ball at Kenmuir House had been anticipated for a long time. Lady Marsden was one of the beauties of the past London season. She had been a *débutante* at the beginning of the season, and before the end had become engaged to Lord Marsden—one of the best matches of the year. During the period when London is supposed to be empty she had married him, and now stood a bride of dazzling youth and fairness in one of her husband's noble houses, receiving her guests as one so lovely, talented, and high-born knew how.

The nuns and the cavaliers, the savages with tomahawks and the fair ladies of the time of Marie Antoinette, went off in couples, and the spacious rooms beyond the great staircase filled fast; the sweet, spirited music of the Blue Hungarian Band sounded through all the rooms, and the dance went merrily forward. But no one guessed, as the fair girls and the gallant men danced together, or met together, or talked together, that in those rooms and through those most lovely grounds stalked also a gaunt figure. It is true a few saw him in imagination, but no one fully recognized him. He was the god of war. For war had been declared between England and the Transvaal, and already the best of her sons, the flower of her young manhood, were preparing to go south. So the aching hearts which some wore that night, and the dread which encompassed others, and the longing for glory and fame and greatness which swelled the breasts of others, were all due to the god of war. He had been quiet, sleeping for a long time; but he was awake at last, and he came to gloat over his victims at Kenmuir House that evening.

The dance was essentially a dance for the military; for Lord Marsden belonged to a family of soldiers, and three of his own young brothers were amongst those who were to go to Africa immediately.

In the midst of the throng there came slowly up the stairs a slender young figure—a girl with a pale face, large and sorrowful dark eyes, and lips slightly, very slightly rouged; those lips revealed white teeth, and constantly smiled, and gave the lie to the sorrowful and anxious eyes. The girl was spoken of in the list of guests as the Silver Queen, her real name being Katherine Hepworth. She came in the company of a titled lady, who had promised to chaperon her to the great fancy ball; and following her at a slight distance, accompanied by her father, Hunt the millionaire, came Anne Boleyn. For some extraordinary reason, the bold, bright, dark eyes of Anne Boleyn followed the slender figure of the Silver Queen. She did not even know who the young lady was, but her face attracted her. Presently, leaning on the arm of an Armenian slave, she pointed in the direction where the Silver Queen was standing in the midst of a glittering throng.

"Who is that young lady?" asked Anne Boleyn.

Her companion followed her eyes, looked at the Silver Queen, and said in a tone of admiration,—

"What a lovely girl she is! quite one of the belles on this most auspicious evening."

"She is a beautiful girl. But I am not interested in her looks," said Katherine Hunt; "I want to know her name."

"If you will let me take you to this chair, I will endeavour to find out," replied the Armenian slave.

She sank into a seat near an open window, and he went to do her bidding. He came back after a minute or two.

"The fair lady's name is Miss Katherine Hepworth. I cannot find out much about her. She has been in society a little, not a great deal. She is acknowledged to be quite a beauty wherever she goes."

"Katherine Hepworth," whispered Katherine Hunt to herself. "K.H., Katherine Hepworth—K.H."

"What do you mean?" asked the Armenian slave.

"She has my initials," replied the girl. "I am interested in her. I should like to know her."

"Well, I have no doubt we can manage an introduction. I will try to find a mutual friend."

"Oh, there is no special hurry. I am not inclined to dance just at present; I want to watch the people. Sit down near me, will you, and tell me who's who."

The Armenian slave was well known in society as a certain Mr. Roy, an inveterate gossip, and a man who never failed to secure an *entrée* into the best houses. He was not in love with Katherine Hunt; but he was considerably in love with her money, and in consequence was only too anxious to do anything to please the young lady. He stood near her now, bent towards her, and answered her different questions. Yes, he knew everybody; through all their disguises he recognized the well-known features of the ladies of fashion. Even under their dominoes he knew who the men were who walked about to-night in their foreign characters. The only guest he neither knew nor recognized was the god of war, who made no sound as he peered into the faces of the guests. Beside the god of war might also have been seen by those who had very keen vision—by those who had that penetration which amounts to second sight—the grim, very grim form of the god of death. And the god of death marked his victims that night, scoring the name of one young gallant after another in his book of fate, for many met that evening who were never to meet again. The fancy ball at Kenmuir House was something like the celebrated dance in Brussels before the battle of Waterloo—

"Bright eyes looked love to eyes that spake again,
And all went merry as a marriage bell."

Miss Katherine Hunt enjoyed herself on the whole. She had by no means got over her curiosity with regard to the handsome young man who had brought her back her hundred pounds. Not that she had been specially struck with that young man's beauty; but she had penetration—a good deal, all things considered—and she read beneath his light words, and made a very shrewd guess with regard to the truth. Never, even for a single instant, did she accuse him in her own mind of having taken her money. When he denied all chivalry in the matter, she became certain that his action had been caused by chivalry of a rare quality; and now she, who had never before been seriously interested in any man except her father, was anxious to see Captain Keith again. He was one of the few men present who wore his uniform only on the auspicious occasion. He wore the full and very becoming uniform of the North Essex Light Infantry, and he came into the ballroom with a smiling face, and looked around him for the Silver Queen. He was a little late in arriving, and the rooms were very full. Katherine Hunt saw him long before Katherine Hepworth did, for Katherine Hunt still retained her cool point of vantage near a window; and as the Armenian slave had long ceased to interest her, and was only standing on sufferance by her side, she was able to give her full attention to all the new arrivals; and when she saw Captain Keith, who walked across the room with that upright and graceful step which always characterized him, the colour rose in her cheeks under all her rouge, and she half started forward, as though she would speak to him. As she did so she caught his eyes. Her own—dark, brilliant, daring—fell beneath his gaze. He looked at her as if he would recognize her, but under the guise of Anne Boleyn he did not see the slim girl to whom he had spoken a few days before, and was passing on, when she called his name.

"Captain Keith!" said Katherine Hunt.

He turned at once.

"Don't you know me?" she said. "I am Anne Boleyn in this room. When I return home to-night I shall be Katherine Hunt. Don't you remember me?"

"Of course I do now," replied Keith. He did not offer to shake hands with her, nor did she hold out her hand to him, but he stood near her without speaking for a minute.

The Armenian slave, seeing he was not wanted, went off in quest of another partner, and Katherine made way for Keith to sit by her side.

"I am interested in you," she said frankly. "What you did the other day struck me as particularly un-nineteenth century. Why are you not in costume to-night?"

"I wear my Queen's colours," he replied.

She laughed, but it was evident that his remark pleased her.

"You are one of those who go south?" she said, dropping her voice.

"I am glad to say yes."

She did not speak at all for a minute. Then she said slowly,—

"My card is not full." She handed it to him, smiling as she did so.

He took it, and scribbled his name for a waltz.

"The third from now," she said, looking at him. "Yes, I can give it you."

He sat with her for a few minutes longer, then bowed and left her. A partner came up to claim her hand. She glided away in the mazes of the waltz. As she flew round and round with her companion, a cavalier of the time of King Charles, she saw Captain Keith leaning idly against one of the massive doors. He was not dancing; his face looked moody. It seemed to her that his eyes were watching for some one. Presently she saw the girl in white and silver glide by in the arms of a handsome partner. At the same moment she noticed that Captain Keith drew himself up, and stood like one at attention. He seemed to stiffen all over, and his face wore an expression which was almost akin to pain. His eyes were fixed full on the girl in white and silver. Katherine Hunt began to feel that the plot was thickening.

"What intuition has seized me?" she said to herself. "He knows her— beyond doubt, he knows her. I wait with impatience for the third waltz."

It came, and with it Captain Keith.

"Don't dance," she said suddenly; "come and sit in the garden. I am too hot to dance."

"Shall I fetch you an ice?" he asked.

"No; I only want air. It is cool out of doors. Come."

She led the way, and he followed her. They sat down together. Katherine Hunt was not sorry to perceive that the white and silver dress was in view— that another girl, bearing the same initials as her own, was also resting under the shade of a sycamore. The light from a Chinese lantern fell softly on her face. This girl had her cavalier, of course, but her attitude was weary, and she was scarcely speaking. Katherine Hunt, impelled by an ardent curiosity, determined to see this game, as she termed it, through. She chose a seat which would keep the Silver Queen full in view, and she contrived that Captain Keith should sit near her, and in such a position that he could see each movement of the Silver Queen. They talked for a moment or two upon indifferent matters; then she turned her head, looked full up at him, and watched until his eyes rested on the hem of the dress of the other girl.

"How pretty she is!" said Katherine Hunt.

"Who?" he asked, with a start.

"The young lady whom they call Katherine Hepworth. I have been told that is her name. Do you know her, Captain Keith?"

"Yes, I know her," replied Keith.

"I have not seen you dancing with her."

"I shall dance with her next time. Her name is on my card."

Katherine Hunt tapped the ground with the heel of her white satin shoe. She was silent for a minute; then she said,—

"It is strange, her initials are the same as my own."

"Are they?" answered Keith.

"Yes. My name is Katherine Hunt; her name is Katherine Hepworth. I presume she spells her name with a 'K'?"

"She does; we call her Kitty at home."

"At home! Do you know her very well?"

"Miss Hepworth lives with my mother; she is my mother's adopted daughter."

"How interesting! What a charming face she has! Are you engaged to her, Captain Keith?"

"What do you mean?" he asked, in astonishment.

"You are not married, are you?"

"No," he replied; and his face seemed to stiffen, and he moved a little away from Katherine Hunt.

"I hope you will forgive me," she added, noticing this movement. "I am a daring girl, but it seems to me that to be in the same house with a girl like the Silver Queen, to see her daily, would make it almost impossible to any man not to have a good try for her. I wonder if you have tried, and if you are going to succeed! I know you like her—I see it in your face."

Captain Keith turned and looked at the audacious girl with an expression of utter astonishment. She gazed back at him with bright, laughing eyes, and his own fell under her glance.

"I read your secret in your face," she said then. As she spoke she rose and laid her hand on the back of her chair. "Take me back to the ballroom, please," she said.

As he was leading her back she continued in a light tone,—

"Thank you for returning the money; only I miss the purse. It was given to me by a very dear friend. The initials on the purse were 'K.H.,' and I miss it; I should like to have it back."

He looked then as if he wished to speak, but not a word passed his lips. The waltz had come to an end, and Katherine's partner came to claim her. Keith was released. He went back to the garden to find Katherine Hepworth. She was waiting for him. She was standing in an expectant attitude; her face was very white. There was a moon in the sky, and some of its light fell with silver radiance across the slender figure of the Silver Queen, and made her beautiful face look almost unearthly. As Keith approached her lips trembled.

"This is our dance," he said.

He took her hand, and was about to lead her into the ballroom, when she interrupted.

"I cannot dance," she said, in a husky voice.

Then he knew that his hour had come, and that he must go through with something which would crush the joy out of his life.

CHAPTER XII.
KATHERINE HUNT'S STRATEGY.

"Is there any place where we can be alone?" said Kitty.

"Why?" asked Keith.

"I cannot dance," she said again; "my heart beats too fast."

Keith could observe through the cobweb lace which was fastened across her neck that her heart was beating far too fast for health and prudence. He looked at her earnestly. Her eyes were raised to his, and something of the passion which blazed in them was communicated to his breast. His intense unwillingness to fling himself at her feet—his almost aversion to her when he had learned a few days ago that she had committed a crime punishable by the law—left him. He said in a choking voice,—

"You want supper; I will get you a glass of champagne. Come with me."

He led her through the throng, put her into a cool seat by an open window, and brought her some champagne. She drank a glassful, and then handed the glass back to him. He laid it down. From where they sat the dreamy music of the band, the rhythmic steps of the dancers, the buzz of conversation, seemed far off and almost unreal. A curtain, gracefully arranged, almost concealed the figure of Kitty Hepworth; but the reflection of some fairy lamps in the wide balcony outside fell across her face, and Keith thought he had never seen such dark and such lovely eyes before.

Close to them, unseen and unnoticed, stalked the god of war. If it were given to him to smile, he must have smiled then as he saw the young pair, for Keith suddenly bent forward and took Kitty's hand in his own.

"This is Monday," he said, "and I go on Saturday."

She tried to speak, but found herself unable.

"Will you wait for me until I come back?" he said then.

His words were like an electric shock to the girl. Notwithstanding all her beauty, her attitude had been one which denoted extreme weariness, not to say despair; but now there shot through every fibre of her being the most rosy and golden hope.

"Will I wait for you, Gavon! Do you mean it?" she asked.

"I mean it," he said slowly. "Will you be my wife when I return home, Kitty?"

"I will go with you," she said. She took his hand in both her own and clasped it with feverish intensity. "You must not go alone. I will go with you."

"We cannot be married between now and Saturday," was his next remark.

"We can," she said, "by special licence. And what is money worth? I will go with you; you shall not go into danger alone."

"Wives are not expected to go with their husbands."

"With you, or without you, I will go south," she said. "And is it true that you really love me, Gavon?"

"I have always cared for you," he said then, very slowly, "and I will marry you when I return, Katharine."

"Before you go," she replied.

He shook his head.

For a wonder, Katherine Hunt was standing alone on a balcony; she had no cavalier close at hand—the daughter of the millionaire was to all appearance, for the time being, neglected. A man came close to her; she turned, and saw Captain Keith. There was a change in his face. She did not know whether he looked glad or sorry. He just came up to her and said briefly,—

"I should like to tell you something,"

"What is it?" she answered.

"I am going to marry the Silver Queen. Will you congratulate me?"

She gave a quick start; then she said quietly,—

"I congratulate you with all my heart. I trust she will make you happy."

"She is very fond of me," he said. "I hope we shall be happy. Thank you for your congratulations."

"Will you marry before you go south?" was her next remark.

"Certainly not. Can I take you anywhere?"

"No. I came out here to be alone. Don't tell anybody where I am. It is delightful to be in a crowd like this, and yet to be alone. I congratulate you again, Captain Keith. You said the other day that you were without chivalry. I think you have a great deal. Good-bye. Will you think I am taking a liberty if I say, 'God bless you'?"

"Indeed I do not," was his answer.

She held out her hand; he wrung it and went away. A moment later he had left the ballroom.

Katherine Hunt sat on alone.

"This dazes me," she said to herself. "He doesn't love her. Is she worthy of him? I must find out something else too," she thought impatiently, and now she looked towards the crowded ballroom.

Presently a man appeared—a tall man, with a florid face.

"Major Strause!" said the girl.

He came towards her at once. He had paid court to her assiduously for some time, always without the slightest result. She detested the man, reading his character well enough. He was delighted at the welcoming tone in her voice, and went quickly to her side.

"Is there the most remote chance of your giving me a dance?" was his first query.

"I think not," she answered. "My card has been full for a long time."

"Then may I at least have the privilege of staying with you until your next partner arrives?"

She was silent for a minute; then she said quickly,—

"You may stay on one condition."

"What is that?"

"I want to be introduced to a young lady, one of the guests."

"What young lady?"

"She is known as the Silver Queen. Her real name is Katherine Hepworth."

"What! Keith's young lady?" said Major Strause.

"Captain Keith," corrected Katherine Hunt.

"Captain Keith, if you like. We happened to be brother officers for a time in the same regiment. I thought he seemed very much taken with her the other day. But what can I do for you with regard to Miss Hepworth?"

"Will you bring her to me to be introduced, or shall I go with you? I want to see her, to speak to her, to look at her."

"Why this romantic interest?" queried Strause. "I do not know that there is anything very special about Miss Hepworth. She has a sister worth twenty of herself—a very fine girl indeed. Still, she is pretty, and, I believe, will have money."

"What has money to do with it?" asked Katharine Hunt. "I don't want to see her because she has money. I want to see her in order to speak to her. Can you introduce me?"

"I will try. Will you stay where you are? and I will, if possible, bring her back to you."

Major Strause re-entered one of the reception rooms Katherine Hunt waited in the balcony. Her heart was beating fast.

"I am curious—wonderfully curious," she said to herself. "I want to find out."

A moment later she heard a man's voice and a girl's silvery laughter. She turned. A girl with a radiant face—a face which beamed happiness on all around her—stood by her side. Major Strause performed the necessary introduction.

"I wanted to see you so badly," said Anne Boleyn. "Will you come with me, beautiful Silver Queen?—Major Strause, will you keep guard? I shall be everlastingly indebted to you." The major frowned; he evidently did not care for the rôle assigned to him. "And will you dine with us to-morrow night?" added Katherine. Whereupon his face cleared. He liked his dinners at the Hunts', and Katherine was quite cordial.

The two girls retired into a little alcove close at hand. They were in comparative solitude in this position, and what they said to each other could not be overheard. Katherine Hunt looked full at the excited, beaming, happy face of the Silver Queen.

"I am going to leap over conventionalities, and come direct to a subject which must be very near your heart," she said.

"What is that?" asked Kitty.

She looked with interest at Katherine Hunt. She had never seen her before, but she liked her face.

"You are one of those blessed ones," continued Miss Hunt, "whose privilege it is to help a man in a great emergency. All we girls in these ballrooms know that many of those we love best will soon be exposed to danger, to hardship—perhaps to death."

"Why do you remind me of it?" asked Kitty. She trembled as she spoke.

"Because such thoughts must have come to you: because I guess—nay, I know—your secret. I met Captain Keith a few days ago. He is engaged to you. He asked me for my congratulations."

"Did he?" replied Kitty. She held out her soft hand impulsively. "Congratulate me too," she said. "I can scarcely realize my great happiness. Yes, I am engaged to him, and if possible we will be married before Saturday, and I mean to go south with him."

"I don't know whether to admire or to upbraid you," said Katherine Hunt. "Sometimes a woman best shows her love by effacing herself."

"Mine is not that sort of love. It is selfish; I don't pretend to deny it," replied Kitty.

"I am sorry to hear you say so, for Captain Keith deserves an unselfish devotion. Shall I tell you how I first became acquainted with him?"

"Please do." Kitty leaned back as she spoke. She felt quite restful and very happy. All was right at last—her daring step had been crowned with success. Even the dress of the Silver Queen had been worth buying at the cost of honesty, for was not the prize she had coveted in her hand?

Katherine Hunt read the eager and charming face as though she would sift all its thoughts to the very bottom. She noticed, even in that moment of bliss and exultation, certain lines about the lips, certain weaknesses in the contour of chin and neck, which would develop into something more than weakness by-and-by. She felt a curious desire to wring this girl's secret from her. She knew that she was in a measure cruel, but she could not desist.

"I will tell you," she said, "it is such an exciting story. Do you know that on Thursday of last week—yes, I remember quite well, it was Thursday—I lost my purse."

"Your purse!" said Kitty. She half rose; but Katherine, with a very light, detaining hand, kept her seated.

"When your partner wants you he will find you out. Major Strause will be sure to see to that," she said.

"I beg your pardon," said Kitty. She sat back again. "Your purse!" she said. "I think the present style of pockets very unsafe."

"I did not lose it in that way. I had gone to my bank and drawn a hundred pounds. I had a few shillings in the purse at the time. My purse had the initials 'K.H.' in silver on it. It was a Russian leather purse. I left it in a hansom. Curious to say, I, who am one of the most reckless of girls, took the number of the hansom. It was 22,461. I had just got an invitation to go to Kenmuir House. My father had been angling for the invitation for some time. I was most anxious to go. I was wild with delight, and hurried off to my dressmaker, Madame Dupuys. Did you say anything?"

"Curious," said Kitty. "I—oh, nothing."

"Nothing! Do speak."

"She happens to be my dressmaker too—that is, if you mean Madame Dupuys in Bond Street."

"I mean the same. She made your exquisite dress, did she not?"

"Yes. I am sure I ought to go back to the ballroom."

"How uninteresting of you not to listen to the end of my story! But I will be quick. And I have not yet come to Captain Keith's part."

"But Gavon—"

"Who is Gavon?"

"Captain Keith's name is Gavon. But Gavon can have nothing to do with the story of your purse."

"You would certainly think not; but wait until you hear. I went to Madame

Dupuys and put my hand in my pocket. The purse was gone! I made a great fuss, and said that I would go straight to Scotland Yard, as I happened to remember the number of the cab. I went there, but could get no tidings. The cabman had not brought the purse there; but as the number of his cab was known, the police said that they would look him up. I gave full particulars and returned home. I hoped to get my money back, and I expected some one to come to me from Scotland Yard with tidings at any moment. The hours passed, however, and no one came, and I was considerably annoyed. I am rich, but my father would be angry if I lost so much money. In the afternoon Captain Keith called to see me. I saw him. He said that he had called to restore me my lost money. He was sorry he could not let me have the purse as well. What is the matter?"

"My partner must be waiting for me," said Kitty. "And this place is too close," she added. "I cannot breathe comfortably."

She staggered out of the little retreat, and Katherine Hunt noticed that her face was as white as death. Major Strause was within view. Katherine led Kitty on to the balcony. She did not say anything more about the purse.

CHAPTER XIII.
KITTY'S PROPOSAL.

A week after the events related in the last chapter Katherine Hunt was standing in her pretty sitting-room. It was about eleven o'clock in the morning. She had ordered her carriage to come round at half-past eleven. She meant to do a round of shopping, and afterwards to visit a hospital in which she took an interest, in East London. She was already dressed, in a smart jacket and pretty hat. She was drawing on her gloves, when the servant threw open the door and announced Miss Hepworth, and Kitty Hepworth came in.

Kitty's face was white, and all the joy and happiness which had beamed in it when Katherine first made its acquaintance, on the night of the fancy ball, had left it. She came up to Katherine, clasped both her hands, and said impulsively,—

"If you cannot help me, no one can."

"Do sit down, Miss Hepworth. Your visit astonishes me very much," said Katherine.

"When I tell you what I have come about, you will be still more astonished. I want you to do something great—tremendous. I dreamt of you last night. I dreamt of you three times running, and every time yours was the helping hand, yours the sustaining touch. I came to you without telling Aunt Louisa. I have come alone. Are you going out?"

"Yes; will you come with me?"

"You must not go out; we can talk best here. Countermand your carriage—that is, if you are going to drive. I claim this morning from you. You have forced yourself into my affairs, and I claim this morning; it is my right."

"I have forced myself into your affairs!" said Katherine Hunt. "What do you mean?"

For answer Kitty plunged her hand into her pocket.

"Here is your purse," she said. "You got back the money, and now here is the purse. Pretty, is it not?—soft Russian leather, and your initials in silver! Here it is back."

"My pretty, pretty purse!" said Katherine. She took it up, handling it with affection, and then put it down. "Now, what does this mean, Miss Hepworth?"

"Call me Kitty. We must be friends in future. Don't you want to ask me something?"

Miss Hunt thought for a moment; then she crossed the room and rang the bell. The servant appeared.

"Send a message to the stables, Jameson, and say that I shall not require the brougham this morning," said the young lady. "And, Jameson," she added, as the servant was about to withdraw, "don't admit any one. I shall be particularly engaged for the next hour or so."

The man promised compliance, and left the room.

"Now, Miss Hepworth, I am at your service," said Katherine Hunt.

Kitty was still standing. She was a forlorn-looking little figure. Without a word, she now raised her hand, pulled the pin from her hat, and put the hat on the table. Her pretty, curly hair was all tossed and untidy. The pallor in her small face was very marked, the black shadows under her big, dark eyes very apparent. Her sweet lips, too, had a sorrowful droop. But there was a queer, strange determination about the little creature which Katherine Hunt, knowing her story, as to a great extent she did, could not help, in a curious manner, respecting.

"You saw me a little over a week ago at Kenmuir House," continued Kitty. "You saw me on the happiest, the greatest night of my life—the night of my engagement."

"Ah! did Captain Keith propose for you that night?"

"He did; and I accepted him. I hoped he would propose that night. I hoped the dress would do the business. That was why I—" she turned very white, but her words came out bravely—"that was why I stole your purse."

"Sit down, Kitty," said Katherine, "sit down. If you grow any whiter you will faint, and I don't want you to faint on my hands."

"You knew that I stole the purse, and that was why you told me the story of it," said Kitty then.

"I did not know, but I wanted to know. I beg your pardon for my unwarrantable and cruel curiosity."

"Another person would have been still more cruel. And you may know; I don't mind your knowing. I did it because I love him."

"You will forgive me, Miss Hepworth, but it was a strange way of showing your love! Were you so poor—in such distress—that you must take my purse? Did you realize that you might get the driver of the hansom into serious trouble?"

"I never thought of the driver of the hansom; I only thought that the money which I needed was put into my hands by Providence."

"Rather say by the devil!"

"Very likely. And yet," said Kitty, "it did achieve its purpose."

Katherine Hunt was silent.

"Shall we agree," she said then, after a long pause, "not to speak of this any more? You know, and I know, and Captain Keith knows. Whatever your motive was, the deed is done. The money has been restored to me; even the purse has been restored. Shall I forget, and will you forget? I think he at least will act as if he forgets."

"But he can never forget—never, never!" said Kitty Hepworth.

"We must all act—we three who know must act as if we forgot," continued Katherine Hunt. "You may rest assured with regard to me. I did not respect you the other night—I will own it—but I respect you now. You were brave to bring back the purse, and you were still braver to acknowledge that you did what you did. I respect you, and I will act as if I quite forgot. Is that why you have come? If so, rest assured—all is well."

"I came for this; but this is only a small matter compared with what I want to say now," said the girl. "Don't you wonder—that is, if you think of anything at all in connection with me—why I am here to-day?"

"No; why should I wonder?"

"And yet I told you I was engaged to Captain Keith!"

"You told me, and he told me. By-the-way," continued Katherine Hunt, "of course I ought to wonder. He has left, has he not?"

"He sailed on Saturday, and my sister Mollie, who is one of the nursing sisters, has gone too. Gavon is ordered to Dundee, in the neighbourhood of Ladysmith, and Mollie is ordered straight to Ladysmith, where there is a hospital, and where the wounded are to be taken. I wanted to go with Mollie, but she would not hear of it; I wanted to go with Gavon, but that also was impossible."

"I thought there was a possibility of your being married before he left?"

"I wanted it, but Aunt Louisa would not hear of it. Gavon left me to her care, and he left her to my care. I have said good-bye to him, and he thinks I shall not see him until the war is over; and he knows that there is a great, a dreadful possibility of his never coming back. But he does not know me after all, for I cannot rest under such terrible conditions. I must follow him."

"But, Miss Hepworth, surely this is madness! If you love him, you will sacrifice your own feelings rather than put him to needless pain."

"I love him," said Kitty, and there was an obstinate note in her voice, "but not in that noble, heroic sort of fashion. I love him—I suppose selfishly. I cannot keep away from him; I must be close to him—by his side. Sometimes I am visited by a fear—oh, I won't tell you; there may be nothing in it—but I don't want him to be alone with—with *Mollie*. And I want to go—to be close to him! I will go to Ladysmith. He is certain to get to Ladysmith sooner or later. I shall sail in the next ship that goes to Durban, and get to Ladysmith by hook or by crook!"

"You are plucky," said Katherine, "only I don't think you are right. On the contrary, I think you are wrong; but, all the same, you are plucky."

"I am glad you think me plucky," replied Kitty. "And now I come to my great request—my request—and the reason of this visit."

"Well, my dear?"

"I want you to come with me."

"I!" said Katherine Hunt. "What in the world do you mean?"

"Oh, you must, you must! I have thought it all out, and I am determined to win you over; for women like you, strong, and brave, and daring, are wanted in a time of war. You must go in some capacity—in some fashion. Oh, won't you, Miss Hunt, won't you? And won't you take me with you? You are rich, and strong, and young. Won't you, won't you go?"

"You are mad, Kitty Hepworth!"

"Perhaps I am. Anyhow, I want you to go. If you don't, I will go alone, and then perhaps I shall fail. I may never get to Ladysmith, for the country is already, they say, in the hands of the enemy; but if you come with me I shall succeed. Think of it; think it over for twenty-four hours. We must leave here on Friday. Oh, will you come? You have nothing, surely, to keep you at home; and it means so much to me. Will you promise?"

"You ask me, calmly and coolly, a girl whom you scarcely know, to leave my father and go with you on a wild-goose chase!"

"It is not a wild-goose chase. It would be in your case an act of nobility. You can make some excuse to your father; you can arrange things. I will give you just twenty-four hours; then I will come for your answer. If you go with me, I shall be all right; if you don't go with me, I shall go alone. Now think it over; don't say no at present." As Kitty spoke she rose. "I dreamed of you three times last night," she said, "and you seemed to be the way out—the only way out. I feel, somehow, that you will go."

As she said the last words she held out her hand to Katherine Hunt. Katherine grasped it; then she looked into the little face, so childish, so obstinate, so weak, and yet so strong. She drew Kitty towards her, and laid a light kiss on her forehead.

"Although you stole my purse I kiss you," she said. "Now, never again will we allude to this."

"And you will think it over?"

"You certainly are the most startling, original, impossible child!"

"But you will think it over?"

"I will think it over."

"And may I come to see you to-morrow?"

"Come at this hour; but don't be too terribly disappointed, Kitty, if I am obliged to say no."

Kitty smiled; her smile was radiant. She raised Katherine's hand, pressed it to her lips, and ran out of the room.

Kitty let herself out of the great house. Katherine Hunt was so stunned that she forgot the ordinary duties of hostess. It was only when she heard the slight bang of the hall door, which Kitty made in shutting it after her, that she seemed to awake from a sort of dream. She sank down on a sofa, clasped her long, slender fingers together, and was lost in thought. How long she thought she never knew, but she was roused at last by the servant announcing lunch.

She went into the dining-room. Her father often came home to lunch, and he was present to-day.

"My dear Kate," he said, "are you well? Is anything the matter?"

"I am well," replied Katherine, "but there is a great deal the matter."

"My child, what?"

"I will tell you to-night, father. Shall you be dining at home to-night?"

"Yes, if you wish it. I had thought of dining at the club; but if you wish it, Kate, I will come home."

"I should like you to come home; I may have something to talk over."

Mr. Hunt agreed.

"Just as you like, of course," he said. He looked hard at her, and an uneasy sensation stirred within him.

She was the idol of his life; she was all the child he had ever had; she represented everything that made his money valuable. He was a rough diamond—a rough sort of man in every sense of the word. But he was tender, and gentle, and chivalrous to Katherine. He had always been tender and chivalrous to her. He respected her; she was a good girl, and he knew it. He trusted her implicitly. If he had a dread in life, it was that some day she might leave him; she might do what in his opinion all worthy women did—seek a husband and a home of her own. He did not want this. The thought of her marrying did not annoy him, but the thought of her leaving him was almost unbearable. If only he could secure a son-in-law who would be submissive—who would be satisfied to live at home, to share the big house with Katherine and himself—then, indeed, he would consider himself a lucky man. But no such son-in-law had ever loomed across his horizon, and he was not the man to seek one. He was a keen business man, but he could do nothing towards making an establishment for Katherine. His dread now, as he looked into her face, was that a son-in-law of the undesirable sort—a man who would want to take his one ewe lamb away from him—had appeared; that Katherine had found her mate, and was going to leave him.

"For if she does want to go, I can't refuse her," he thought. "Although it break my heart, I can't refuse her anything."

So he went away a little anxious and slightly perturbed. Katherine would not ask him to come home to dinner for a mere nothing.

Meanwhile that young lady thought out her thoughts, and having arranged them compactly and neatly to her own satisfaction, she proceeded to act. She was very sensible, very wise. She was also very clever. From her earliest days she had possessed a talent for writing. She had written smart articles more than once for the different newspapers. She was rather in request as society correspondent to a weekly, which, for the purposes of this story, we will call *The Snowball*. *The Snowball* had on several occasions published a series of papers by this young lady, and now Katherine Hunt drove straight to the office in order to interview the editor.

Times were busy for newspaper people. Newspaper proprietors and editors were at their wits' end as to how to shove and push into their papers all the interesting items with regard to the war which were pouring in by Reuters and every other telegraphic agency. The editor of *The Snowball* would not have seen any other outside correspondent that day; but Katherine Hunt was a valuable contributor to his paper, and he sent a message that he would spare her a few moments. She entered his office in her usual bright, brisk fashion, and came to the point at once.

"I want to make a request, Mr. Henderson," she said.

"What is that, Miss Hunt? We have no room for your special line of work just now; every scrap of available space is required for war intelligence. Where this war will end God only knows! The impression amongst most people is that with a small force we shall bring the Boers to their senses; but I, for one, think that the future of the war is larger, and involves more serious issues, than most of my *confrères* seem to think. What can I do for you?"

"I called to say that I am going to South Africa on Friday," said Katherine Hunt.

"You!"

"Yes. I want you to give me the proud position of your war correspondent at Ladysmith."

"Miss Hunt!"

"I should make a good correspondent, and will send you the news as direct as I can."

The editor hesitated.

"Our circulation is scarcely large enough to warrant our meeting your expenses," he said then. "I could not pay much for the articles."

"It is not a question of money," said Katherine, rising. "Pay me what you think fair; but the remuneration need not stand in the way. If you decline my offer, I shall go to the office of *The Sparrow* and make the same proposal to its editor. I should like to write for you, or for some paper, because I should go out to South Africa in a more assured position as a war correspondent.

That is all."

A moment or two later Katherine left the office, having got the post she coveted. The editor knew that he would be a madman to refuse so golden a chance.

CHAPTER XIV.
AWAY TO THE WARS.

Mr. Hunt came home in good time. Katherine was an excellent housekeeper, and she had the sort of dinner which he loved. Rich as they were, Katherine was not by any means too proud to see after small domestic matters herself. It is true she had a *chef* as cook, but that did not matter. He and she consulted every morning with regard to the bill of fare. The man respected the girl, and the girl was not unreasonable to the man; they pulled well together. Such was the case with all Katherine's servants. She was free-handed, but firm; she was liberal, not extravagant. They liked her because they respected her, and they respected her because they liked her. The wheels of the establishment were well oiled, and went smoothly. Katherine never parted with her servants except for marriage or ill-health.

The father and daughter now sat down to their nicely-appointed meal.

They were alone. Hunt had resisted the temptation to bring home a couple of his own special cronies to dinner. Katherine and her father always dressed in the evening. Katherine's dress was simple and girlish, but her neck was bare, and she wore short sleeves. Hunt, in his immaculate white tie and expanse of shirt front, looked imposing, and even handsome. He was the sort of man who may be described as lion-like. He had a big head and a bushy beard. His eyebrows were bushy also, and his dark, well-open eyes were very like his daughter's. He had a firm, massive sort of appearance altogether, and looked what he was—a John Bull of the old type. During dinner he was hungry and a little tired, and while enjoying his meal he did not talk much. Towards the end of dinner, however, he was sufficiently refreshed to look across the table at his handsome daughter.

Certainly Kate was looking her best to-night—the colour in her face was absolutely brilliant; she did not often have such a mantle of crimson to add to her charms. Her eyes were very bright and very dark, and her lips were remarkably firm.

"There's something in the wind," thought Hunt; "she does not wear that mouth for nothing. What can it be?"

The uneasiness which visited him destroyed his appetite for the rest of the dinner.

"By George," he said to himself, "if she is going to come over me with the news of some impossible marriage, I'll—I'll oppose it tooth and nail."

But as Hunt thought of opposing the child so like himself in all her characteristics, he owned to himself that he would have a tough time before him.

Dessert was placed on the table, and the servants withdrew. The moment they had done so Hunt looked straight across at his daughter.

"Have it out, Katie," he said; "don't beat about the bush. What's up? what's wrong? Why are you wearing your mouth in that particular angle? I know you. You are up to mischief, Katie. But out with it, for any sake! Don't beat about the bush."

"It isn't what you think, father," replied Katherine.

"And how do you know what I think, miss?"

"You are imagining," said Katherine, and she gave a smile which was very sad, and which took on the instant all the hardness, and almost all the firmness, out of her mouth—"you are imagining that I am going to tell you that I love somebody better than you, dear old man, and that I am going to

102

leave you for him. But that's not the case, daddy mine—that is by no means the case."

"Then nothing matters," said David Hunt—"nothing." He took out his large white silk handkerchief and mopped his forehead. "I got a bit of a fright," he said. "I will own it—I got a considerable bit of a fright. You don't wear that mouth for nothing."

"I wish you would leave my mouth alone, father. My lips must form themselves into any curves they like."

"They don't go down at the corners for nothing," said the obstinate old man.

"If they were down at the corners during dinner, they had good reason to be," she replied. "I am not going to do what you feared, but I am going to do something else you won't like."

"You are always doing things I don't like. You are at once my worry and my blessing. I don't like your going out so late in the evening to visit the slums; don't like your having those old women from the workhouse to tea once a week; I don't like your—"

"Don't go on, father. You know you do like me to visit the slums, and you do like the old women to come to tea. And perhaps, father, we might arrange for them to come in my absence. Marshall, my maid, knows them almost as well as I do; and on their day out from the workhouse they have nowhere to go, poor darlings, and they do so love their cup of tea and their chat with me, and to sit in a warm room and look at a bright fire."

Katherine paused abruptly; in the midst of her glowing picture she caught sight of her father's face.

"In your absence!" he said—"your absence! What does this mean?"

Katherine paused for a moment. Hunt jumped to his feet.

"I tell you," he said, "you are not to beat about the bush. You have got something at the back of your head. Out with it!"

"I have a very big thing," answered the girl—"the biggest thing in all my life; and there's no going back on it, father. There's no changing my mind. It's got to be done, and I am not prepared with any special reasons. You've got to bear it, daddy."

"What in all the world have I got to bear?"

"I am going out to South Africa, father, as special war correspondent to *The Snowball*."

Katherine made her announcement quietly after all. The beating about the bush had ceased. The blow had fallen with a vengeance! As she spoke she rose, and now she stood a foot or so away from her father, confronting him. Her long arms hung at her sides; her slim figure was drawn up to its fullest height; her eyes flashed defiance and resistance into the eyes of the old man. But the hard lips were no longer hard—they trembled. Hunt's face turned from red to white, and from white to red again, and then he put his hand with a sudden gesture over his heart, and sank into a chair.

"Wha—what did you say?" was his first remark.

Katherine repeated her intelligence. Then she said, after a pause,—

"We sail on Friday."

"Whom do you mean by 'we'? I cannot go with you."

"No; you must stay at home and look after the dollars. You were always a dear old daddy, and the dollars are necessary to our existence. I shall want a good few to take with me. 'We' means Miss Katherine Hepworth and myself."

"Who is Katherine Hepworth?"

"A girl I met at Lady Marsden's—a girl I am interested in. She is also going to Ladysmith, and I am going with her."

"But why to Ladysmith?"

"Because a considerable contingent of our army is assembled in that neighbourhood. We go to be in the thick of—the fun."

"Fun, Katherine!"

"Oh, it is only a word, father. It means one thing to you and another to me."

"And you leave me—you absolutely leave me for this?"

"For no slight thing I leave you," said the girl.

"You are of age; I don't suppose I can legally prevent you."

"You cannot. But, all the same, I would ask your blessing before I go."

"You would leave me, really?"

"For no light thing do I leave you, daddy. Our men, the flower of our manhood, are going to encounter a tough time, and every woman who has a spark of womanly feeling in her ought to help them if she can. I am one of the women who can."

"You are not a nurse," he answered. "This is all tomfoolery—mere sentiment. I am surprised at you, Katherine."

"I am not a nurse; but I have got what every nurse does not possess— enormous health, enormous animal spirits, enormous courage—and I won't fail; I will succeed. And oh, daddy, daddy darling, I am going! Yes, I am going on Friday; and you can't—no, daddy, even if you cried to me—even if you went on your knees to me—you can't keep me back."

"Leave the room," said Hunt.

He pointed towards the door. Katherine, who had come close to him, started back.

"What does this mean?"

"Leave the room; I cannot bear your presence just now. I will come to you by-and-by."

Then she saw that she had caused some emotion within him too mighty to be held down. She knew he wanted solitude, and she left him. She went into her little private sitting-room—the one where she had seen Kitty Hepworth that morning—and there she fell on her knees. She did not sob, but she prayed.

In about a quarter of an hour Hunt came in. His face was quite white.

"Let us talk about *pros* and *cons*," he said.

Katherine pushed a chair towards him.

"What a dear daddy you are!" she said. "Few would treat my wilfulness as you are doing."

He winced when she said a tender word.

"There's a thing that I want to say," he remarked then, "and afterwards I'll be silent."

"What is it, father?"

"You think you are doing your duty. You are very—*painfully* modern. The old ideas with regard to 'Honour thy father and mother' are exploded in this end of the nineteenth century. It is a dull sort of task to stay at home with the old man, and it is heroic, and glorious, and grand to step out of your place and go where God knows you may not be wanted. It is a grand thing to make a fuss, and think that you can help, when all the time you are only hindering. It's a mistaken idea of duty, according to my way of thinking. The old man wants you far more than the army wants you. The old man may—break down." He paused as he spoke, and looked full at Katherine.

She clasped her hands together, and her nails were hurting her tender skin; but the colour in her face did not alter, nor did her eyes fall beneath her father's gaze. He gave a quick sigh, and then resumed his remarks.

"God knows why you go, but you yourself think it heroic—you think you will help?"

"I shall help," she answered. "There is a task to be done, and if I do not undertake it, two lives may be ruined."

"Why don't you confide in me fully, Katherine?"

"Because I can't. Up to the present you have always taken me on trust; you must take me on trust now."

Hunt jumped to his feet.

"I have had my say," he remarked. "To me it is the reverse of filial; to me it savours of sentiment, not of duty. But you go, I take it, in spite of my feelings."

"I am sorry, father, but I do go in spite of your feelings."

"Then we will cease to talk over why you go. We have too little time to talk of the way in which you go. You are a rich woman, Katherine."

"I know it, father."

"Since your mother died I have toiled for you; I have added pound to pound, and hundred to hundred, and thousand to thousand—and all has been for you. And if I died to-morrow, you would find yourself one of the greatest heiresses in London. You would have a cool million of your own—yes, a cool million—to do exactly what you liked with. And if I live another ten years, God only knows how many millions you may have. The American heiresses will be nothing to you. And it's money in consols, mind you, as safe as the Bank of England. And I have done it—I, your father, David Hunt."

"There never was such a daddy," said the girl.

"It seems to me that you don't think much of him. But there, I am getting personal, and I don't wish to be that. But you will understand that, as you have made up your mind to do this foolhardy, mad, and reckless thing, you must do it comfortably—you must do it in the best possible way. There is to be no stint, mind you. When you want to draw on me, draw. I will give you a cheque book, and I'll sign every cheque, and you can fill in any amount you fancy. Can I do more than that?"

"No one else would do as much," she said.

"And you will take care of yourself, Kate? you won't run needlessly into risk? you won't try to catch that abominable fever, which they say tracks our armies like the plague, will you, Kate?"

"I will do my utmost to keep well for two reasons: first, because of you— because I want to come back to you; because each single hour I spend away from you, my heart will be drawn and drawn, as if a great pain were pulling me to your side."

"Don't, Kate; you are abominably sentimental."

But Hunt stretched out his big hand as he spoke, and patted his daughter on her shoulder.

"And also I will take care of myself because I honestly wish to live. I wish to do big things if I can; if not, small ones. But anyhow I want to live, and not to die. And I want to make my life as useful as possible."

"Then sit down, and let us go over the list of things you will require," said Hunt.

When Kitty Hepworth came to see Katherine Hunt the next morning, Katherine Hunt told her that she was going with her.

"And you will never know—never to your dying day—what it has cost me," said Katherine Hunt. "Don't keep me now. Go and make your preparations."

Kitty's face, which had been white when she entered the room, grew rosy as the dawn. She rushed to Katherine, clasped her hands, and kissed them frantically.

"You are so big and so strong," she said, "you are as good as a man. And you are going with me! There are no words in the English language to tell you how passionately I love you!"

"Love me as much as you like, Kitty; all I ask is that, you should not be foolish, and that you should keep yourself straight. If you mean to marry a man like Captain Keith, you have great reason to keep yourself straight. And now go and make your preparations. We leave here on Friday; we have only to-day and to-morrow in which to do what is necessary."

Kitty hurried back to Mrs. Keith, and Katherine began the arduous task of getting ready to leave the country in about forty-eight hours. Without unlimited money it would have been almost impossible, but with boundless resources the task was comparatively easy. And Hunt, having given his consent to his daughter's going, suddenly became almost mild and certainly thoroughly amiable on the point.

He insisted on being with her during those two days. He accompanied her from shop to shop, and made, with the marvellous common-sense which always characterized him, and which his daughter inherited, the most useful purchases. It was necessary to take as little luggage as possible, so "condensation" was his favourite word. "Boil down, condense. Do the thing in the most expensive, but also in the tiniest compass," he would say; and he planned the sort of trunks she ought to have, and the luggage which should go into them: and not one single thing which was necessary to the comfort of a girl travelling through an enemy's country did he neglect.

Finally, on Friday morning, the two girls, both bearing the same initials, met at Waterloo Station, *en route* for Southampton. Hunt was there, and also Mrs. Keith. Mrs. Keith looked broken down and very sorrowful; but whatever Hunt's feelings were, he kept them to himself. Kitty's face was radiant, and Katherine's face was strong. Katherine clasped Kitty's small hand, and bent towards Mrs. Keith, and said earnestly,—

"I will take great care of her. It is a venturesome thing that she is doing; but, on the whole, perhaps she is right."

"Her presence may keep Gavon from risking too much," said the widow; "that fact is my only consolation."

Then the train moved out of the station, and the deed was done.

CHAPTER XV.
THE GIRL HAD KITTY'S FACE.

Two girls were standing in a plain, barely-furnished room in the best hotel in Ladysmith. A trunk made of condensed cane was open, and the taller of the two was bending over it and taking out a white muslin dress. She shook it as she removed it from its place in the trunk, and then laid it on a tiny bed which stood in one corner of the room.

"I will put this on," she said; "then perhaps I shall feel cool. I never knew anything like the heat."

"It is the dust that tries me," said the other girl. "See, I put this blouse on not half an hour ago; and look at it now."

The white blouse looked no longer white; it was speckled all over with a sort of red dust.

"It blinds my eyes," said Kitty Hepworth, "and it makes my throat sore. I tasted it on the bread and butter and in the tea we had downstairs. But after all," she added, "it does not matter; nothing matters now that we are safe here."

"We were very lucky to get through," said Katherine Hunt. "They have moved the camp into Ladysmith, and the siege has practically begun."

"You have not heard, have you, whether Captain Keith is here?" asked Kitty.

The words seemed to stick in her throat. She looked full up at Katherine with a pathetic and longing expression in her pretty eyes.

"I don't know. If he is not here, he will be soon. All the forces are to collect in Ladysmith. We are lucky to have arrived safely. Don't let us think of anything else just now."

"I cannot help thinking of him; you know I have come out for his sake."

"I will make inquiries about him as soon as possible, dear. Now, do lie down and rest. Try to have a little faith too, Kitty. Remember how lucky we were to have got here at all. We should not have been able to do it were I not one of the special war correspondents. There was an awful moment at Durban when I thought we could not go forward another mile. Don't you want to see your sister? I am told that she is occupied all day long in the central hospital. I will go over there presently, and tell her that we have arrived."

"She will be very much startled," replied Kitty. "I don't know that I want her to hear anything about us just yet. I am anxious to see Gavon. Oh, if only I could find out something about him!"

"I will find out all I can about him, and also about your sister. Now, do lie down and rest."

"I suppose I must. How imperious you are getting!"

"I said I would take care of you; and yours is a character which must be subdued, or you will get into trouble. Now lie flat down and shut your eyes."

Kitty made a show of resistance, but was, all the same, rather glad to yield to Katherine's entreaties. She had not been an hour in Ladysmith, and she was as tired as a delicately-nurtured girl could be who had gone through a terrible time in the armoured train. She had been frightened on her dreadful journey from Durban to Ladysmith; she had been hot and choked with dust; she had wondered if her life was to be the forfeit of her rashness. But, strange to say, although some of the convoy were killed, the passengers in the train remained unhurt. And here she was now in the midst of the enemy's forces, having come forward, and being unable to go back. She was in Ladysmith, knowing little of the perils and trials which lay before her. She was tired—dead tired; and as she lay with her eyes closed, she thought with a feeling of satisfaction,

—

"Not all the tears of every soul who ever cared for me could take me back to England. Did not the men who brought us here in the train say that in perhaps twenty-four hours no one would be able to get out of Ladysmith? Well, we are in—in for everything now—and Gavon cannot be far away."

In a few moments the tired girl fell asleep. Katherine, who was moving softly about the room, drew down a blind, opened the door, and went out. She was anxious to consider the position. She herself would have been more than delighted to see Mollie. She had not yet seen her; but Kitty's description of her sister was very emphatic, and she believed that she would recognize her if they were to meet.

She ran down to the entrance of the hotel, where some officers of the 5th Lancers and the Imperial Light Horse were eagerly talking. They all looked at her with some curiosity, and suddenly a familiar face started out of the crowd. A man came quickly forward, and Katherine found herself shaking hands with Major Strause.

"By all that's wonderful," he said, "what has brought you here, Miss Hunt?"

"What brings many another Englishwoman," was her answer—"a *soupçon* of curiosity, a *soupçon* of common-sense, and a *soupçon* of folly."

"Well answered," he replied, and he laughed. He brought one or two of his brother officers and introduced them to Katherine. "I believe," he said then, "that the common-sense will be in the ascendant, and that you will be useful to us. But how did you get here, and when did you arrive?"

A young lieutenant rushed into an adjoining room and brought out a camp stool.

"Sit down," he said. "We all honour you for coming here. We are very glad to see you, and if you are fresh from home, perhaps you can give us some news."

They all looked eagerly at her. A cloud of the horrible red dust entered at the open door. Katherine coughed, and took out her handkerchief to wipe the dust from her face.

"You will find it as beastly as we all do," said the young fellow who had brought the camp stool: "but in time you will get accustomed to it. One does get accustomed to everything, particularly in Ladysmith. We breathe and eat that dust, and we wash our faces in it. In some ways it is capable of doing more mischief even than Long Tom."

He laughed as he spoke, and the words had scarcely passed his lips before a loud report, followed by a screaming noise, filled the air. There was an explosion not far off, but still out of sight. Katherine, unprepared, started to her feet.

"That comes from Long Tom's ugly muzzle," said the young officer; "I call it one of his kisses. He has been very affectionate for the last few hours. But our battery is turned on him now, and will pour deadly shrapnel on him hour after hour. He shall have kiss for kiss."

They chatted a little longer on different matters. The young men were very cheerful, and although it was all too plain to every one that Ladysmith was practically besieged, they did not think that the siege would last long.

By-and-by the other officers went out, and Katharine found herself alone with Major Strause. Strause was looking thinner than when last she saw him, and his face wore a worried expression. Leaning against the nearest wall, he gave her a sentimental glance.

"Well," he said, "it is strange that we should meet here. When last we saw each other, was it not at Lady Marsden's ball?"

"It was," replied Katherine.

"Had you any idea then of flinging yourself into the heart of this war?"

"Not the remotest idea; why should I?"

"Then why have you come? What does Hunt think about it?"

"My father is a brave Englishman, and after the first disappointment he is not sorry that his only child should do her little best for her country. But, Major Strause, you must treat me with respect. I am here as one of the special war correspondents. Without that delightful occupation I doubt if my friend and I could have got here."

"Oh, you have not come alone?"

"No; I have come with a girl, a friend of mine."

Strause looked his curiosity. Katherine had no idea of gratifying it at the present moment. After a time she spoke.

"I am glad to see an old friend," she said, and her big brown eyes had never looked more kindly than they did as they rested on Strause's face at that moment. "I am glad to see an old friend, and when I write to my father, which I mean to do immediately, I shall tell him you are here."

"Do," said Strause, a look of gratification causing his face to look almost good-natured for the time being. "And tell him also that as far as Major Strause can, he will try to make things endurable for you. And now, pray let me know if there is anything I can do at the present moment? You have of course, secured rooms for yourself and your friend here?"

"I have. We are accommodated with the best bedroom in the house, and a very tolerable sitting-room."

"I am glad of that, and this hotel is as comfortable as any. But we are in for an exciting time, Miss Hunt. There is no doubt whatever of that. Our enemy is not to be despised; he has pluck and perseverance, and he is about the best marksman in the world. How long we shall have to stay in this horrid place Heaven only knows. I do declare I think the red dust is our greatest trial."

"Are there many cases of illness here at present, and is the nursing staff well supplied?" Katherine next asked.

"I don't know anything about that. I fancy there are a few nurses, but probably nothing like as many as will soon be required. Many of our men are suffering from the change of life and food, and Ladysmith has an evil reputation besides. Last year there was a good deal of enteric, and there is fever now, and dysentery even, among the regulars. Of course wounded soldiers are being brought in every day, and the central hospital has a good many cases already."

"Have you Red Cross nurses here?"

"One or two. I only know one personally—the finest woman I ever met in my life."

"Her name, please?" said Katherine.

"Hepworth. She is a sister of the pretty little girl whom I always associate with Gavon Keith. By-the-way, we are expecting him with his company any day. Well, this nurse is sister to the little girl Keith is engaged to."

"May I trust you with a secret, Major Strause?" said Katherine suddenly. "That girl is here."

"What!"

"Yes, Kitty Hepworth is here. She has come out with me. She is devoted to Captain Keith; and as she could not come with him, it being against the rules of warfare, she has followed him. Now, I should like to see her sister, and just at first I don't want to say anything to her about Kitty's arrival. Do you think you can help me?"

"Bless me, this is news indeed!" said Strause. "I don't know whether I am glad or sorry."

He paused, and a peculiar expression flitted across his face. He was wondering how he could use Katherine's somewhat startling information for his own benefit. It seemed to him that he saw daylight.

"On the whole, I am thoroughly pleased," he said. "And you want to see Miss Hepworth—Sister Mollie, as we call her? That is a very easy matter. There is no infectious illness at the hospital. If you like to come with me now, I will walk across to it with you and introduce you to her."

Katherine jumped up with alacrity.

"I shall be greatly obliged to you," she said.

She and Major Strause went down the long, irregular street, and entered the hastily put up military hospital. There was at that early stage of the siege a special ward for the enteric cases; surgical cases were attended to in a ward by themselves. The stores and ammunition, and the different comforts for the sick, had arrived, and the nurses were flitting noiselessly about, attending to one case after another.

Katherine entered the long ward, where about a dozen poor fellows were lying in different stages of enteric fever. A girl in a nurse's uniform, carrying a basin of gruel in her hand, was coming down the ward towards her. The girl had Kitty's face, and Katherine recognized her at once. Kitty's face, but with a difference. All the beauty was there, and none of the weakness. The full, dark eyes, the curving sweet lips, the delicate contour of the finely-marked brows, the chiselled and delicate features, were all present. But on Mollie's brow and in Mollie's eyes might have been seen that perfect and absolute self-abnegation which always brings out the noblest qualities of a true woman. She was deeply interested in her cases, and scarcely saw Katherine as she stood in the entrance of the long ward.

Major Strause went softly down the ward, and said a word to the nurse. Katherine saw her give a slight start of surprise; then she handed to the major the basin of gruel which she was carrying. He carried it across the ward, and seating himself on a low stool, began to feed, spoonful by spoonful, a young subaltern who, alas, would never live to see his twentieth year! Mollie came eagerly forward to where Katherine was standing.

"You are Mollie Hepworth; how do you do?" said Katherine Hunt.

"And you are a brave Englishwoman who has come over here to share our ill fortunes and our good," replied Mollie.

She looked Katherine all over. She noted the strength of Katherine's face, and the girl's upright, bold carriage.

"You will be invaluable," said Sister Mollie. "Welcome to Ladysmith. We are sure to have a tough time, but I think in the end we shall be victorious. Anyhow, there is that in us which will never say die. If it were not for these poor fellows—my boys I call them—I think I could bear anything. I am in charge of this ward, but, of course, I have nurses to work under me. I shall claim your services, Miss Hunt."

"And most gladly will I give them," replied Katherine. "I can come to you almost at any time. When shall it be?"

"The sooner the better. But Major Strause tells me that you have not come here alone—that there is another lady."

"So there is."

"Will she help us also?"

"I don't know. Perhaps. I will tell you about her presently."

CHAPTER XVI.
WELCOME HER, WON'T YOU?

Ladysmith was hemmed in. Sir George White sent a message to Joubert, asking leave for the non-combatants, women, and children, to go to

Maritzburg. Joubert refused. The wounded, women, and children, and other non-combatants, might be collected in a place about four miles from the town, but would not be allowed to go further. All those who remained would be treated as combatants. Sir George White advised the town to accept the proposal, but his advice was indignantly rejected. Everybody's life was in danger, therefore, for the Queen. The proposal to leave the town was flung back with defiance. There was no more going out. Until help came, the inhabitants of Ladysmith were besieged by the enemy.

Meanwhile, day after day, Long Tom did his deadly work. Shell after shell entered Ladysmith and exploded, carrying consternation and death with it. Then people became quiet and submissive. Even to danger one can get accustomed. The excitement had subsided to something not exactly like despair, and not resembling indifference, but to a state of mind midway between the two. The inhabitants of Ladysmith tried to go about their usual occupations. The women still kept their houses tidy, and their children washed and well fed; and every one hoped that relief would come any day or any hour. And the soldiers fought as only English soldiers can fight; and the Boers were brave as enemy could be, and more and more closely surrounded the town. Even the Naval Brigade, splendid fellows all of them, could not deliver Ladysmith, although beyond doubt they kept the enemy in check.

Meanwhile Kitty remained in her rooms. She became a sort of mystery to the other people in the hotel. Mollie Hepworth had not the slightest idea that her sister was close to her. Gavon Keith, with a contingent of his men, had arrived. Kitty longed to see him; but the strangest nervousness was over her. What with the dust and the heat, and all her fears, and the dangers through which she had travelled, the girl was suddenly prostrated with a kind of malarial fever. There was a time when Katherine feared that it would turn to enteric; but watching Mollie Hepworth's patients, she soon saw that she had nothing to apprehend on that score, and resolved to nurse Kitty herself.

She could not understand the wayward girl, so plucky, so determined to join her lover while in England, and yet now so overcome with nervous terrors that she dreaded him to know of her arrival. Whenever a shell exploded in Ladysmith, Kitty screamed, covered her face with her hands, sat up in bed trembling all over, and asked Katherine, who seldom left her, if the hotel were still intact.

Katherine had much ado to put up with Kitty's fears, and quite longed for the time when the girl would be well enough to leave her enforced imprisonment and take what small pleasure lay before her in the beleaguered city.

There had come a day of general attack. Early in the morning Long Tom

116

had spoken, and Lady Anne and all the other Naval Brigade guns replied at once. The firing went on for hours, and finally the enemy were repulsed. But it was a day of horror to all in the brave little town; and when night came, Katherine, who had been busy helping Mollie with the sick and wounded, and doing all that woman, could to lighten the strained situation, came into Kitty's room. She had left Kitty much better—had given her all that was absolutely necessary for her comfort; had cheered her up as best she could; had offered her a yellow-backed novel to read, and left her, hoping that she would drop asleep. She came back to find the frightened girl partly dressed, half fainting, and leaning against the wall of the room.

"Now, Kitty, what is it?" said Katherine, in a tone of expostulation. "You know you are not fit to get up. What is the matter?"

"I had an awful dream," said Kitty. "After you went I fell asleep as you meant me to do, and I dreamed a long, terrible dream all about Gavon. I thought he was killed. Is he killed? Is it true? I believe it is. Oh, I was so terrified! Is it true?"

"It is not true," replied Katherine.

"But I am so frightened; and there is something in your face which makes me think you are hiding something. He has been wounded!"

"Kitty, sit down," said Katherine. "Sit down and stay quiet. You had no right to try to get up; you are too weak."

"I am a miserable, good-for-nothing girl, but I will be good if only you will tell me that he is safe."

"You ought to have seen him long ago. Now that you are here, I cannot understand your attitude. Your illness has made you nervous."

"I will be good if only you will tell me the truth. Is he—is he wounded?"

"I will tell you the truth," said Katherine, in a brave voice. She looked at the trembling, weak, terrified creature with eyes large with compassion. "Here, drink this," she said. She poured out a restorative which had always a soothing effect on Kitty, and brought it to her. "Drink it, my dear; you will want your courage. But things are by no means so very bad. Captain Keith has had a slight wound—nothing at all dangerous. He is in hospital. He must remain there for a few days, and—"

"And Mollie is nursing him?"

"Thank God, your brave sister is there, doing all she can for every one."

"Don't look at me as if you meant to despise me, Katherine. I sometimes see that look in your eyes, and it makes me so sick."

"I don't understand you, Kitty. I admired you in London, for I thought that, whatever happened, yours was a true and a great love, and I always respect sincerity in anybody or in anything. But since you came here—"

"It is all my nerves," said the poor girl. "It is the bursting of the horrible shells, and the terror that one will come through the roof."

"Well, and if it does come through the roof?"

"Katherine! Why, we should all be killed."

"What of that? we can but die once. Oh, you must lose your fear of death if you are to be any good at all in Ladysmith. And look here, Kitty, I mean you to be good—I mean you to be of use. What is a woman, strong and in her youth, doing in a place of this sort if she is not of use? We are going to have a very terrible time; I don't pretend to deny it. We are hemmed in closer every day. The enemy are coming up in greater and greater numbers. The Boers are no fools, let me tell you. They know how to fight, and they know how to endure. They have the courage, some of them, of ten men, and they are fighting for their country. And they mean—yes, Kitty, they mean to take Ladysmith if they can. Of course they won't take it, for we will never, never give in. But if there were many of us like you in this place, why, we'd be indeed a poor lot!"

Kitty turned white. Her handkerchief was lying near; she took it up and wiped the moisture off her brow.

"I wish I was not so—shaky," she said, in a tremulous voice.

"You poor little thing! I am sorry I spoke harshly, but I have been seeing so very much of real life all day. Those poor fellows—not a murmur out of them! And oh, the agony some of them have endured! And then I come here, and I see you with a whole skin, in a comfortable room with food and water within reach, crying because you have a fit of the nerves. But I know people who get these nervous attacks are to be pitied. And I do pity you, poor little Kitty; only I want to stimulate you to courage."

"I will be good," said Kitty faintly. "Help me to dress."

Katherine hesitated for a moment. It was between nine and ten at night; the heat of the day was mitigated. Long Tom had ceased firing; until morning there would be comparative peace. She took Kitty's wrist between her finger and thumb, and felt her pulse.

"Your fever has gone," she said; "you are only weak, I have got some bovril here. I will make you a cup, and then—"

"Yes, what?"

"Then I am going to take you to the hospital."

"O Katherine!"

"Yes; to see Captain Keith and your sister Mollie. I hope you will be helping Mollie this time to-morrow night."

Kitty was so excited at Katherine's daring proposal that the colour mounted at once into her pale cheeks.

"I wonder if I dare," she said.

"Dare or not, you have got to come—and to-night. Here's your bovril." Katherine brought her a cup. She had heated the water with her spirit-lamp. "Drink it. That is a good girl."

"Things are so horrid!" Kitty moaned; "I have no appetite for the coarse food here."

"O Kitty, you are very lucky to have any food. The supplies are by no means unlimited, although at present we have not felt the stint. Now, then, I will help you to dress."

She went to one of the trunks of crushed cane and brought out a white skirt and white blouse. She helped Kitty to put them on, and she herself brushed out the girl's dark, pretty hair, and arranged it becomingly around her head.

"There, now," she said. "Have you got a blue sash anywhere? A girl in white with a blue sash will be a sort of angel in the wards to-night. The moment you enter one of the wards, if you are worth anything at all, Kitty Hepworth, you will forget yourself."

"And you are quite, quite certain that none of the awful shells will come into Ladysmith to-night?"

"Quite certain; we have some hours of peace and safety."

Kitty looked fragile and lovely when Katherine had dressed her. She herself also put on a neat and becoming dress, but she took care that Kitty's beauty should be the chief focus of attraction. She then took the girl's hand and led her downstairs. The mystery about the sick English girl had come almost to fever height amongst the officers and nurses, who principally inhabited the hotel. Many people glanced now at Katherine, whose face was quite familiar, and at Kitty, whose face was unknown, as they went slowly by. Major Strause suddenly burst out of the smoking-room.

"I say!" he exclaimed. "Miss Hepworth, you here!"

He pretended that he had not until now known of Kitty's arrival in

Ladysmith.

She gave him her hand indifferently, raised her pretty eyes to his face, and then dropped them.

"I am going to Gavon," she said. "He is wounded, and I must go to him."

"Only a flesh wound—nothing of any importance. He must lie up for a day or two.—Shall I go across to the hospital with you, Miss Hunt?"

"No, thank you," replied Katherine; "Kitty and I can manage nicely alone. —Now, Kitty," she said, as the girls went down the street, "you must remember that Sister Mollie knows nothing of your arrival here. She will be very much astonished when you walk into the ward, and perhaps a little hurt with you for keeping things dark from her."

"I shall like to see her," replied Kitty; "and if she is nursing Gavon, I of course will help her. It is my place to nurse him, is it not, Katherine?"

"I should say yes. I am glad you feel it in that way."

Katherine could not help a note of sarcasm coming into her voice.

She and Kitty entered the hospital. A moment later they found themselves in the long ward. Kitty's face turned white. Had she thought of herself, she might have fainted; but just then her eyes were arrested by seeing a girl bending over a sick man, holding a stimulant to his lips, and speaking cheering words. The girl was her sister; the man she was bending over was Captain Keith.

With a cry—a curious mingling of delight, and suffering, and absolute self-forgetfulness—Kitty, in her white dress and blue sash, looking something like a fashionable London girl and also something like an angel, ran down the long ward and approached the side of the sick man.

"Gavon," she said, "Gavon, I am here! I have come.—Mollie, I have come —Kitty has come."

Mollie Hepworth had often said that nothing could ever take her by surprise—that she was, owing to her education, and perhaps also to her temperament, prepared for any emergency—but she was sorely tested at the present moment. Her first wild thought was that Kitty was dead, and that this was her wraith come to visit the sick ward in the beleaguered town of Ladysmith; but one glance at Kitty showed her that it was a very living girl with whom she had to deal. She stifled the inclination to cry out; she showed no surprise, and putting her finger to her lips, gave a warning glance at the excited girl.

"He is very weak from loss of blood," she said; "don't startle him."

120

Gavon Keith had been looking full up at Mollie while she was ministering to him. Her touch brought him comfort, the look in her eyes brought him strength. The next instant he encountered eyes like hers, a face like hers, but without the strength, without the power to give comfort. He had a sick feeling all over him that in his heart of hearts he had no welcome for Kitty; and then, weak as he was, he struggled to subdue it. His eyes lit up with a faint smile; but the effort was too much—he fainted away.

"Sit down quietly," said Mollie—"there, in that corner, where he can't see you when he comes to. Of course you shall be with him. But I have no time to ask any questions now.—Miss Hunt, give me the brandy, please, and that bottle of smelling-salts."

Katherine Hunt brought the necessary restoratives, and Mollie bent over the wounded man just as if Kitty did not exist. The faint was a bad one, but after a time he recovered consciousness. Mollie held his hand and stroked it gently.

"Did I dream anything? Was it all a mistake?" he said, in a low whisper.

She bent over him.

"It is no dream," she said. "Your little Kitty, whom you are engaged to marry, is here. She has come out all the way from England for love of you. She has encountered grave danger and difficulty and the possibility either of death or imprisonment all for love of you. She will stay by you part of to-night. Welcome her, won't you?"

"Kitty!" said the wounded man; and then Kitty bent forward, and he smiled at her, this time without fainting.

After this incident Kitty Hepworth was established as one of the extra nurses in the central hospital. Mollie secured her this post, and on the whole it did her good. There was no time in Ladysmith for fainting or hysterics. The minor ills of life had to be put out of sight, for the men and women in that town were face to face with a great tragedy.

CHAPTER XVII.
MAJOR STRAUSE.

Just about this time there was a curious change observable in Major Strause. Hitherto his character had been all that was contemptible. He was deep in debt; he was met at every turn by money difficulties. He was also a confirmed gambler. In order to keep himself in any degree straight, he had stooped to the lowest of crimes, and was in every sense of the word a most selfish man. Nevertheless, at the present moment no one could consider Major Strause selfish. When he was not absolutely engaged in his military duties, he spent his time in the hospital. He turned out to be not only a clever but also a tender nurse. He did exactly what Sister Mollie told him; he even sat with her worst cases at night; and was, she could not help expressing it, invaluable.

The fact was, two things had happened to Major Strause. In the first place, at Ladysmith his most pressing creditors could not trouble him; therefore, for the time being at any rate, he was not up to his ears in money difficulties. The second thing was this: he had fallen in love, passionately in love, with Sister Mollie. He was not a particularly young man—in fact, his years were very little short of forty—but until he met Mollie he had never honestly and truly, and as he thought unselfishly, cared for any one. He was not a marrying man, and if he thought of matrimony at all, he certainly thought of it as an aid to a fortune. If he met a rich, very rich girl who would have him, why, then, his money troubles might cease to exist. He certainly would not, under any circumstances, marry a poor one.

But love will work wonders even in natures like Major Strause's, and he no longer thought of money in connection with a possible wife. He knew well that Sister Mollie had little or no private means. He was fond of saying to himself that, when he looked at her brave and noble face, he ceased to think of money. The more he thought of her, the more deeply did he love her. He dreamed of her at night; to be in her society by day was heaven to him.

This was the real secret of the change in the major. It was because of Mollie he had become unselfish, a useful nurse, an invaluable servant of the Queen. Mollie improved him not only as a nurse, but also as an officer. He would rather do anything than catch the scorn in her eyes. So he fought bravely, and led his men to the front in the sorties made against the Boers. His brother officers began to like him, and even Keith, who quickly recovered from his wound, wondered what had come to the major. He was an old enough man to keep his emotions to himself, and neither Mollie herself nor Keith—who listened for Mollie's slightest footfall, who lived on her smile, who was consoled by her touch—guessed for a single moment that Strause cared for her.

Both Keith and Strause just then were playing a difficult game: for Keith, while engaged to one girl, devotedly loved another; and Strause was endeavouring by every means in his power to hide that part of him which was unworthy from Sister Mollie's eyes. Both men, after a fashion, were succeeding. Mollie, in the stress and strain of her present life, had more or less forgotten the curious story Keith had told her with regard to Strause. She was destined to remember it all too vividly by-and-by, but just then she was glad of his help. She learned to lean upon him, and to consult him with regard to those cases of delirium and extreme danger which were brought into the little hospital day by day.

The other nurses all depended more or less on Mollie, and she took the lead in this time of great peril.

As to Keith, his task was even more difficult than that the major had assigned to himself; for if ever there was an *exigeante* and jealous girl on the face of God's earth, it was Kitty Hepworth. She expected the undivided attention of the man she was engaged to. He liked her, and was intensely sorry for her. He was touched by her devotion to himself, and he did all that man could to render her stay in the beleaguered town as happy as it could be. He did not know until afterwards how much he was indebted to Katherine Hunt for his measure of success. She was possessed of enormous tact. She had the wisdom of ten ordinary women. When she was not writing accounts of the siege for *The Snowball*, she was attending on the sick and wounded, visiting the inhabitants of the town, cheering up the frightened mothers, comforting the children, helping to give out the rations. There was nothing that this clever and unselfish girl could not put her hand to; there was nothing she did not do more or less well.

As to Keith, he rejoiced when he saw her entering the hotel. He could be affectionate to Kitty, who had very little to say, and listen to Katherine's brilliant conversation; and Kitty could not be jealous of Katherine, try hard as she might. After the first week she got a fresh return of the malarial fever, and was from that moment more or less exempt from giving her services to the sick men in the hospital. Thus she seldom saw Keith in her sister's presence, and in consequence her fears slumbered, and she tried to believe that she was the happiest girl on earth, and that no one could be more loved than she.

But with such dangerous elements at work it was scarcely to be expected that this time of peace and apparent security could be of long continuance. Strause was not the man to hold himself in check long, and Keith began to find the yoke which tied him to Kitty more galling every day. When all was still at night he often went across to the hospital; he felt safe to go there then. Kitty was asleep in her room in the hotel, Long Tom was not troubling anybody; but the sick and dying were wanting help and consolation, and, what was more important to Keith, although he did not dare to whisper it even to himself, Mollie was there. He might do some trifle for her; he might help her in an hour of need.

There came a night after one of the many battles when such a number of wounded had been brought to the hospital that every nurse in the town was requisitioned to look after them. The enteric cases were also getting more and more numerous; there was not a bed to spare. Keith resolved to sit up all night in order to give what help he could. He met Mollie at the door of the enteric ward.

"I am at your service for to-night," he said.

"Thank God," she answered. "We shall need all the help we can get."

"Which ward shall I go to—the surgical or enteric?"

She looked around her. They were standing just then at the entrance to the surgical ward: the doctors, two or three of whom were present, were busy attending to the suffering patients; an amputation was going on behind a screen in a distant corner; the groans of the dying reached the ears of the man and woman as they stood so close together, and yet so truly far from each other. Keith, even at that extreme moment, thought of the tie which bound him to Kitty; and Mollie, as she raised her eyes to look into his face, felt a great throb of her heart. How manly he was, how brave, how all that a woman could love and worship!

Just at this instant she raised her hand and laid it on his arm.

"Will you not go and rest for an hour?" she said; "you look terribly spent."

"And you?" he answered, "are you never tired out?"

"Oh, don't think of me; I am happy in my work."

"And I in mine," he replied. "It is for our country and our Queen. I can hold out; I won't leave you."

"Thank God!" she could not help saying; and as she said the words, Keith for one instant, carried out of himself, laid his hand on hers.

She coloured all over her face, looked full up at him, and her brown eyes filled with tears.

Strause, who for the last hour had been busy and invaluable in the enteric ward, came upon this scene. His deep-set, dark eyes grew suddenly bloodshot. He gave an evil glance full at Keith, looked at Mollie, who did not even see him, and went back again to his duties. But the sleeping devil was awakened; and the man, although he did not fail for one instant during the livelong night to do what was necessary, and no sufferer within reach missed his accustomed nourishment or his necessary medicine, was all the time plotting and planning how he could best foil his enemy, Captain Keith. Having injured Keith for his own purposes—having cast the blackest of imputations upon his character—he was naturally the young man's enemy. And now Keith had dared to look with unmistakable fervour into the clear brown eyes of Nurse Mollie! Strause trembled all over as he thought of it.

"He is a scoundrel. I need no longer feel remorse. He is engaged to one sister, but he loves the other," thought the major. "I will spoil his game for him. He shall never have my Mollie; she shall be engaged to me before

125

twenty-four hours are over."

In the early dawn of the coming day, just before Long Tom began his murderous work, Mollie stood for a moment outside the hospital. She was feeling faint after a night of great anguish and terror. Many souls had gone up above the clear stars to meet their Maker during the hours which had passed away. Mollie thought of the anguish which would fill hearts at home for the gallant and the brave who had given up their lives for their country. One poor young fellow, in particular, had given her a last message to his mother.

"Cut off a bit of my hair," he had said, "and give it to me to kiss. Ah, thanks! that is all right. Tell her I was not a bit afraid, that I remembered the —*prayer* she used to teach me, and I feel somehow that—that it is all right, you know. Put the hair in a bit of paper and send it to her. Be sure you tell her it is all right. You know it is, don't you? *Be sure* you tell her."

And Mollie had promised, and the boy had closed his blue eyes and gone off to sleep like a baby. Now he was dead, and Mollie had the little lock of hair pinned inside the bosom of her dress. She was standing so when Strause came up and stood by her side. He gave her a look, saw that she was very faint and tired, and rushed into the little surgery, where restoratives, beef tea, bovril, etc., were to be found.

He mixed a cup of bovril, and brought it to her.

"Drink this," he said. "You are doing more than mortal woman can be expected to do. You must go and lie down for a few hours."

She drank the bovril and returned him the empty cup.

"Thank you. How good you are!" she said.

"Who would not be good to you?" he replied.

She did not answer; she was looking far away. He doubted if she heard him. The utter calm, the quietness of her attitude, impressed while it maddened him. His passion rose in a great tide. He suddenly took her hand.

"Don't you know?" he said—"don't you know?"

"Don't I know what, Major Strause? I don't understand," she said, and she gave him a bewildered glance.

"O Mollie!" he cried, "don't you know what I think of you? Don't you know that there is not in all this world a more magnificent woman than you? Mollie, I love you. Mollie, don't turn away. I worship you—I love you—I would die for you. I can't do more. Just give me a vestige of hope, and there is not a thing I would not do—not a thing. Say you love me back—say you love me back! Look at me. O my darling, my darling, how I love you!"

"Hush!" she said then; "you have no right to use such words. And now, who can think of such things? Major Strause, forget you ever said them."

"Forget," he said, "when my heart is on fire! I cannot see you without the maddest passion rising up in my heart. I have loved you from the first hour we met. Only give me hope, and I won't worry you until we are out of this horrid place."

She turned white, and leaned against the wall. His words were just the straw too much, and the next instant she burst into a flood of tears. When the strong and the brave give way, it is always a painful sight, and now Mollie's tears were as the final straw to Strause. He could not stand them. The next instant he swept his strong arms round her.

"You shall give me what I want," he said—"one kiss. Give it to me at once. You will drive me mad if you refuse."

These words acted as a cold douche: she recovered her self-control in a moment. Disengaging herself from his embrace, she backed away from him.

"I am sorry for you," she said. "You are mistaken. I could never by any possibility love you. Forget that you have spoken."

"You can never love me!" he said. "Do you mean to tell me that you—reject me?"

"We won't talk of it, Major Strause. But yes, it is only kind to put you out of your pain. I am sorry for you, very sorry, but I can never marry you."

"Has any one been maligning me?"

"No; and you have done splendidly since you came here. We have all admired you. You don't know what the nurses think of you, and how loud they are in your praise. Don't, don't spoil everything now, just for a personal feeling. Who can think of himself at moments like these. Be brave right on to the end, and let your conscience be your reward."

"That is all too high for me," he cried. "It may suit you, Sister Mollie, but I am not made of that stuff. I came to the wards because of you, and for nothing else. Do you think I wanted to give my strength nursing those fellows, and sitting in those beastly smelling wards, drinking in enteric poison and all the rest? No; I did what I did for you, Sister Mollie, and you are bound to give me something as my reward. You had no right to encourage me."

"I never did," replied the girl.

"Didn't you though? Yes, and what's more, I believe you would have had me but for— Oh, I know what's up: you care for that other chap."

"What do you mean?"

"You are in love with Keith, although he is engaged to your sister. Now listen."

"Hush!" replied Mollie. She was not white any longer; she was strong and rosy, and there was a proud light in her eyes and a firmness about her lips. "I won't listen to you," she said—"no, not another single word. I am utterly ashamed of you!"

There was a scorn in her tone which stung him. He held out his hand to detain her, but she re-entered the hospital. For the rest of that day he saw nothing of her. He did not attempt to go back to the hospital. He retired to his own tin hut, where he cursed and swore, and finally drank himself into a state of oblivion.

In the evening four companies marched across the open grass land towards Observatory Hill, and Major Strause was amongst them. They marched in fours towards the foot of the hill, and then began to climb up. Not a word was spoken, and the Boers did not give a sign till the men were within twenty feet of the top. Then the firing began. Our men fixed swords and charged to the top with splendid cheers. Major Strause was amongst the bravest of that gallant band, but all the time, while he fought and rushed forward and appeared to forget himself, he was thinking of Mollie Hepworth. What mattered his bodily sensations? There was a thirst which raged round his heart greater than any danger. He was determined to get Mollie. She must be his even if she did not love him.

"I shall frighten her into it," he said to himself. "I have a good case, and I will put it to her. She cares for Keith; any one can see it. What are women made of? A spiritless chap without funds—I have drained most of that wretched legacy—and yet there are two women madly in love with him! It can't only be his handsome phiz; a woman like Mollie Hepworth wants more than mere beauty. Keith, in my opinion, is not half a man. If he were, he would never sit down under the imputation I have fastened on him. Well, he has done for himself now. It will stick like a burr when the time comes, and come it will if I can't get Mollie without its help."

As Strause thought these thoughts he raised his eyes, and saw Keith with a company of his men a little way off. Keith was rushing forward—he and his men with their swords fixed. The Boers were firing heavily. Just by sheer dash and consummate bravery Keith and his men took the position, and the Boers were driven back.

"It is because he believes that she loves him," thought the major. "If a man were sure of that, it would give him such courage that there would be nothing he would not dare. All the same, he did it bravely; I am the last to deny that fact. He will get his V.C., and then he'll be more a hero than ever with those two women. Once I get her I'll leave him alone. There are two things which I can do—two strong levers which must be brought to bear upon the position. They are like great siege guns in their way, and they will carry the fort, the fort of a woman's heart—yes, if I am not greatly mistaken."

The major bided his time; and as though to aid him just then, there came an incident which certainly was in his favour. He had come unscratched out of the sortie, but he had caught a chill, and fever of a slight character supervened. He immediately suggested that he should be moved into hospital. There happened to be a vacant bed, and the major occupied it. Now Mollie would nurse him; she could not avoid him when he was ill and suffering. His eyes followed her as she walked about the ward. To his distress and dismay, however, she appointed Katherine Hunt to look after the angry major.

Katherine was now almost as often in the ward as one of the trained nurses. She had a head on her shoulders, and could do anything that a girl might be supposed capable of doing. When the major was brought in, she had gone to Mollie and told her.

"Your friend Major Strause is down with fever," she said: "I suppose you will take his case?"

Mollie coloured, and a wistful look came into her eyes.

"I think not," she answered.

"I will look after him if you wish," said Katherine eagerly.

"I should be so much obliged. I don't suppose he is very ill, and I cannot leave the surgical cases to-night."

Accordingly Katherine was the one who gave Major Strause his medicines, his cooling drinks and his other comforts. He bore with her for a time. There had been a moment when he would have given ten years of his life to have Katherine Hunt, the daughter of the millionaire, waiting on him. But his passion made him impervious to money just now, and he felt that if all the riches of the world were to be offered him with Katherine, and Mollie were to come to him penniless, he would choose her. But next best to Mollie was Katherine Hunt, and he determined, if possible, to make her his friend.

"Why does not Miss Kitty Hepworth do her share of the nursing?" he said towards morning, when Katherine had time to linger by his bedside for a moment.

"Because she is not strong enough. We have had to forbid her to come to

129

the hospital," replied Katherine.

"She is a poor sort; don't you think so?" said the major.

"I certainly do not," replied Katherine, with some indignation.

He looked at her, and gave the ghost of a smile.

"I know why she doesn't come," he said.

"There is no mystery about it," replied Katherine. "She is anything but strong. We have to look after her."

"When is she going to marry Keith? Why don't you hurry on the wedding?"

"We don't have weddings in Ladysmith," was the girl's reply.

"I don't see why you should not; there are parsons here, and all the rest. It would be about the best thing possible for Miss Kitty. I'll let her know as much when I see her."

"I hope you won't do so much mischief, Major Strause. Kitty is content to be close to Gavon. No wedding could be contemplated for a moment."

"She's likely to lose him if she doesn't look out."

Katherine did not even ask him what he meant; she stood and fixed her eyes upon him. He shuffled under their clear gaze.

"Look here," he said, "I'd like to do you a good turn. You are very fond of Miss Kitty Hepworth, are you not?"

"Of course I am," replied Katherine.

"You would not like her heart to be broken?"

"Certainly not."

"And in the most insufferable way," he added. "But I won't explain myself now, Miss Hunt. You and I have been good friends at home."

"We have been acquaintances at home," replied Katherine. "I am afraid, Major Strause, I have no more time to give you just at present."

"Oh, don't go, for mercy's sake!" He stretched out his hand and tried to catch her dress. She moved away from him.

"You forget yourself," she said haughtily.

"I don't," he replied. "But stoop down. I am a desperate man. Why are you nursing me?"

"Why am I nursing you!"

"Yes, why?"

"Do you disapprove of my services?"

"No; you are first-rate—a grand girl! I did not know it was in you when I saw you in town. I thought you were just one that was well supplied with worldly pelf. I did not know you had what I see you have. Now, Miss Hunt, if you will do me a good turn—why, one good turn deserves another, and you will never regret it, never. I want to see Sister Mollie. I have something that I wish to say to her—something which will save a great deal of trouble. Will you send her to me? At this hour most of the patients are quiet: anyhow, you can stay in the surgical ward. All I want you to do is to send her, and just keep the other nurses a little away. Will you?"

"You are disturbing the patients, talking so much."

"But will you?"

"I will do nothing of the sort."

"I'll get up then myself and find her."

"Oh, don't talk nonsense, Major Strause. I believe you are delirious."

"Yes, I am. I am very bad indeed—very bad. You are a good nurse, but you don't understand all cases of illness. Send Sister Mollie to me."

His face was nearly purple, his eyes bloodshot. Katherine touched his arm —it burnt like a coal. She suddenly felt alarmed.

"All right. Do stay quiet," she said. "Don't wake the other poor fellows. Ah! there's that poor boy Hudson; he has only just dropped asleep. Oh, I will do anything rather than disturb the ward. Stay quiet, and I will bring her to you."

CHAPTER XVIII.
PEACE AFTER STORM.

"You must go to him," said Katherine.

"To whom?" asked Mollie.

She was looking very white: she had gone through a night of intense anxiety and ceaseless work. The poor fellows around were dying fast. One man after another succumbed to his wounds and to the hardships of the last battle. Those who were still living were very ill indeed. Mollie felt as if all her world were hemmed in by the shadow of death. The mysteries of life and of death were close to her, and all the trivial things of daily existence seemed miles and miles away. She raised her big and beautiful eyes now, and fixed them on Katherine's face.

"Who wants me?" she repeated.

"Major Strause," was Katherine's reply.

"I had forgotten about him," said Mollie. She put up her hand to her forehead. "Must I see him?" she asked.

"He seems to be very ill. His temperature has gone up; he is in for a sharp attack of fever. Nothing will quiet him but your presence."

Mollie gave a sigh.

"I will go to him," she said. "Will you stay here until I return?"

Katherine nodded, and Mollie went slowly down the ward. One ward led into another. The dying men looked at her as she walked. She had a slow and dignified step; there was never any undue haste or hurry about her. It calmed the delirious men even to look at her. Her hand was always cool, too—her touch always firm. She entered the ward. Hudson was weak and very, very ill, but his face lit up when he saw the girl.

"Come here, you angel, come here," he said in a whisper, under his breath.

"Come here, come here," said Major Strause.

The face of the lad who was soon to see his Maker, and the face of the angry, worldly-minded major, were both visible to Mollie as she approached.

"Hush!" she said to Major Strause. She raised her finger warningly, and bent over Hudson.

"I am better," he said, with a smile.

"Yes, I think you are," she said. But as she spoke she swallowed something in her throat; for she had learned by this time to discern, and she saw on the white face, and on the worn brow which illness had made so prominent and thin, the unmistakable shadow. The great wings loomed above the dying man; soon he would be folded in their embrace, and all the sorrows of earth would pass away from him.

"I am sorry for the folks at home," he said in a whisper. "If I die they will grieve; but I shall not die—I am better."

"Yes," said Mollie. She spoke firmly, and he did not see in her face any of the knowledge which she dreaded.

"I don't want to die," he said; "I want to live. Last night I thought I'd like to die, for the pain did grind so; but now I want to live. There are my father and mother, and I have a young sister. Her name is Ethel. She is so pretty. You remind me of her. She is only sixteen, and she is very clever and very pretty; and she has a look of you—or, rather, you have a look of her. It will be all right. I'll get well, won't I, Nurse Mollie?"

"Drink this," said Mollie. She poured a restorative into a teaspoon.

He shook his head.

"I'll get well," he repeated. "But I cannot swallow; my throat is closed up. All the same, I am much better."

"Yes, dear," she said.

She knelt down by him and took his hand. She laid her finger on his pulse —it scarcely beat. There was a cold dew all over him.

"Oh, I am much, much better," he said, smiling, "and—where am I? Where's mother? Where are you, governor? I am back home. George, your son, has come back. We have had a grand victory—the Boers utterly routed.

Hurrah for the British flag! Where am I? Oh, here in the sick ward at Ladysmith. Sister Mollie?"

"Yes, my dear lad."

"Sing to me."

"Oh, I can't," came to her lips. But she never uttered the words. "What shall I sing?" she asked.

"My mother's favourite hymn, 'Peace, perfect peace.' It is peace, you know—wonderful—all the pain gone—not a bit thirsty—sure to get well—going—home; invalided home, you know. Peace! Yes, sing it, won't you?"

Mollie sang the first verse,—

    "Peace, perfect peace, in this dark world of sin."

"Sing it louder," said the poor lad; "I can't hear you. Wonderful! how quiet it is! And it is dark—night—yes, it is night."

"No, dear," she answered; "it is morning."

"Morning! then I am much better," he said "Peace—yes, the morning brings peace." The words died away. "Much better," he said again, after a pause. "Going to—get—*well*."

As he uttered the last words Mollie bent forward. She laid her fingers on his eyelids and closed them down. Then she motioned to a nurse who stood a little way off. She turned to Major Strause. His eyes were shining—there were tears in them.

"God bless you! God bless you!" he said

"What do you want with me?" she answered.

"Nothing now. You have quieted me; you have stilled my evil passions. Do you want to go on stilling them? Do you want still to be an angel in the ward?"

"You are very ill, Major Strause," said Mollie. "Let me take your temperature."

She did so. His temperature was high—104°. She laid her hand on his forehead.

"You have been exciting yourself," she said. "I don't believe you have got enteric; it is just a bad chill. I am going to give you a soothing draught and a compress. Now stay perfectly quiet."

"Won't you nurse me, instead of Miss Hunt?"

"I cannot; my place is in the surgical ward."

"Can't I be moved in there?"

"No, you must not; there is too much noise, and some of the sights are— You must stay here, Major Strause. Try to control yourself, won't you?"

"If you will come to see me twice or three times a day I will. What's that?" He looked around him in a frightened way.

A nurse had brought a screen, and was putting it round the bed where the lad Hudson had breathed his last.

Mollie took the major's hand.

"I will come to see you," she said; "and you will try to be good?"

"For such an angel I would do anything. Oh, I have been bad—yes, I have been very bad; you don't know half. Is there any chance for a worldly chap like me? Not young, either. When I heard you talk to that boy, I felt I would give all the world to be that boy myself."

"If there was a dear lad on this earth, it was George Hudson," she answered.

"I know—so different from what I am! I am not even young, you know, and I have led a—"

"I cannot stay now, Major Strause.—Sister Eugenia, will you look after Major Strause, please? he wants—"

Mollie gave quick directions. The young sister bowed her head. The major made a wry face. He could be good in Mollie's presence, but he did not think he could be good with Sister Eugenia, who was small, and plain, and awkward.

Mollie left the room. All that day the effect of Hudson's death remained with the major, and as Mollie did come into the ward two or three times in the course of the morning, he tried to believe himself satisfied. But when the dead man had been removed for burial, and when his place was occupied by another man, uninteresting, coarse, not particularly ill, Major Strause forgot his good resolutions. He grumbled, and gave the nurses who looked after him a bad time. When Mollie came in he was soothed and comforted, and he could express his feelings to Katherine Hunt. In a day or two the fever left him, and he was able to crawl about a little, and then, as his bed was wanted, to get back to his own hut. Still, the memory of what he had seen Mollie do when Hudson was dying remained with him, and, for the time at least, he gave up all idea of persecuting her, or forcing her, as he expressed it, to listen to his suit. He had no intention, however, of giving Mollie up.

"I will live for her sake, and try to lead a clean life for her sake, and in the end I must win her," he thought. "She is better than any money—she is worth her price in rubies. She is the finest woman God ever made."

The major might for a time have had strength to keep these resolves, had he not once again seen Mollie and Gavon Keith together. They were talking just at the door of one of the wards, and they did not touch hands this time. But the major saw the light in Mollie's eyes, and could not mistake its import. The moment he observed this there fell away from him, like a mantle, all the good resolves of the last few days. He would do something, and at once.

He passed the couple, who started aside when they saw him, and strode away to the hotel where Kitty lived. He asked boldly to see Miss Hepworth. The servants of the hotel were busy in those days, when every one had his or her special duty to perform. One of them said carelessly,—

"You will find Miss Hepworth in her sitting-room;" and he ran upstairs and knocked at the door.

A girlish voice said, "Come in." He turned the handle and entered.

Kitty was lying on a sofa, in just the position where she could get what little air there was. The heat was intense, and the red dust was more irritating than ever. It lay on the table, and made a pink shade over the cup and saucer out of which she had taken her last meal; it made a pink shade also on the girl's dark hair and on her white blouse; but it did not take any of the prettiness out of her big brown eyes, nor any of the refined delicacy from her beautifully-chiselled features. The strong likeness to her sister Mollie was very apparent at this moment, and Strause uttered an exclamation, which he suddenly checked.

"I never guessed it," he said to himself.

"How do you do, Major Strause?" said the girl. "Do you want anything? I am quite alone."

"I called to see you, Miss Hepworth, because I thought you would be alone," was his reply.

Already his anger against Mollie was more or less abated; but he lashed it up again, for he said to himself,—

"If I don't take extreme steps I shall lose her. I have a great deal to tell this little miss, and tell it I will."

"Why did you utter that exclamation when you came into the room?" said

Kitty.

"Because you are so like your sister," he replied. "You know I have been in hospital for the last fortnight. I am better, but I am confoundedly weak. Would you think me very rude if I dropped into a chair?"

"Oh, please seat yourself," said the girl. She gave a dreary sigh and looked out of the window. "It will soon be dark," she said. "The only peaceful time in Ladysmith is when it is dark! Do you think the enemy will make an assault and try to take the town at night, Major Strause?"

"Oh, bless you, no," said the major. "The Boers like to fight under cover. They won't attack us; at least that is my belief."

"But I heard some of the officers saying to-day at dinner that the Boers did fight sometimes in the open, and that they might make an assault on the town. I heard them say so—I did really," said Kitty.

"Well, they talked nonsense; don't you believe a word of it," said the major.

He felt himself quite manly as he sat not far away from Kitty and looked avariciously at her face. Her likeness to Mollie made this quite an agreeable task. She shuffled uneasily under his stare, and turned once more to look out of the window.

"It is so dull in Ladysmith," she said then, with a sigh. "I never knew a siege meant this."

"What did you think it meant?" asked the major.

"Oh, nothing like this," she repeated. "I thought there was great excitement, and that everybody kept close together, and that—"

"There is plenty of excitement, if that is what you want," said Major Strause.

"Well, it doesn't come to me," answered the girl. "I spend all my days here. I am awfully frightened, too. I am terribly afraid of the shells. Do you think one of them will strike the hotel, Major Strause?"

"Can't tell you; hope not."

"Well, that is poor comfort," said Kitty, and she gave a dreary laugh.

The major was not getting any nearer the object of his visit. This would never do.

"If I were you," he said, "I would go into the hospital and make myself useful."

"I cannot; they have turned me out."

"Who have?"

"Why, Mollie, my sister, and—and Gavon."

"Oh, indeed! And did they give you a reason?"

"They said that I was nervous and would not make a good nurse. And they are right," she added. "I am nervous. I quite screamed when I saw a poor man brought in one morning with his leg shattered. He was unconscious, and my scream awoke him, and he looked at me. Oh, I see his face still! He was dead in an hour, and I never saw anything like the reproach that was in his eyes! They haunt me. He thought I was afraid of him—and I was—and his eyes haunt me! No, I am not fit to be a nurse."

"I don't think you are," said Strause. "You are a delicate little thing, not a bit like your sister."

"Oh, Mollie is so strong—she is almost coarse," said Kitty.

"I don't think there is anything coarse about her. I wish you could have seen her the other morning. It was quite early, before daylight, and a poor chap was dying, and she sang to him."

"Oh, please don't tell me about dying people, it is so melancholy."

"May I ask, Miss Hepworth," said Strause, "why you came here at all?"

"Can't you guess?" she answered, and she flushed a very rosy red. "To be near Gavon."

"Do you see much of Captain Keith?"

"Yes, a good deal. He comes in most evenings. He has not been in yet to-night."

"You are desperately in love with him, aren't you?"

Kitty sighed, then she smiled, then she put up her hand to sweep away the curls from her forehead.

"Oh yes," she said then; "of course I am. We are going to be married."

"I wonder," said the major, "if you would thank me for a piece of information?"

"What? what?" she asked eagerly.

"Something to do with Captain Keith."

"What do you know about Gavon?"

"Something. Would you thank me if I told you?"

"I'd like to hear it very much. I don't believe you know anything bad of him."

"Nothing exactly bad, and yet something important—at least for you. I can tell you if you will make me a promise. I think you ought to know it, too, but I can only tell you if you make me a promise."

"And what is that?"

"That you will keep it dark that I told you. I must have your promise; then I have something of great interest to say."

"You quite frighten me," said the girl. "What can it be? Something about Gavon, and something, I see by your manner, not quite good. And I am to make you a promise."

"You can act in any way you like, but you are never to tell who told you. And if you give me your promise, I will take you a little bit into my confidence, and you and I can work together. You won't find it dull in Ladysmith when you and I have made our little plot to stick together and work together."

"But I don't at all know that I want to work with you, Major Strause."

"Oh, it isn't a love business—nothing of that sort."

Kitty flushed and looked annoyed.

"It simply means that you and I want to hold what we have got."

"To hold what we have got!" repeated the girl.

"Yes, that's about it. You and I want to hold our possessions tightly; and I think we can if we make a little league to work together."

"All right; let's make a league," said Kitty. "It really is exciting, and while you talk to me I forget Long Tom."

"Before we do anything you have got to make me your promise."

"Yes; what is it?"

"That you will never, under any circumstances, tell anybody that I have informed you of that thing which I know."

"Of course I won't."

"That kind of loose way of answering won't suit me. You must answer me solemnly; and remember, before you make the promise which I am going to make you give me, that if you break it you bring a great deal of bad luck not only upon yourself, but upon Keith."

"Oh, I would not do him harm, my darling, for all the world!"

"Well, see you don't. You will if you break your vow."

"Vow!" said Kitty; "must I make a vow?"

"You must, and pretty sharp, too, if you want me to tell you what I know."

"All right," said Kitty, who was now overcome with curiosity. "Of course I'll do what you require."

"Then say these words after me: 'I promise that whatever happens—'"

"'I promise that whatever happens,'" she repeated.

"'I will never tell that Major Strause was my informant with regard to Gavon Keith and Mollie Hepworth.'"

As Strause uttered the last words Kitty's face turned white as a sheet. She sprang from her reclining position, and stood before the major with both her hands tightly clasped.

"'Gavon Keith and Mollie Hepworth.' Oh yes, I will make a thousand promises if necessary. I will never, never tell. Thank you, Major Strause, thank you. And now, please tell me."

"You will do him an injury if you break your vow. You must say, 'So help me, God.'"

"'So help me, God,' I will never tell."

"Then this is my information: it will pain you, but not more than it has pained me. I have been in the hospital, and I know. You can find out for yourself. Your sister Mollie is in love with Captain Keith, and Captain Keith is in love with her."

CHAPTER XIX.
IN THE HOSPITAL.

Kitty was supposed to be weak; but when this information was quietly given her by Major Strause, she showed no weakness. Even the pallor left her face, giving place to a rosy red. Just for an instant she staggered; then she regained her self-control, and sat down on her sofa.

"Don't sit on that chair," she said; "come near me and tell me why—why you said such an awful thing as that to me."

Major Strause replied by giving Kitty a full account of the two occasions on which he had seen Mollie and Keith together. He described with vividness and power that hand-clasp and those few words, and then with greater power he got his excitable hearer to understand the look which filled Gavon's eyes and the look which filled Mollie's eyes on the next occasion when he had seen them together. And Kitty, who had been jealous of her sister from the first, gave a heavy, very heavy sigh.

"You need not tell me any more," she said. "I know you are right. I know you have just said what is the truth."

"And you are satisfied to sit down under it?" was the major's remark.

"No, I am not."

"Yet you must be. You are willing to give up your lover to your sister. Your sister is a very fine woman, a very noble woman, and you are willing, for your sister's sake, to submit to this act of extreme renunciation."

"Never!" said Kitty, "never!

"Ah, now you speak with spirit. And the renunciation is not necessary, believe me. You can, if you will take my advice, keep your lover for yourself."

"Yes!"

"I know a way in which you can not only keep him, but get him to love you just as passionately as he now loves Nurse Mollie."

"Do you indeed, Major Strause? If there is such a way, believe me I will take it."

"I think you will. You must listen attentively."

"I will listen," said Kitty.

"In the first place, you must completely change your mode of life. You must not shrink any longer from terrible sights, nor from unselfish actions; you must not spend all your time in this dull, wretched room—any one would get hipped who lived in a place of this sort; you must show your pluck and spirit; you must go back to the hospital; you must learn the duties of a nurse; and you must not leave your sister and Keith alone."

"I will not," said Kitty. Her cheeks were flaming and her eyes shining.

"That is right. You will be twice the girl you are now. You will cease to fear Long Tom when you have so many other things to fear."

"I don't really mind Long Tom," answered Kitty, and as she spoke she gave a shudder. "I think," she added, "that I would almost like a shell to come in and—end everything; for oh, your words have made me so very miserable!"

"I was obliged to speak; but, after all, the very pain you now suffer may be your means of deliverance. It is necessary, absolutely necessary for your sake, to take extreme steps. The thing is serious; it can only be combated by extreme measures."

"What way is that? oh, do tell me! I shall always look upon you as my greatest friend if you save me from the terrible fate which seems hanging over me."

"Remember you are never to breathe that I was your informant."

"I never will."

"Well, you must act with guile. In the first place, you must go back to the hospital. You will soon have proof that your sister loves Keith, and that Keith loves her. Tell your sister, or Miss Hunt, that you are very much better, and that you are going back to the hospital to do what little good you can. If you show tact and spirit, you will soon learn your duties, and your sister will be pleased with you; and what is far more important, Captain Keith will be pleased with you. You will be no longer the pretty nonentity who has come to Ladysmith to be a trouble and a worry. No woman ought to be a trouble and a worry who lives in Ladysmith now."

"Yes, but I don't care to be a heroine. You may think nothing of me, but I really don't. If I act as you suggest, how will it get me back Gavon's love?"

"In the first place, he will cease to despise you."

"Oh, he cannot despise me—my darling cannot despise me!" said Kitty, and her lips trembled.

"I am sorry to have to say it, but I greatly fear he does despise you. If you were to look into his heart, you would find that he does. He has his faults—no one has more reason to know that than myself—but he is not a nonentity. He is a brave soldier, and he would not like the girl he marries to be a coward. Now, while you stay in this room, you are acting a coward's part. Go back to the hospital, reinstate yourself, and see that what I tell you is the truth. You will not be very long before you know. Not that Captain Keith makes love to your sister in so many words—he would not do that sort of thing for worlds— but there is a love which fills the eyes when the lips never speak; and if you watch you will see it, and you will also see the same expression in your sister's eyes, although she also would not speak of her love for worlds. When you see that love in her eyes and in Keith's eyes, the time will have come for you to speak openly to your sister, and that is what I am coming to."

"Yes!" said Kitty.

"Now, Miss Hepworth, I am really going to confide in you. There is one way, and only one, to save the position."

"What is that, Major Strause?"

"Your sister Mollie must marry me."

"O Major Strause!"

"Yes; I love her madly. I love her with the most pure, self-sacrificing passion. I would do anything on earth for her. She must become my wife here, in Ladysmith, and thus *you* are saved. Captain Keith is not the man to love her after she is my wife."

"But if Mollie doesn't love you?" said Kitty, trembling very much, and fixing her eyes full on the major's flushed face.

"She shall love me; and you must bring it about. I am determined to win her. If she won't have me after you have spoken, I have another lever to bring to bear. It will be her mission to save you and to save Captain Keith; for if she doesn't, as there is a God in heaven, you go under, and he goes under. Now I

143

have spoken; now I think you understand."

As the major spoke he rose to his feet.

"But I don't understand," said Kitty.

"That is all you are to understand to-night. Go to the hospital to-morrow. I have spoken the truth. The way to save the situation is to get your sister Mollie to marry me."

"If she doesn't love you, she will not marry you."

"Watch Miss Hepworth; be silent, be wary, watch! and when you see what I know you will see, then speak to her—tell her to her face that she loves him. She will deny it, perhaps, or perhaps she will confess it. If she does, you are to tell her there is only one way out—*she must marry me*! If she refuses, let me know. I shall have another lever to bring to bear. Now, good-night, Miss Hepworth."

The major strode from the room. Kitty looked wildly round her. She was alone, and night was over the scene. Even over the doomed city of Ladysmith the moon shone, and there was a white sort of fragrance in the air, and the dust no longer covered everything. The beleaguered town lay quiet under the wing of sleep—that is, all those slept who were not suffering from enteric, or from deadly wounds, or from the slow, the slow, cruel death of starvation; for already rations were short, and food was precious. The uneasy neighing of half-fed horses came to Kitty's ears as she went and stood by the open window. She did not heed, she did not care; she was selfishly absorbed in her own mad thoughts, her own wild grief.

The door was opened, and Katherine Hunt came in.

"Well, Kitty," she said, "any better?"

"Yes, much better," said Kitty. She turned, and faced Katherine.

"Come over here and let me look at you," said Katherine suddenly.

She took Kitty's hand and drew her towards the lamp. She looked full into her face. Kitty's face was very white, her eyes were too big, and the black marks under them too dark for health. But just now the eyes were bright and the lips were firm, and there was a hectic flush on each thin cheek.

"I thought you looked well, but I doubt if you do," said Katherine. "You look strange. Is anything the matter?"

"No," said Kitty, "no; only, Kate—"

"Yes!"

"I am going to turn over a new leaf."

"I wish you would, with all my heart. Oh, I have brought you something nice for supper!"

"What?"

"A little, precious, precious pot of bovril. You must make it go as far as you can. I doubt if I can get you another."

"I was hungry at dinner-time—we had a very poor dinner—but I am not hungry now," said Kitty; "only I am thirsty," she added.

"Well, you shall have a drink, but you must eat too. A cup of bovril and some bread will make quite a nice supper for you. Don't throw away good food now."

"Is food really scarce in Ladysmith?" said the girl.

"Not yet; but we don't know how long the siege will last. I think Sir George White is anxious; he wants relief to come quickly. It is being strangely delayed. Oh, we are all right, of course, but our enemies are the sort who will sit down and wait for any length of time. They are not a foe to be despised. We are hemmed in, and the provisions cannot last for ever. Milk is the most pressing want just now. I was passing a house, when a mother came out and asked me if I could get her even a very little milk. She said her baby was dying for want of it. I went in and looked at the poor little thing. It had lived for a week on sugar and water. And the orders now are that all the milk is to be kept for the sick, I could not get her any. While I was with her the child had a slight convulsion, and died. That is the sixth baby that has died in Ladysmith to-day."

"How gloomy!" said Kitty.

"Why do you speak in that tone? Aren't you sorry?"

"No, I don't think I am. No; it is best for the little babies. Oh, oh, oh, I am so unhappy!"

She burst into tears. Katherine kissed her.

"Now, cheer up!" she said. "You stay so much alone! You would be much better if you did what I do. Just go about and fling yourself into the trouble, and do your very best for those who are in distress and suffering, and misery and fear—the deadly fear of death. And yet why should people be afraid?"

"I am not," said Kitty; "I was, but I am not. I was going to tell you that I am about to turn over a new leaf. I am going back to the hospital to-morrow."

"Are you really, Kitten?" said Kate, looking with interest at the girl. "And are you going to be a brave kitten—not to cry out if you are hurt, not to be troubled if everything is not quite your way? Are you going really to help? For if so, you can, and you will be all the better for it."

"Yes, I am going to help," answered the girl; "but I don't at all know that I am brave, and I don't at all know that I shan't cry out. Anything is better than sitting in this room and waiting for Long Tom's kisses."

"Mollie will be pleased."

Kitty gave a shudder.

"I never met a finer woman than your sister. Try to copy her, and you will be a blessing in Ladysmith."

Kitty's shudder this time was invisible. She knew that she must act with guile if she would follow out Major Strause's wishes.

Early next morning she put on a clean white dress, tied a big apron round her slim waist, and followed Katherine into the hospital. Katherine took her in with a certain air of triumph. She brought her straight up to Mollie, who was busily engaged dealing out the food necessary for the sick during the coming twenty-four hours. Nurse Eugenia was waiting for instructions; another nurse, who was called in the ward Nurse Helen, was not far off. The two nurses narrowed their eyes, and looked with anything but favour at Kitty as she came in.

"That little hysterical girl! we don't want her here," thought Nurse Eugenia.

"She's too pretty to be useful," thought Nurse Helen. "But, all the same, the men, poor fellows, like to look at her. I wouldn't trust her out of my sight for a moment. But she's pretty, and even that's something."

Kitty did look very pretty. There was a pink flush on her cheeks, and her eyes were very bright. She had scarcely slept all the night before. Long Tom was sending shells at intervals into Ladysmith, and the noise of a great explosion fell upon Kitty's ears now as Katherine took her up to her sister.

"This is the Kitten, and she's going to do more than a kitten's work to-day," said Katherine.

"Ah, Kitty!" said Mollie, "I am glad to see you. But are you strong enough, darling?"

"Of course I am," said Kitty—"quite strong enough. I want to do something. Give me some work please, Mollie. I mean to stay in the hospital."

"There's a poor young man who has been badly hurt in his leg. He is discontented and nervous. Sit down by him and talk to him," said Mollie. "Here, bed number five."

She took Kitty's hand, and they crossed the ward. The young man was a private in one of the infantry regiments. His ankle bone was badly shattered. He had gone through great agonies, but was feeling comparatively easy now.

"This is my sister, Lawson," said Mollie. "She will sit with you for a little. She would like to read you your home letters, and she can write a letter at your dictation if you wish it. Anyhow, she will try to amuse you."

Kitty sat down very shyly. She had her mission full in view. She was not forgetting herself for a single instant, but, all the same, the cases in the surgical ward made her nervous. She hoped no fresh wounded men would be brought in while she was present, and that no operations would take place anywhere within earshot. She felt that her own courage was of the poorest quality, and that if Long Tom sent any kisses in her direction she might shrink.

"But I must not," she said, "for if I do they would turn me out; and it is my only chance to stay here, and—and use my eyes."

"Shall I read you anything?" she said, raising her pretty eyes, as the thought came to her, to Lawson's face.

"If you would, miss," he answered. "I'd like to hear all the home letters read over one by one. Here they are, miss."

He indicated a pile of letters which were pushed under his pillow. Kitty took them out. They were tied with a bit of red ribbon.

"They are from my mother, miss, and my—the young woman I keep company with."

"Oh!" answered Kitty. She looked with interest at Lawson. His mother was nothing to her; but his sweetheart! A fellow-feeling made her kind. "Is she very fond of you?" she asked suddenly.

"Is Annie fond of me, miss?" he replied. "I should think she is just; and I —oh, I adore her, miss! She wanted us to marry afore I come out; but I said best not—best wait till I get back with my V.C. I won't never get that now, miss; and they say I'll limp all the rest of my days."

"I don't suppose she will mind that," answered Kitty.

"Indeed and she won't, miss. Annie wouldn't mind nothing if only she had me with her. Bless her, she's as fine a girl as ever walked. I'm fair hungering to hear from her. It's such a long time since we had any letters. Sometimes I think that's about the worst of anything in the siege. I wouldn't mind having a bullet in my other ankle and starving half my time, if only I had a long, long letter from mother and my brother and Annie. But we don't get letters, nor news of any sort. That's the hardest part of the siege."

"I suppose it is," answered Kitty.

It was not the hardest to her, for those she cared for most were with her in Ladysmith. Nevertheless she appreciated some of the hunger she saw shining out of Lawson's keen grey eyes.

"You'd like me to show you Annie's picture, perhaps, miss?"

"I would like to see it very much," answered Kitty.

Lawson was too ill to move, but he directed Kitty where to slip her hand, and where to find, under his bolster, a photograph-case. She opened it under his orders, and saw a full-faced girl of a common type, with frowsy hair and a showily-made dress.

"Ain't she a beauty?" said the young man. "And she's mine, too—mine. I think a lot of her when I lie awake at night. She'll make me a right good wife. She'll take in washing—Annie's grand at the laundry."

Kitty drew him on to talk. He forgot his pain when he talked of his sweetheart. Kitty did not care to hear him speak of his mother, whom he also loved very much; she thought this kind of conversation dull. All the time, while she listened, her restless eyes darted here and there. She felt certain that she would get very white if Captain Keith came into the ward.

But Keith was not coming into the ward that day. He was fighting for dear life and country outside Ladysmith against the Boers. Had Kitty known this, even the small measure of tranquillity which was hers would have deserted her.

Long Tom continued to send in shells, and Puffing Billy helped him. But Lady Anne answered back, and managed, after a time, to silence Long Tom. With each explosion Kitty gave a start.

"Be you afeard of the firing, miss?" asked Lawson.

"Yes," she answered, with a shudder; "but please don't tell any one."

"I won't, miss; but you ain't no cause to be frightened while you are here. 'Tain't likely they'll send a shell right over the orspital. They know the orspital by the Red Cross flag. No one would be mean enough for that."

"I think they are mean enough for anything," replied Kitty.

"Not so mean as that," answered Lawson, and he shook his head as one who knew.

The firing went on, and presently Kitty, in her alarm, found herself clasping the hand of Private Lawson. He held her little hand tightly in his. He was fond of saying during the next day that the feel of that little warm hand had supported him during the extreme of his pain; for his ankle became dreadfully inflamed, and the agony was intense. After that interview he took a great interest in Kitty. She was the pretty little lady, who was no nurse, bless her, but who was so very human, so very like what he pictured his own girl in his dreams to be. Only his own girl would not have been afraid of the shells, and would have turned to, there and then, to do a lot of laundry work for the sick soldiers. There was no one in the world less like Kitty than this girl, who was brusque, and determined, and strong in character, and faithful and unselfish to her backbone. But Kitty had her uses that day in the hospital, all the same. She supported Jim Lawson through his darkest hour, and just because she was nervous and frightened, for her sake he must keep brave and calm; and God only knew what a hero the little girl made of him for the time being.

CHAPTER XX.
PRIVATE LAWSON.

Kitty was praised by Mollie that night for her endurance during the trying day. Kitty replied with what affection she could, and Mollie said she would come and see her that evening if possible; and tired, excited, but on the whole happier than she had been the day before, the little girl went back to her rooms at the hotel. She slept well, and early the next day returned to the hospital.

The first person she saw there was Gavon Keith. He smiled when he saw her. He was seated on a stool near one of the entrances; his leg was stretched out, and Mollie was bathing it with Condy and water.

"So you are wounded!" said Kitty, white as a sheet. "Is it dangerous?"

"Dangerous," said the young man, smiling, "when I can sit up! My dear Kit, what are you made of? It is a mere scratch,—isn't it, Nurse Mollie?"

"Nothing more," she answered; "but you ought to keep the leg up until to-morrow at any rate."

"I cannot do that; we are safe to have another skirmish with the Boers in the course of the day. They are getting desperate. I am glad they are moving. Anything is better than the terrible quiet of the last few weeks. If we can only induce them to come out of their shelter and fight us in the open, I believe we could force them to retreat. There is that in every mother's son of us which can't be beaten; that's my belief."

Keith smiled as he spoke, and his dark eyes looked away from Kitty across the long ward. Every mother's son of the men looked back at him. Were they not giving up their very lives? On every face was that indomitable look which the British soldier will wear in his time of need—the look which says to the foe, "Come on; I am waiting for you. I am ready; I am not going to cave in. Come on; do your worst." And Keith, whose spirit was boiling within him, forgot Kitty at that supreme moment. But though he forgot Kitty, he did not forget the soothing, very soothing touch of Mollie's light fingers as she bathed the ugly scratch on his leg. She bathed and bathed, and Keith lay back contented. He was very tired and very dusty; and it was delicious to have his wound attended to, and by her. As to Kitty, she was, of course, his betrothed wife; but—he could not help it—she was not in touch with him at that moment.

As to Kitty herself, the curious mingling of emotions which filled her little frame made her almost incapable of speech. Mollie certainly made the very sweetest nurse. She was never untidy; she never looked flushed, or hurried, or discomposed. Her face was as calm when she was breathing comfort to the last moments of a dying soldier as it was at this instant when she was making a brave young officer more comfortable. Nothing ever seemed to disturb Mollie's calm. Kitty sat and watched her. Just at that instant Major Strause strolled through the ward; he was going into the enteric ward. He had leisure, and meant to spend a good morning helping brave Mollie in her work. As he passed through, his eyes lighted on the little group. First at Keith he looked, then with a lingering gaze of awakening passion at Mollie, then with an expression of great meaning at Kitty. Kitty could not bear to feel that there was an understanding between herself and the major. She turned away, but nevertheless his glance had done its poisoned work.

"I wish," she said, trembling a little—"I wish, Mollie—"

"Yes?" said Mollie, looking up. She had just changed the Condy and water for a fresh supply, and the warm, comforting application was causing Keith delicious ease.

"I wish you would let me do that. I could, you know. It seems as if it was my—right."

She said the last words in a whisper. Mollie looked up, startled at her tone. Keith also glanced at her. He seemed to awake to the true position. He shook himself and sat up.

"I forgot things, Kitty," he said. "Yes, of course you shall bathe my leg if you like."

Mollie rose immediately.

"Here is a fresh jug of water," she said; "and you must throw that Condy and water away in a few minutes, and apply a little more.—Then you had better have a cold compress over the wound, Captain Keith; otherwise some of the red dust may get in, and it may get really inflamed."

"All right," said Keith. "I leave myself in your hands.—Now then, Kitty, bathe away."

Mollie looked at her sister in some wonder. Kitty had put a white linen apron over her dainty dress. She stooped down, looking at Mollie as if she wished her to go. Mollie read the expression on Kitty's face aright. She turned aside and went to attend to a young soldier who was lying in great discomfort in a bed opposite.

Kitty began to bathe. Her white fingers were loaded with rings; she had a gold chain bracelet on her wrist. The bracelet dipped into the lotion, the rings became wet, the little fingers were slightly stained. Keith watched her with a growing sense of amusement. What a baby she was! How pretty! how ignorant! How dared she play with matters of life and death? Nevertheless it interested him that she should do so.

"What has brought you back to the hospital again, Kit?" he said. "Are you better?"

"Oh, much better," she answered.

"And you seriously mean to help the nurses?"

"Yes, seriously. Isn't the lotion rather cold?"

"No; it does very nicely. Please don't dab the sponge quite so hard against my leg. Ah! that is better. You would make quite a good nurse if you practised, Kitty."

"I mean to try," answered Kitty, encouraged and cheered by his words of praise.

"But you ought not to wear rings or bracelets."

"Don't you like me to wear my rings?" she said, her lips quivering as she raised a perfectly childish face to his.

"Anything you fancy, little girl."

"I am sure this is too cold now," she said.

He did not reply. She threw the used-up lotion away, and made a fresh one. She was very ignorant, and he was as much so. Instead of two or three drops, she put in a liberal supply of Condy. The water also was hot—too hot for the inflamed leg. She filled the sponge, and put it on. Keith, in spite of himself, uttered a cry. Then he bit his lip and turned very white.

"I don't think, somehow, that is quite right," he said, and he had scarcely uttered the words before he fainted away. Kitty's lotion had burned his wound badly.

Mollie heard his cry, and rushed towards him. She applied restoratives quickly, and spoke to Kitty in a voice rendered sharp with annoyance.

"You did not make the lotion right," she said. "How much Condy did you put in?"

Kitty lifted the bottle.

"Oh, how it discolours my hand!" she said. "It is horrid stuff; why do you use it?"

"It is the right thing to use. Go away, please Kitty; I will see to this."

"No, I won't go away," answered Kitty.

She stood sullenly by. Keith opened his eyes. He could not suppress a groan of pain. Mollie had made a fresh lotion; she applied it, cool and tender and refreshing, to the inflamed leg.

"After all, Kitty's measures were a little stringent," she said; "but perhaps they will do you good in the long run, only you must bear an hour or so of pain. Now, I will get an orderly to help me, and we will put you on one of the empty beds, and by the afternoon your leg ought to be much better."

"I can help, can't I?" said Kitty.

"I think not; you are not strong enough,"

"O don't, Kit," remarked Keith, with a laugh; "your ministrations are just a trifle too violent."

She frowned with annoyance. Her jealous heart was becoming very sore. Keith was considerably hurt by the powerful lotion, and he lay for some time indifferent to Kitty's presence. Once she went up to him and asked if she might do something.

"You do something!" he replied. "No, thank you; send your sister to me."

"It is true," thought Kitty to herself. "He hates me, and he loves her. Why should he turn me away just because I made a tiny mistake?"

She choked down a sob in her throat, and went to fetch Mollie. Mollie returned instantly. Keith smiled when he saw her.

"Your very presence gives me strength," he said; and Kitty, silly, foolish Kitty, heard the words.

Her mind was made up now; surely she had seen for herself.

"But I won't give him up," she thought. "Mollie shall not have him. She aims at being so high, and yet she does the very lowest, meanest things. She tries to take my Gavon from me, but she shan't have him."

Kitty went across the ward. Lawson called out to her.

"Have you anything special to do, miss?"

"Yes, I have a great deal to do," said Kitty, in a cross voice. "But do you want anything?" she added.

"I thought maybe, miss, I might dictate a letter to my young woman, so be as you'd write it for me. I don't mind saying out my mind afore you, miss."

Kitty hesitated.

"I will write it for you after dinner," she said.

"I may not be so well then, miss. I ain't been the thing to-day, My mind keeps wandering, and I shouldn't be surprised if I had a touch of enteric. I feel like it, somehow."

"Oh, you are getting on very well," said Kitty. "You are just nervous.—Isn't Lawson just nervous, Sister Eugenia?"

Sister Eugenia came up to Lawson's bed and looked at him.

"You don't seem quite comfortable," she said. "What do you complain of? Ankle very painful?"

"Yes, rather," said the poor fellow.

"I am afraid, Lawson, you must submit to amputation," said Sister Eugenia. "It is sharp and short, and puts things right."

"Couldn't stand it; it would kill me. I couldn't go back home with only a stump instead of a leg. I couldn't do it, and I won't."

"Well, we'll see what the doctor says," replied Sister Eugenia.

"If I were you," she said in a low voice to Kitty, "I would do what he asks. I don't at all like his look. He has been suffering a lot of pain, poor fellow, and he is very bad now."

Kitty hesitated; her heart was on fire with her own imaginary wrongs. Why should she worry about a man like Lawson? True, he was a nice fellow—very nice—and she sympathized with him about his girl. But that girl was happier than she, for Lawson loved her well, and saw no blemish in her. For him she was surrounded by a halo; he looked at her through blue glasses, and her coarse and common nature was refined and rendered beautiful. She was his dream, and he had no room in his heart for any other woman. If only Keith might be as true, thought the girl.

"May I dictate a bit of a letter to you, miss?" said Lawson again.

"After dinner. I'll come back after dinner," replied Kitty.

She went away, and returned to her own room. She dined with some of the officers and nurses at the hotel. All during dinner the talk was of the short rations which must in future be the portion of the beleaguered city. The strongest pity was expressed for the horses, which were not half fed. There was to be a consultation that very day as to whether the cavalry horses were to be destroyed or not. Kitty was too full of herself really to sympathize with the woes of Ladysmith; but she heard the conversation, and it depressed her more than ever. After dinner she yawned feebly, went slowly up to her own room, and stood looking out of the window.

"Oh, it is all so miserable," she thought. "I suppose I must do what Major Strause wants," and just as the thought came to her she saw his broad figure crossing the street.

He entered the hotel, and the next instant was tapping at her door. Kitty said, "Come in," and he entered.

"Well?" he said, the moment he saw her face. "I haven't a minute to stay. Was I right, or was I wrong?"

"You were right," said Kitty. "And I," she added, "am nearly mad."

"No wonder, poor little girl. You will adopt my suggestion?"

"I certainly will. I mean to talk to Mollie to-night."

"By-the-way, I believe you are wanted at the hospital; your sister told me to ask you to go back as soon as possible. A private of the name of Lawson is very bad. The doctors are with him. He wants you to do something. Sister Mollie offered to do it, but he seems to have taken a fancy to you."

"Oh, I will go presently," said Kitty. "It is nothing much."

"Nothing much! but the poor chap is in danger."

"It really isn't much," said Kitty. "He only wants me to write a letter to the girl he is engaged to. But I will go; any time to-day will do, I suppose."

"I would be quick if I were you. I didn't like the account I got of him. I can't stay now. Any time you want me you have only to send for me; my hut is just round the corner. Good-bye for the present."

The major went away, and Kitty sank on to a sofa. Should she go to see Lawson? She was tired, and the afternoon was hot. She dreaded walking down the street, fearing one of Long Tom's kisses. In the hotel she felt comparatively safe; in the Town Hall she was quite certain she was safe, but the way to the Town Hall was a way of danger. She did not wish to die now. When she was Keith's wife nothing else would matter; but until she was his wife she would not leave him, if only to show him that she was determined to claim her rights. She forgot about Lawson: she sank on the sofa, rested her head against a pillow, and dropped off asleep.

When she awoke it was past five o'clock. She started up with an uneasy, guilty sense that she had neglected something. Suddenly she remembered Lawson. She would go to him now. She would write his letter now if he wanted it. She felt much better for her sleep—much calmer; she would not be frightened now to go down the street. Long Tom would not kiss her this time. Taking her broad linen apron with her, she quickly reached her destination. Mollie was standing by the door. Kitty ran up to her.

"I am sorry I am a little late," she said, "but I can do what Lawson wants now."

"Why didn't you come when you were asked?" replied Mollie.

"I didn't know it was important."

"I would have sent for you, but I had no one to send. Major Strause said he would tell you."

"He did, only—somehow I was drowsy, and I went to sleep. What is the matter, Mollie? Why do you look at me with that strange expression? I tell you I will do what Lawson wants now. His bed is number five. Don't keep me."

She was pushing past Mollie, but Mollie held out a hand to detain her.

"You are too late," she said.

"Too late!" cried Kitty. "What do you mean?"

"He is past your help. Mortification set in in the wounded leg. The foot and ankle were amputated not an hour ago, but he is sinking fast. He won't see the night out."

"Oh," said Kitty—"oh! and he wanted the letter written! I'm sure it can't be too late."

"Why didn't you come after dinner? Even then he might have said what he wanted to say. He kept calling for you."

"Don't keep me," said Kitty. "I don't—I won't—believe it is too late."

She pushed her sister aside, and went to bed number five. They had put a screen round the bed; but Kitty pushed the screen open and went in. Sister Eugenia was standing by the bedside. She turned when she saw Kitty, and the dislike she felt for her shone in her calm blue eyes.

"If you were coming, why didn't you come before?" she said. "You can do no good now. You had better go away."

"I won't go away," answered Kitty; "and you have no right to speak to me in those tones."

Then her eyes fell upon Private Lawson, and she became silent. Her face turned the colour of chalk. Her lips trembled. Lawson was breathing rapidly in a shallow way. Kitty went to him; she bent down over him.

"Lawson," she said, "Lawson, I have come at last. I have come to write the letter."

He did not hear her. He breathed on rapidly, and the pallor on his face was terrible to see.

"I have come, Lawson," said Kitty, in a louder tone, "and I will write the letter to the girl you love faithfully."

Then he did open his eyes. Something in her words had arrested him. He looked full up at the white face of the girl. He looked straight into her eyes, so full of self-reproach.

"The girl I love faithfully," he murmured.

"Yes, I'll write a letter for you to the girl you love."

"Ay, will you?" he asked. "She's a beauty. There ain't no one like her. And she'll—take in laundry work, and she—won't—mind whether—I've got—one or—two—feet; no—she—won't. God bless—her."

"You want to write to her," said Kitty, bending over him. "Tell me now, tell me what to say; I'll write it for you now."

"Ay, ay, you write. Tell—her—tell—her—"

But what Private Lawson had to tell his sweetheart was never known on this side eternity!

CHAPTER XXI.
KITTY'S REQUEST.

Kitty was terribly upset when Lawson breathed his last. She made a painful scene by the deathbed. Her nerve gave way, and she went off into violent hysterics. The angry nurses made short work with her; two of them carried her right out of the hospital. Sister Eugenia said she would see her home.

"I will walk with you," she said, "as far as the hotel. A girl like you is worse than useless in Ladysmith."

The stinging words recalled Kitty to herself.

"Why won't you have any pity for me?" she gasped.

"No one has pity for moral weakness in Ladysmith," replied the sister. "You are worse than a coward; you are selfish. If you had come into the ward when you were asked for, you might have done some good, and the poor fellow would have died happy. But nothing can be done now. All the tears in the world won't alter things. And to make a fuss when there are soldiers dying, soldiers of the Queen—oh, I could shake you!"

Sister Eugenia's words were so full of passion that Kitty was aroused to be ashamed of herself. She turned when they were half-way up the street.

"I don't think I'll be afraid of the kisses," she said. "You can go back."

"Afraid of what?"

"Of Long Tom's shells."

"They are not likely to touch you," said the sister, in contempt. "They don't touch the selfish and the useless. You are safe. If you don't want me, I will go back."

She turned, and Kitty, putting wings to her feet, re-entered the hotel. For the rest of the day she was as miserable and remorseful as girl could be, but towards evening she began to recover. Once again her selfish nature came to the fore. She began to consider herself ill-used and neglected. Nothing would have been wrong had Mollie only loved her as she used to love her, and were Gavon only as true to her as he ought to be to his promised wife. Yes, she must see Mollie that evening. Things could not go on as they were doing any longer. Accordingly she wrote a tiny note, and sent it to the hospital.

The large hospital for the sick and wounded was at Intombi, a sheltered position about four miles away; but the Town Hall was largely used during the siege, and another hospital was in the Congregational Chapel. Mollie, with a few nurses under her, had charge of the Town Hall hospital. She received her sister's note late that evening, and went to her during the hour which she usually devoted to her supper.

Captain Keith was better. He sat up as Mollie passed his side.

"How white and tired you look!" he said. "Is anything troubling you?"

"I have had a note from Kitty. She wants me to go to her."

"I am sorry Kitty came out here," said Keith, in a grave tone. "I am sorry Miss Hunt brought her."

159

"Katherine Hunt is of immense use," said Mollie. "She is as good as any trained nurse."

"I know; but my poor little Kit is different."

"We all have different natures," replied Mollie, in a gentle tone. "Kitty was never accustomed to nursing. She has been very tenderly treated all her life, and perhaps just a little bit spoiled. We must have patience with her."

"You have patience with every one, I think," said the young man, and his eyes shone brightly as he spoke.

Mollie looked gently back at him.

"Are you better?" she asked.

"I am always better when you are by. You don't know what you are to me."

"Hush!" said Mollie. "I know exactly what I am—your sister, your friend, and nurse."

"You are far, far more. Oh, I can't help it!" he said under his breath. "You must know what you are to me; you must know what I feel for you. I am a coward to speak of it, but just now I—your presence, the look in your eyes, unmans me."

"Think of Kitty, and you will recover your manhood."

Mollie spoke hurriedly. She did not want him to say any more. She went out into the night. She was very tired, and the healing and comforting stars shone down upon her. The Boers were sending a searchlight over Ladysmith, and as Mollie quickened her steps she wondered whether they meant to send shells into the little town during the night. But no firing was heard. An orderly going past suddenly stopped and spoke quickly.

"Have you noticed anything, nurse?" he said.

"No," she replied; "what do you mean?"

The words had scarcely passed her lips before there came a sharp report, a screaming noise, and a loud explosion. Mollie turned in some astonishment.

"Pepworth Hill knows Long Tom no more," was the orderly's next remark. "He now reigns on Little Bulwan, below Lombard's Kop. His range is nearer. If this sort of thing goes on, Ladysmith will soon be taken."

"I don't believe it," answered Mollie.

She hurried past the orderly and went into the hotel. She ran upstairs at once to Kitty's room. Kitty was standing in the middle of the floor. Her face looked ghastly.

"What is the matter?" she said, the moment she saw her sister.

"Oh, I am so terribly frightened!"

"What of?" asked Mollie, speaking in a soothing tone.

"That awful report—the bursting of a shell at night. Oh, what does it mean?"

"I hope nothing to frighten you, Kitty; but, of course, you quite understand that all our lives are in danger. They are all in His hands, Kitty—in His hands who does nothing wrong; who has ordered the day and the hour, and the manner of our deaths, when death comes."

"I wish you wouldn't talk like that," said Kitty. "You terrify me—oh, how you terrify me!"

"You sent for me, Kitty," said Mollie.

She sat down by her trembling little sister, and took one of her small hands in hers.

"What have you done with your rings?" was her next remark.

"Gavon said that I ought not to wear them in the siege. I have taken off my bracelets too. Nothing matters. See how terribly my hand is stained, Mollie."

"Yes," said Mollie, "You did a very dangerous thing this morning. You made the lotion far and away too strong. It was lucky that Gavon is so healthy and that his skin is healing. It is healing, so you need not trouble."

"And you will let me go back to the hospital again, Mollie, and—and nurse the poor fellows. Oh, I promise—I really will promise—to be good. Will Gavon be at the hospital to-morrow, Mollie?"

"I hope not. He is much better to-night. Our soldiers do not stay in hospital for trifles, Kitty. My dear Kitty, why don't you too become a soldier of the Queen? A real soldier, I mean—one who fights as a woman should fight, with such brave weapons, my dear, such sympathy, such courage, such faith. Such a woman in Ladysmith now would be an angel of light. Why don't you try to become one, my poor little Kit?"

"I can't," said the girl, sobbing; "I am all selfish. I know I am. Mollie, when you hear why I really sent for you, you will hate me."

"I can never hate my only little sister."

"But you are so different," sobbed Kitty. "You are so brave and strong, and all—yes, all that constitutes an angel of light. Why were you made the way

161

you are, Mollie? and why was I made the way I am? Oh, it was wrong of God, it was wrong!"

"Don't say that, Kitty. I feel God to be so near me now it hurts me to have even one word said in His dishonour. He made you for His glory, He made you for His praise, He made you for your own best, best happiness. Lift up your head, little Kitty, and take courage. Take courage, darling, and do better in the future."

"But you know how badly I behaved to-day. I was so selfish I would not go back to the hospital in time to receive poor Lawson's message."

"Perhaps he is able to give it himself now," said Mollie.

"What do you mean?"

"Nothing—it is only a thought; he may be able himself to convey the comfort he wanted to give to his poor sweetheart. Anyhow, Kitty, there is no looking back over that. In Ladysmith we have no time to look back. There are other poor fellows with sweethearts and mothers and sisters—others who are either dying now or who will have to die before this terrible siege is over— and you can comfort them."

As Mollie spoke she clasped Kitty in her arms, and laid the girl's tired, frightened head on her breast. There came another sharp, very sharp report, and the searchlight suddenly lit up the windows of Kitty's room. She gave a terrified scream.

"I wish I had never come to Ladysmith. I wish I could get away."

"Too late for that now; you are a little soldier, and must stand to your guns."

"I am a coward; I am the sort of soldier who runs away," said the girl.

Mollie was silent until the noise of the explosion ceased; then she said quietly,—

"This may mean more patients for me; I must hurry off again. What did you really want with me?"

Kitty raised her head and looked full at her sister.

"I have got something to confess," she said.

"What is that?"

"I came back to the hospital to-day because—not because I am a soldier of the Queen, not because I wanted to help anybody, but because—"

"Well, child, speak," said Mollie.

"Because I wished to watch you."

"What do you mean? To watch me, your sister!"

"Yes; to watch you and—and Gavon."

As Kitty said the last words, she forgot her fears with regard to Long Tom; she forgot everything but the wild passion, the jealous, miserable rage, which filled her. She sprang to her feet and faced her sister, she clasped her little stained fingers together and looked with her white face into Mollie's face, and then she hurled out her words impulsively.

"You love him—you know you do! And he loves you, and he—he is engaged to me. You have taken him from me. Oh, how I hate you! Oh, I shall die with misery!"

"' You love him—you know you do !'"

Page 163

"'You love him—you know you do!'"

Mollie's face turned very nearly as white as Kitty's; she did not speak at all for a moment. Kitty, having hurled out her reproaches, waited, expecting Mollie to speak. Mollie still was silent. There came another screaming report, another explosion. Kitty was deaf to it. That fact alone impressed Mollie. She looked with almost reverence at her sister now. How great and strong, after all, were her love and her passion!

"It is true," said Kitty. "Why don't you speak? why don't you speak? You

164

know it is true. I saw it in your eyes, and I saw it in his eyes; and if you were to tell me a thousand, thousand times that you don't love him, I would not believe you."

"But I am not going to tell you any such thing," replied Mollie.

"Then it is true," said Kitty; "you have confessed that it is true."

"No, I have not confessed it; I have said nothing."

"How can I bear you? I wonder I don't even try to kill you."

"Why so, Kitty? I have never done you any harm."

"You have: you have taken away the love of the man I am engaged to—the man I worship."

"Now listen to me, Kitty. You really must allow your common-sense to come to the fore. I am not going to tell you a lie. As you have put the question to me, I shall answer you frankly. Were you not engaged to Gavon Keith, did you not love Gavon, it is just possible—I do not say any more—that I might love him. But as you are engaged to him, the thought to me of taking him from you is as impossible as that I should be faithless now in Ladysmith to the Queen. Won't you understand that, little sister? won't you believe it? Have I ever to your knowledge done a downright mean thing, that you should think me capable of doing this greatest of all sins now?"

"Oh dear!" gasped Kitty. "But he is often in the ward with you, and I know that he—he cares for you."

"He has never been unfaithful to you; and what you have got to do is to keep well for his sake, and to be brave for his sake. You must try to learn so to live that he shall not think small things of you. Believe me, I am right in saying this. Your character must grow too, and your love shall make you noble. Won't you try, dear, to live differently in the future?"

"I can't! I can't! And your words don't comfort me a bit. What are words, after all? It is actions that I want."

"You want me to prove my words; in what way?"

"You must do something for me; you must do something to put matters straight between Gavon and me. Will you?"

"I will do anything in my power," replied Mollie, but her voice had grown suddenly tired and faint.

"Will you really and truly, and from your very heart, prove your love for me in that way?"

"Really and truly, and from my very heart."

"Then there is something you can do."

"What is it?"

"He has never told you that he loves you?"

"Never."

"But you think he does?"

Mollie was silent.

"But you think he does?" Kitty repeated.

"You have no right to ask that question, Kitty."

"I know without your telling me," replied Kitty. "He must learn to unlove you."

"What do you mean?"

"You must do something which will upset his faith in you—something which will astonish him very much."

Mollie's face now indeed turned pale. She ceased to regard her sister as a weak, hysterical girl. She stared at her with her wide-open brown eyes.

"Some one has been putting you up to this," she said. "Those words are not the words of my sister. Kitty, what is the matter?"

"There is so much the matter that only by doing exactly what I ask can you put things right. There is a man in Ladysmith who loves you. No, that man is not Gavon; I speak of another. He loves you, and you must marry him. You must marry him for my sake."

"Whom am I to marry?"

"Major Strause."

"Kitty, are you mad?"

"I am not mad; I am sane, It is the only possible way out. If you will marry him, I shall be saved; if you marry him, all will be right. Gavon is not the sort of man to love you as Major Strause's wife. Gavon does not like Major Strause, and I hope he won't like his wife, and he will turn back to me. Mollie, you must marry him. O Mollie, only thus can you save me—only thus, by marrying Major Strause."

"Kitty!"

"Yes; and you must marry him now, and here."

166

"I marry Major Strause now, and here—now, in this time of war, and famine, and siege, and misery! My dear little sister, you ask too much. If that is what you have sent for me for, I must leave you, and I cannot do what you ask. The sick and wounded are wanting me. This is not the time for personal feelings, or for marrying and giving in marriage."

"Then I am the most miserable girl in all the world," cried Kitty.

She fell on her knees, and looked passionately up in her sister's face.

"I can't give you the promise, Kitty. It is too much; you had no right to ask it."

With a quick movement Mollie tore herself from Kitty's embrace and rushed from the room.

CHAPTER XXII.
MOLLIE'S PERSECUTOR.

The next day the bombardment was severe. Long Tom at his nearer range was more formidable than ever, and no less than two hundred and fifty shells burst in the town and forts. Only the cave dwellers felt safe. Even the cattle were beginning to suffer. The noise caused by the constant firing was incessant. The wounded could not sleep, and the doctors and nurses found it impossible to do their difficult work properly. Rations for the sick, too, were running terribly short, and comforts and dainties for the convalescent were far to seek and impossible to find.

Mollie dreaded the time when the town hospital would be shut up, and she might be forced to go to the hospital at Intombi. This, for many reasons, she did not at all wish to do. The discomforts there were indescribable. The dust lay like a thick layer over everything. The noise of the firing was even more incessant than in the town of Ladysmith. The place was low, too, and damp, and in no possible sense of the word a fit situation for a hospital for men down with enteric or with gunshot wounds. Nevertheless at that moment there were nine hundred patients down with enteric at Intombi. Mollie hoped that her work might keep her in the town itself.

All the beds in the Town Hall hospital were now full. She ministered to the sick and dying as calmly and gently as though this were just an ordinary hospital in London or any other part of England. Her nerve was little short of marvellous. Mollie took complete control of the surgical ward; the enteric ward she did not often enter—she had not time. Kitty did not return to the hospital.

Captain Keith was much better, and went back to his usual work. Mollie was glad of that. After Kitty's revelation and her unreasonable jealousy, she felt that she must see as little as possible of Gavon Keith. Major Strause came early to the hospital. He looked anxious. There was an expression in his eyes which Mollie did not care to meet. He looked at her, but did not speak to her. He went straight into the enteric ward. He was coming to be regarded as quite a power among the nurses and doctors, and more than one poor fellow breathed his last and uttered his farewell words into the major's ears. The man was changed in spite of himself, and it was Mollie's doing.

"But I cannot marry him," thought the poor girl, "even to relieve Kitty's fears. That is quite impossible."

And then she was angry with herself for having any personal thoughts in those fateful days.

On this special day the dust was terrible. It came in thick showers through the windows, and disturbed the patients as much as the screams of Long Tom. About half-past five p.m. came the climax to all their woes. A shell burst into the roof of the hospital. It flung its bullets far and wide over the sick and wounded. One bullet hit one poor fellow right on the chest, went through his heart, and killed him immediately. Nine others were hit, and many were seriously wounded. The shock to the patients was terrible. There was no doubt whatever that the Boer gunners had deliberately aimed at the Red Cross flag, which, flying from the turret of the Town Hall, was visible for miles.

Mollie was standing close to the part of the hospital over which the shell burst, but, wonderful to relate, she was not hurt. Major Strause, however, was badly injured in the thigh. From being a help and support to the overworked nurses, he was now himself one of the wounded. It was no longer safe to remain in the Town Hall hospital, and the sick and wounded were conveyed to the Congregational Chapel, which was hastily turned into a hospital. Major Strause found himself here, and in the surgical ward.

"You are bound to see me now," he said to Mollie, and he smiled up into her face.

"I will do my best for you," she answered. "You are a very brave man."

A surgeon removed the splinters from the wound, and Major Strause bore the agonies without having recourse to chloroform. Alas! the supplies of chloroform were getting terribly short, and it was now only used for extreme cases. Mollie bent over the major when the operation was at an end, and did her best to make him comfortable. She was holding a refreshing drink to his lips, when he suddenly seized her hand.

"Oh, if you would only make me the happiest of men!"

"Don't, Major Strause," she answered. "How can you talk of these things now?"

"I only want your promise," he pleaded. "Oh, won't you promise me? I was a man almost lost, but you are saving me."

She tore her hand away, and went off to see to another patient. But now began a series of persecutions which tested the brave girl's courage to the very utmost. Major Strause seemed determined to carry on the siege by incessant small firing. He hardly ever let Mollie alone. He was always calling her on one pretence or another, and whenever she approached his side he told her how ardently he loved her, and what a good man she would make him if she fielded to his solicitations. Mollie, however, was firm. All this time he had never once alluded to her sister, nor to Captain Keith, nor to anything but the all-important fact that he loved Mollie, that he loved her with a true and constant heart, and that he wanted her to return his love.

One day when he had spoken in this tone she suddenly burst into tears. He was instantly full of contrition.

"What is the matter?" he said. "You cry! you, the brave, the constant, the indefatigable, give way!"

"You are making me cry; you are wearing me out," said the girl. "I can stand everything else—yes, everything else—but it lowers me when you talk to me as you do."

He looked at her with a world of consternation and self-reproach in his eyes.

"Is that true?" he said.

"Yes," she answered, sinking her voice to a whisper. A soldier in a bed opposite was looking at her; she observed that he did so, and turned her back on him. He turned away also, with the chivalry which belongs to most brave soldiers. "You make me a spectacle before the others," she continued. "Why do you make my life so wretched? Can't you be generous? Can't you see that you are showing the reverse of love when you act as you do?"

"Is there no hope at all for me?" he said.

"There is no hope—none," she answered. "I will be good to you; I would marry you even, if I could, just to make you happy, but I can't. Were I to marry you, you would be a very miserable man. I have no love for you; on the contrary—"

"Yes!" he said; "speak."

"I will not say what I was going to say; but no woman who feels as I do for you ought to marry you. It would be a mistake, and I will not do wrong that right may come."

"Is that your firm resolve?" he said. "Ah, but you may do wrong that right may come yet; you don't know all!"

She did not even ask him what he meant. He held out his hand.

"Take my hand," he said slowly.

There was something in his tone which made her obey him. She gave her small, white hand into his clasp for a moment.

"I promise that as long as I am ill I will not persecute you by word or deed," he said; and then, before she could prevent him, he raised her hand to his lips and kissed it.

No one saw the action. The Sister of the Red Cross went away with her cheeks on fire.

Meanwhile things were getting more and more gloomy in Ladysmith. The real privations of the siege had now well begun. Enteric fever and dysentery were steadily increasing, and food for both men and horses was becoming very scarce. Ammunition also would have to be used with care. The suffering amongst those who had no stores of their own to fall back upon was getting

170

more and more serious. Eggs were half a guinea a dozen, potatoes one and six a pound, candles a shilling each. Nothing could be bought in the way of drink except lemonade and soda water, and the question of all questions was, what was to be done with the horses. The difficulty amongst the sick was not so much to carry them through their different crises, but to build up their strength afterwards. All the milk in Ladysmith had long been reserved for use in the hospitals, but even for the sick it was now running out. Those who were ill began to say that convalescence was the hardest time of all—there was nothing fit for them to eat. The question which agitated the nurses and all those who had the ordering of supplies was whether or not the horses should be boiled down for food.

Throughout all, however, Major Strause got steadily better. There came a day when he was well enough to leave the hospital. Mollie herself brought his things, and helped him once more to get into his uniform. He had faithfully kept his word, and since the day when he had kissed her hand, had never, even by a look, shown Mollie that he thought more of her than of any other woman. Nevertheless she had a feeling that he was only biding his time. She was too busy just then to see all she might have seen of Kitty, but whenever she met her little sister, Kitty invariably asked the same question—"Are you engaged yet to Major Strause?" And Mollie invariably replied in the negative; whereupon Kitty sighed and turned her head away.

The events of the last few weeks had affected not only Kitty, but Mollie. Kitty indeed seemed to get thinner and thinner, and her small face more and more white. There was a weary, very weary expression about her eyes. She was *exigeante* to Captain Keith when he came to see her or she was sullen, and scarcely spoke at all. It was with difficulty she could keep the words back from her lips: "You have never loved me; you love my sister, not me." But hitherto she had refrained from uttering these mad, wild words, and she hoped she would have self-control until the end.

Mollie was also looking pale and fagged. It was not the nursing; it was not the personal privations; it was not the long, weary hours when she knew no sleep, and was indefatigable in looking after the sick and wounded; but it was the trouble of her mind—the knowledge that she did love Gavon Keith, the further assurance deep down in her heart that he loved her, the dread fear that she was, after all, breaking Kitty's heart—the dim outlook in the future. What was she to do? Oh, she could not set things right by doing wrong—she could not do it!

On the day that Major Strause quitted the hospital Gavon Keith went to see Kitty. He had not been with her for two or three days. He had been very much occupied. The sorties against the Boers were more and more frequent; and when in camp he had much to do, for each officer had now to bear his part, if in no other way, in cheering up the soldiers and making the best of things all round. Keith, too, was feeling the effects of the siege. From time to time he had received slight although nasty wounds, and the one on his leg, which Kitty had injured by her application of the too strong lotion, had never quite healed. It gave him incessant pain, and he limped slightly as he came now into the girl's presence. Her heart was in her mouth; all the misery and nervousness of the last few days were reflected in her small, thin face. Keith had come away from a very anxious discussion regarding ways and means with the other officers of his regiment. It had just been decided that the cavalry horses were to be let loose. There was great trouble amongst all the cavalry officers in consequence. Keith, who belonged to an infantry regiment, had not, of course, his own special horse, but he felt the trouble almost as much as the others. When would relief come? When would Buller get any nearer? It was not a moment for a girl's petty jealousy, for a girl's silly fears. The moment he looked at Kitty—Kitty whom he did not really love—and saw the expression on her small face and the discontent round her lips, it seemed to the young officer that this was the last straw.

"Why have you not come in to see me before?" was her first remark.

"You may be thankful that I could come now," was his answer. "I have been too busy. I have not had a single moment to devote to personal matters."

"I am glad you think anything connected with me personal," was her answer, and she went and stood, with her back to him, looking out of the window. A shell burst a few yards away. She started, and glanced nervously at Keith. "Why don't you speak?" said the girl. "It is bad enough to be away for a few days, but then to come and—and to say nothing! And you have not even kissed me!"

He strode up to her, laid a hand on each of her shoulders, drew her towards him, and kissed her lightly on the forehead.

"Poor Kitty!" he said, "you are more to be pitied than any other woman in Ladysmith. There are fifteen thousand people in the town all told, and I don't believe there is a woman here more wretched than yourself!"

"Why do you say that?"

"I say it because I know it. Why won't you do things? You might copy Katherine Hunt, for instance."

"Or Mollie," she said. She coloured crimson as she spoke, and then her face turned white.

"Or Mollie, brave Nurse Mollie," answered Keith, and a rich colour dyed his cheeks and mounted to his brow.

Kitty looked at him. She saw the expression in his eyes, and every remnant of self-control deserted her.

"Gavon," she said, "I will have the truth. Oh, I should not be miserable were it not for you! You come to see me when you cannot help it; but you don't love me—you never loved me!"

He was silent; his lips took that hard, firm line which they wore at times, but which Kitty had seldom seen; his eyelids narrowed slightly, and he watched Kitty with a curious expression on his face. She was too mad with rage and misery to be checked even by that look.

"You are recommended for your V.C.," she said; "and you will get it, I suppose. Oh, I know you are brave, very brave against the Boers, but you can hurt a woman who loves you for all that. You can be false and faithless!"

"That is not true," he answered.

"It is true!" cried the girl. "You are busy, and you don't care; but I am not busy, and I do care. You have no time to think; I have all the long, long hours to think, and I think and think, and I know and know. You don't love me; my heart will break. I came out here to be near you, and ran untold dangers just to be by your side; but I am left in this miserable hotel, and you come to see me only when you must."

"I come to see you when I can," he replied.

"It is not true," she said. "If you loved me as I love you, your heart would be drawn to me. But it never, never is drawn to me; you only come to see me when you must—and you love Mollie, not me. Deny it, Gavon; tell me to my face that I am telling you a lie, and I will believe you. I will believe no one else. But oh, you can't. You love Mollie, and Mollie loves you, and it is cruel —oh, it is cruel! It is the hardest fate that could overtake a poor girl—to love a man, and for that man to love her sister. Oh, I am a miserable, most miserable girl!"

"Stop, Kitty; you have said enough," cried Keith. "Now listen to me." He spoke with great decision and suppressed passion, and there was a power in his voice which arrested the weak, half-hysterical girl. "I forbid you, Kitty, if we are to remain engaged to each other, ever to say again what you have said to-day. I decline to answer your accusation. If you don't wish for me as I am, give me up; but if you do wish for me—and I have thought you did, Kitty—if you do wish for me, you must take me as I am, with my faults, with the measure of love I can give you—just as I am. When this siege is over (if it ever is over), when we leave Ladysmith (if we ever do leave it), I will marry you, and be as good a husband to you as God gives me grace to be; but I will not answer your base accusations. If you believe what you say you believe, why don't you give me back my freedom? why do you remain engaged to me? I decline to answer your insinuations. And now good-bye, Kitty. I will come back to see you, when perhaps you will be in a better frame of mind."

He turned and left the room. He was in his full uniform, and he had never looked more handsome. Kitty was terribly frightened when he left her.

"I never meant to say that to him! Now he will never forgive me! But I mean to marry him whether he loves Mollie or whether he does not," said the desperate girl to herself.

She thought for a minute, and then, carried out of herself, pinned on her hat, and ran, just as she was, to the new hospital. She entered, and stood waiting near the surgical ward. She saw Mollie in the distance. Mollie was very busy; she was attending to several patients. Major Strause had, as she hoped, gone quite away without saying anything. Kitty did not attempt to call her sister; she kept looking at her. To her jealous eyes each movement of Mollie's was torture. She had to admit that beside Mollie she herself cut but a poor figure. Even her very beauty, owing to her selfishness and self-indulgence, was getting to be of the very poorest and shabbiest order. There was no self-renunciation on her face; there was no light of courage in her eyes: there was scarcely another woman in Ladysmith who did not show to advantage against poor Kitty. And Mollie, who had beauty as well, how splendid she looked this morning! How erect was her form, how stately was her step, how firm and courageous and grand her nerve!

"No wonder he loves her; he can't help himself. Oh, I wish I were out of the world!" thought the wretched girl.

Just at this moment Mollie caught sight of her. She had not seen Kitty for two or three days. She gave a brief direction to a nurse who stood near, and walked down the ward.

"Well, Kitty?" she said.

She went up to Kitty and took her hand; the girl pushed her back.

"I have come to say something."

"What is it, dear? Anything wrong?"

"Everything is wrong. I saw Gavon this morning, and he—I know now what I guessed before. There is only one way to save me, and you won't take it. You won't be troubled by me long; I cannot endure this. I have come to say that this is good-bye."

She turned away as she spoke; she did not wait for any remarks from Mollie. Mollie went to the door of the hospital and called the girl's name; but Kitty had put wings to her feet, and was running back to the hotel. Shells fell around her as she ran, but nothing wounded or touched her.

Katherine Hunt was standing in the door of the hospital. She had been up all night, and was tired.

"Aren't you ever going to rest, Sister Mollie?" she said.

"Some day," replied Mollie, with a sigh.

"You are fretting about that silly little sister of yours. She's not worth it."

"I am rather anxious about her," said Mollie. "She is very desperate and very unhappy. I have no time to go over to her, or I would."

"I am off duty for two or three hours. I will go to the hotel and look after her."

"She bade me good-bye. She means something desperate," said Mollie.

"No, you need not be alarmed; that is not Kitty's way. Take care of yourself, and don't yield," said Katherine Hunt.

Katherine put on her hat, and prepared to go back to the hotel. Mollie returned to her duties. About noon there was a brief lull, and she went out to take a little air. She had scarcely been two minutes in her post of observation, where she could watch both her cases and the street beyond, when Major Strause strode up to her side. He looked around, saw that they were alone, and said briefly,—

"The day and the hour have come. As long as I was in hospital I kept my word. Will you marry me, Mollie Hepworth?"

"No, Major Strause," she replied.

"I will ask you once more. Will you, when the siege is over, be my faithful and true wife?"

"I will never be your wife."

"Is that your final answer?"

"Yes."

"I have asked you to be my wife for more than one reason," continued Major Strause. He stood in such a position that she could not get away from him. "I have hitherto not declared my reasons. Now I am prepared to go fully into the matter. You can say 'yes' or 'no' afterwards. I have just seen your sister. She is terribly unhappy. Her brain is not too strong, and it has been very

175

much shaken by the terrors and misery she has undergone since she came to Ladysmith. She loves Captain Keith."

"She is engaged to Captain Keith," interrupted Mollie.

"Yes, yes; but that is a trifle. The fact is that she loves him desperately, as I love you. He does not love her; he loves you."

"You have no right—" began Mollie.

He interrupted her by a hasty ejaculation.

"No right," he said, "when the whole thing is as plain—as plain as that there is a sun in the sky! The man loves you as men will love women like you, Sister Mollie; and you love him back. Your sister is mad with trouble. There is only one way to save her—marry me!"

"And believing such a thing to be true, would you really take me to be your wife?" said Mollie.

"I would."

"Then you would be a very miserable man."

"That would be my affair. I would take you as my wife; and, before God, I would be the best man on earth. Yes, Mollie Hepworth, the best, for you have power over me. I was born, I think, with a devil inside me; but in your presence he lies quiet, he does not trouble. You have the effect of sending him to sleep."

"That is little," said Mollie, "if he is there. I cannot marry a man with a devil in his heart."

"Can you not? will nothing induce you?"

"Nothing."

"Not even to save your sister from suicide?"

"She will not commit suicide," said Mollie, a startled expression crossing her face. "I don't believe that for a single moment. No, you cannot frighten me with that. Kitty will marry Gavon. He will be good to her, and she will be happy, if ever we leave Ladysmith alive."

"The provisions are getting weak, and enteric is gaining strength," said the major gloomily. "Ten fresh cases have been brought into hospital this morning. Do you happen to know that?"

"I had not heard it."

"They are making beds on the floor now; there are not enough bedsteads.

There is a sad lack of nurses, too. These are dark days for Ladysmith. But outside the Boers are rejoicing. Buller does not get any nearer. We are left to our fate. That being the case, may we not be happy while we can? Your sister would be relieved if she knew that you were engaged to me. Keith would scarcely give you another thought when he learned that you were to be the wife of his—" Major Strause bent lower, and hissed the last words into the girl's ear—"his enemy!"

"And why are you Gavon Keith's enemy?" said Mollie.

"Will you say that you will marry me?"

"I will not."

"If you say it, I need never tell you; if you don't say it, I mean to tell you, and now."

"Now, now," said Mollie—"now?"

"Sister Mollie, you are wanted," said Sister Eugenia, coming out of the hospital.

"Oh, for shame!" said Mollie, turning to Major Strause; "for shame, to keep me now to talk of these things.—Yes, Sister Eugenia."

"I will wait till you come out, or it will be the worse for Gavon Keith," said Major Strause, in a very firm voice.

Mollie looked at him in absolute terror. She went back to the hospital, where her services were urgently needed. But all the time, as she attended to this patient and the other, her thoughts were with Major Strause, and she remembered his words—"It will be the worse for Gavon Keith."

Presently she had a moment's leisure, and seeing the major standing outside, she went back to him.

"I am prepared to listen to you to the very end," she said. "All I ask of you is that you will be brief."

"I must tell you something that will pain you very much," he replied. "You think well of Keith? You have no reason to."

"Speak!" said Mollie.

"About a year ago a very shady circumstance occurred in connection with Gavon Keith. A young man, a cousin of mine, was in our regiment. We were stationed near Netley at the time, and this young fellow—he was extremely rich—became a great friend of Keith's. He came of rather a delicate family. His father and mother were both dead. He had unlimited means—"

"Is the story going to be very long?" interrupted Mollie.

"It shall be as short as I can make it. I need not trouble you with many particulars. He was devoted to Keith, and Keith, for reasons of his own, did all he could to keep young Aylmer from my society."

"Why?" asked Mollie.

"He had what he supposed were good reasons, but it was naturally annoying to me, as I was Aylmer's cousin. However, the long and short of it was that Aylmer was devoted to Keith, and the two were inseparable. Aylmer became very ill; I offered to nurse him. Keith arrived suddenly on the scene, and took my patient from me. I could not help myself, for Aylmer loved Keith and disliked me. Aylmer's illness was supposed to be progressing favourably; nevertheless there were reasons to fear the possibility of a fatal result. Keith came to nurse him one afternoon. It was arranged that he was to spend the night with him. In the night Aylmer died suddenly. The doctor gave the usual death certificate, and poor Aylmer was buried. His will was read, and it was found that he had left Captain Keith ten thousand pounds. This was a large legacy; still no one said anything. Keith was a favourite in the regiment, and people were glad that the young man had remembered him. They are glad to this day. They shall be glad, if you so will it, to the end of time; for Keith and I alone know the truth."

"What do you mean?" said Mollie. Her face was very white—white as death. "What do you mean?"

"I happened to go into the sick-room the morning after Aylmer's death. Now listen—listen hard. Aylmer was ordered two medicines: one was what they call an alterative, or fever mixture—you know the kind?"

Mollie nodded.

"Aylmer was to take two tablespoonfuls of the alterative medicine every two hours. He suffered intense pain from some obscure internal inflammation, and a sedative, which contained a large quantity of opium, was also to be given at stated intervals—a teaspoonful at a time. Those were the two medicines. When I went into Aylmer's room on the following morning, I found that Keith had given Aylmer the wrong medicine—he *said* by mistake. Anyhow, Aylmer had taken two tablespoonfuls of the sedative and one teaspoonful of the fever mixture. The consequence was that he died. You must admit that a very ugly finger of suspicion points to Captain Keith, more particularly as I found out, after careful inquiries, that he wanted that ten thousand pounds badly just then."

"And you think—"

178

"I don't think; I know. I have more to say. Keith was very ill after Aylmer's death—shock the doctors called it; but I, having made my discovery, knew better. I carried the bottles away with me. I have them still. When Keith was a little better I went to see him, and told him what had happened. I invited him to take the matter up and make inquiries; but he preferred to hush the whole thing into oblivion."

"And your part, Major Strause?"

"My part is of no consequence. Had I been less soft-hearted, I should have gone straight to the coroner and told him what I had discovered. But I could not bear to ruin the career of a brave soldier, and I let things lie."

"And you—you received nothing?" asked Mollie, her cheeks on fire, her eyes glowing.

"I wanted a little money badly, and Keith gave me some out of his legacy. I could not resist the temptation of asking him for it. I don't want for a moment to pretend that I acted the hero. I did not; but compared with a man who could take the life of another, I was—"

"Very white indeed," said Mollie, with a curious, half-strangled laugh.

"Yes," he answered, "very white. We need not discuss that point. All this time I have lain low, and Keith has got on and forgotten the ghastly thing—he has engaged himself to a pretty young girl, and I have never said a word, and I never will say a word; on the contrary, I will do something else. On your wedding day I will make you, Mollie Hepworth, a present. I will give you those bottles out of which the medicines were taken. You shall destroy them, and so save Gavon Keith for ever. Will you marry me under these conditions?"

"If I say 'no'?"

"If you say 'no,' I never repeat my offer; and to-night the whisper begins in Ladysmith that one of the heroes of the hour, a man who is to be recommended for his V.C., has committed a secret murder."

"You will do that?"

"I will do that for you, Mollie Hepworth; for you, because I want to win you at any cost. If you say 'yes,' Gavon Keith need fear nothing from me. He will marry your sister—he will cease to care for you; he will marry Kitty, and Kitty will be happy, and you will have saved him. You can never marry him, because I mean to *ruin* him if you do not marry me. Now you know what I require. I will come back for my answer to-night. Good-bye for the present."

He left her. She put up her hand to her forehead. She felt it was very wet.

She did not quite know why the heavy moisture stood on it. She was almost incapable of thought.

CHAPTER XXIII.
DARK DAYS.

T hat evening Molly was sent for in a hurry to visit Kitty. One of the servants from the hotel had rushed across to the hospital, and told her that her sister was ill, was in a most nervous condition, and ought not to be left.

"What am I to do?" said Mollie. She turned to Katherine Hunt.

"Don't go to her; leave her to me," said Katherine, her cheeks first flushing and then turning pale. "Yes," she continued, "leave her to me. She could not have come out here but for me. She must not disturb your grand, your magnificent work. I am the one who ought to look after her."

"There are one or two cases that I ought not to leave to-night," said Mollie. "Even if Kitty were dying, I ought not to leave those cases; for I am a servant of the Queen, and her service ought to come first."

"It ought, and must, and shall," replied Katherine Hunt. "Go to her for a few minutes, Mollie; I will follow you."

Mollie went out.

"If I told her now that I was going to marry Major Strause, she would get better," thought Mollie.

But although she knew that, she shrank back—she had shrunk back all day. She had felt the sacrifice demanded of her too terrible. Until this morning, although she had not had one particle of regard for the major, still she had thought that in some ways there were a certain bravery, dash, and fineness about him. She had noticed his tender touch with the sick men—his devotion to her service could not but in a measure touch her; but when he unfolded his scheme, he showed her all the blackness of his heart, and Mollie recoiled from the sight.

"Not only to love another man who is white as snow beside him—not only to love that man, but to hate Major Strause as I must hate all wickedness; and then—then, with that knowledge in my heart, to become his wife—it is too monstrous! I cannot do it!" thought the Red Cross nurse.

She reached the hotel, and went up to Kitty's room. Kitty was lying in bed. She looked very white and feeble; there was a curious expression about her— an absence of excitement and also of life. She was all alone in her bedroom. When Mollie entered, she raised her heavy eyelids; she saw Mollie, and uttered a feeble cry.

"I tried to do it," she said, "but I couldn't. I took some, but not enough. I could not go on. Do you think I am poisoned?"

"O my dear Kitty, my dear Kitty! what has happened?" said Mollie.

"I got some laudanum—I stole it from the hospital—and I swallowed some, but not enough. I could repeat the dose, and then it would be all over, but I am frightened. When I took a certain amount I got frightened. I have been very sick, and I thought I was going to die, and—oh, I couldn't do it. I would have made it all right for you if I could have done—it; but I couldn't."

"My dear, dear Kitty, how wicked and dreadful of you! Oh, God was with you to prevent this most terrible thing! But I am not going to scold you now; only you must not be left alone."

"You won't tell that I tried to do it?" said Kitty.

"No, darling Kitty; but I must take the laudanum away at once."

Mollie's lips were trembling; her strong frame was shaken to its depths. Kitty pointed to a shelf over her bed where a small bottle of laudanum stood. Mollie put it into her pocket. Then she tried to make her sister more comfortable, and talked to her cheerily. When Katherine Hunt arrived, Mollie left her in that young lady's charge, and went downstairs. Her firm nerves were upset. Still, her resolution was fixed to have nothing to do with Major Strause. He was coming for his answer that night; she would not have an interview with him. She went back to the hospital, and wrote him a short note, —

"Don't trouble me any more. Go your own wicked way. God will protect the innocent.

"NURSE MOLLIE."

This note she gave to an orderly, to deliver to the major when he made his appearance. She did not even ask the orderly whether he had come, or whether the note had been given to him; but she did not get it back again.

The next few days passed quietly. There were no messages from the outside world. Rations grew shorter. The stricken town lay quiet, preparing for its death agonies. After a hurried consultation, it was decided to kill only three hundred of the cavalry horses, and to turn the others out on to the flat beyond the racecourse, and let them survive if they could. This was done; and several of the soldiers said that it was one of the most pitiable events in all the war to see the astonishment and terror of the horses, particularly when they were not allowed to come home to their accustomed lines at night. The poor creatures looked like skeletons, and had scarcely strength to hold themselves upright. At night they came back in groups, hoping to get their food and grooming as usual. They had to be driven away by Basutos with long whips; and then they seemed to recognize that it was useless, and wont wearily back to spend the night on the bare hillside. They were too weak and wanting in energy even to look for fodder.

Meanwhile death was busy. Men fell ill daily and hourly. More died from enteric and dysentery and sunstroke than from wounds. Chevral, a preparation of horse meat, was now in daily use. At first the sick and wounded refused to touch it, but afterwards they took it greedily; and it seemed to stem the tide of mortal illness, and to bring back strength.

Mollie had not seen her sister since the dreadful evening when she found her half poisoned in her room. Katherine Hunt gave up nursing the soldiers for the sake of one weak and troublesome girl whom she, in a fit of generosity, had brought to Ladysmith. How often in the days that were at hand did she regret this step!

Meanwhile the major was, to all appearance, silent. What he did only God and his own conscience knew. Nevertheless, it takes but a little whisper to set an evil report circulating; and just about this time—in the midst of the danger, starvation, and anxiety—there was spoken of in the Royal Hotel, at the officers' mess, and wherever groups of Englishmen congregated together, a curious rumour, sufficiently out of the common, even in a moment like the present, to arouse attention. The days were long gone by when any one smiled or laughed much in Ladysmith; the days for recreation, football, races, or any other amusements no longer existed. But the time is never too gloomy for an evil report to find its listeners, and the report now in circulation gained in strength and credence day by day. It had something to do with Gavon Keith. Brave, fearless, handsome Gavon, already recommended for his V.C., had done something shady, very shady in the past. He did not look the thing a bit; even his enemies acknowledged that. He had a clear eye, a frank gaze, an upright look. He did not drink, nor even smoke, to excess. He was unselfish, and willing to share any small comforts he himself possessed with his men. Where his own life was concerned he was reckless. To save a company of his men in the last sortie, he had himself crossed the plain in order to draw off the attention of the enemy and let his men get under cover. The bullets had rained like hail all round him, but none had touched him; and he had got back again to shelter, having done what he intended to do, without so much as a scratch.

Yes, whatever his past, he was a brave soldier now. But what was this dark thing of the past? The old proverbial saying came into force where he was concerned, "There is no smoke without fire." Was it true that Keith had received a large legacy from a brother officer who had died? Was it true that he had officiously undertaken the nursing of this young man, when a proper hospital nurse was wished for by the doctor in attendance? Was it true that the friend had died suddenly, and Keith had secured his legacy? And was it—could it be—true that a wrong medicine had been given to the sick man by Keith—oh, of course, by mistake; yes, only by mistake? Was there any truth at all in this curious story?

Each person to whom it was told said that he, for one, did not believe a word of it; nevertheless, he, for one, was interested in it, and looked askance at Keith the next time he appeared on the scene. The men of Keith's own regiment were eagerly questioned. Yes, they knew something—they knew about Aylmer. He had died, poor chap, quite young, and very suddenly; and he and Keith were tremendous friends. Yes, Strause was Aylmer's cousin. No one liked Strause; they were all glad when he left the regiment. Of course, he was a very brave officer—no one could say a word against him now; but he had not been popular in the North Essex Light Infantry. Keith had certainly received a large legacy, and at the time there was a little cloud over him; he had not been himself—his nerves wrong. People had wondered, but suspicion had long died away. He was very popular. There was nothing in the story; of course there was nothing in it. The man who questioned also said that there was nothing in it; but he looked grave, and whispered it to his brother officer, and the brother officer whispered it to another; and so it came to pass that, except Sir George White and one or two others high in command, every one in Ladysmith knew the rumour about Keith. And even this might not have mattered much if Keith himself had not known it; but he did. The cloud fell about him like a winter fog. It dogged his footsteps; it surrounded him when he lay down and when he rose. At first he could not understand what this cold breath, this dullness in the air, meant; but at mess one day his eyes were cruelly opened. A man who had always sat near him got up and took a seat at the extreme end of the table. Keith asked a brother officer what it meant. This man looked at him hard, and after a slight hesitation said,—

"We have been listening to a story about you."

"A story about me!" said Keith; and then, he did not know why, but the colour rushed up into his face. "What is the story?" he said, after a pause.

"It is not my affair," said the man. "If it is false, you had better never hear it; if it is true—well, I leave it to your conscience."

Keith would have insisted on a further inquiry, but at that instant he received a message from his colonel, and was obliged to go off. He intended to go back afterwards and demand a full explanation; but he was depressed after a very hard day's work and want of sufficient food, and instead of going to the messroom he turned aside and went to see Mollie. He had avoided her since Kitty's all too frank words; but now she drew him, as the wretched and starving are drawn to food, and the cold and miserable to the sun.

Mollie gave him a quick, bright glance, and invited him into a little corner which was curtained off for herself. He sat down, and she spoke quickly,—

"What is the matter? Have you got a fresh wound? Oh, I know—you have had nothing to eat. You must have a cup of bovril."

"Not for the world," he answered. "We shall want every scrap of nourishing food for the sick and dying."

"For the sick, truly; but the dying do not matter," she answered. "But if you won't have bovril, there is plenty of chevral; it isn't bad."

He shuddered.

"I could not bring myself to taste it," he said.

"Don't be sentimental," she answered. "Try it now. Believe me, it is first-rate."

She left him, prepared a cup of the mixture, and brought it to him.

"Shut your eyes," she said, "and drink it off."

He did as she told him, and the trembling which had tried him so inexplicably no longer thrilled through his frame.

"And now tell me what is up," she said.

He was silent for a minute; then he told her just what had occurred in the messroom that day. He started when he saw the expression on her face. It had grown white as death, and her eyes shone with a strange light.

"Do you know anything about this?" he asked, amazed at her look.

"I would rather not say," she replied. "But I have to ask you an urgent question. You know it is false; can you live it down?"

"To be suspected of the most ghastly crime by the men I care for is just the drop too much now," he answered.

"It shall be put right," she replied at once.

A light flashed into her eyes, the colour returned to her face, her lips grew red.

"But you cannot put it right, Nurse Mollie."

"It shall be put right. Don't be afraid."

She laid her hand on his shoulder as she spoke, and looked into his eyes. Then she said, in a hoarse voice which he scarcely recognized as hers,—

"Leave me—you are better; leave me. I have something to do at once."

As soon as ever he had gone, Mollie sent an orderly from the hospital to desire Major Strause to come to see her without a moment's delay. The man said that he had never seen Nurse Mollie so imperative. He rushed off immediately to do her bidding, and in half an hour Major Strause was in her presence.

"I must speak to you where we can be alone," said the girl.

"We can be alone there," he said, and he motioned to a little lobby just outside one of the wards.

"Yes, I think we can," she answered. "Come."

She went before him. He did not know whether he was frightened or whether hope filled his heart at her curious manner and at the expression in her face. As soon as ever they got into the lobby, she turned and faced him.

"Major Strause," she said, "you have won. You have been doing the devil's work, and you have won. On certain conditions I will promise to be your wife."

"Oh!" said the major, "is it true? Will you? Oh, I cannot realize it!"

He trembled all over; his face turned ghastly white. He looked as if he meant to devour her with kisses, but she held up a restraining hand.

"No," she said, "you don't kiss me—you don't make love to me; but I will be your promised wife. When the siege is over, if we are alive, then I will marry you. I am your promised wife—but no courting in Ladysmith. That is one of the conditions."

"I submit," he said. "I shall court you in my own heart; I shall think of you when I lie down and when I rise up. You will be my good angel in the battlefield; you will help me when I am starving; you will bring me luck. I shall escape out of this net spread by the fowler. I shall escape, and so will you, brave Nurse Mollie. And we will marry, and be happy; yes, we will be happy!"

"Leave that to the future," said Mollie; "we have to do with the present. I yield to you because I must, and because the weapon you carry is too mighty —because you are too cruel. But I am not going to reproach you; I am going to give you my conditions. You may not accede to them. On no other conditions do I marry you."

"Make your own conditions, my darling; whatever you say shall be done. I would go through fire and water for you."

"Major Strause, you have spread a black, black lie against one of the bravest officers in Her Majesty's service. You have spread that lie now in Ladysmith. You have got to eat your own words. You have got to go to the sources from whence the ugly lie has arisen, and clean them out, and put them straight, and allow the truth—God's truth—to go through them. You have got to go to every man who now suspects Gavon Keith, and tell those men that it was a foul lie, and that Gavon is as innocent as an unborn babe of the crime you imputed to him."

"You think so?" said Strause.

"I know it, Major Strause. On no other condition do I marry you."

Strause's face turned livid.

"And if you don't go," said Mollie, "then I will go, and I will tell an ugly story where you have told an ugly one. I will tell of a day when I found a young officer of the North Essex Light Infantry lying by the roadside insensible; but not drunk, Major Strause, not drunk, but drugged! I, a nurse, can prove that. I myself saw Captain Keith. It was there I found him, and it was then I first learned to love him. I will tell the story just as he told it to me. Your lie can be refuted with my truth—here, now, in Ladysmith. Choose, Major Strause. Set your ugly lie right; blot it out as though it had never existed. I don't tell you how to do it; I only say it must be done. And if you do it, and the rumour dies away, and Gavon Keith is known to be what he is— brave of the brave, good of the good, pure and honourable of the pure and honourable—then I give myself away. I have done that which God meant me to do, and my pain and my misery mean nothing at all. I marry you, and I do not reproach you; and I try, God helping me, to be a good wife to you, if we get away from Ladysmith. Now go; you know what you have to do. You have to choose. If you don't do it—and I shall soon find out—then I do what I said I would do, and you go under for ever."

CHAPTER XXIV.
TRUE TO HER PROMISE.

After the bursting of the shell over the roof of the Town Hall hospital, it was decided that it was no longer a safe hospital for the sick. Some were removed to the Congregational Chapel; others to a camp specially provided for their safety; and others, again, to the field hospital at Intombi. Mollie, to her great distress, was ordered to Intombi. She went with a number of the sick and wounded, and she tried, in the full absorption of her new duties, to forget the anxieties which surrounded her personal life. In some ways this was easy, in others it was difficult. She was now effactually parted from Katherine Hunt and from Kitty. She was also not likely to see either Captain Keith or Major Strause; for although they might manage to get to Intombi, the way there, lying as it did through the enemy's lines, was difficult.

Meanwhile she wondered what the major had decided to do. She resolved, as far as she was concerned, not to leave a stone unturned to extricate Keith from the dilemma which surrounded him. But having been ordered so unexpectedly to Intombi, the strong step which she had meant to take, supposing the major did not comply with her wishes, was now almost impossible to carry out. Meanwhile her duties absorbed every moment of her time. The hospital at Intombi consisted of about two hundred bell tents, together with one or two marquees which the medical staff used. A train went from the town every day to the hospital camp. It took the wounded to the hospital, and also took what supplies could possibly be spared.

Mollie missed the close companionship which had been hers in the beleaguered town. The site chosen for the hospital was anything but desirable, and the patients were both anxious and flurried. Good news affected them favourably; but if the news was depressing, many more on those days were added to the list of deaths. They were within constant hearing of the guns, and although they were supposed to be safe at Intombi, yet the shock to the nerves was very trying. The comforts needed for the sick were almost impossible to be had. They were terribly short of all wholesome and nourishing food. They wanted changes of linen and all sorts of comforts. Many of the sick were obliged, for lack of camp beds, to lie upon the damp ground. The nurses were at their wits' end to keep things going at all. The deaths increased daily. The enteric cases became more and more numerous. Relief seemed far off. Despair came nigh, and hope sank very low.

The food both in Ladysmith and at Intombi was now of the worst type. In Ladysmith the bread degenerated to ground mealies of maize. It was quite indigestible, and caused inflammation of the stomach.

Meanwhile Major Strause considered his strange position, and for a time did nothing. Should he or should he not secure Mollie Hepworth on her own terms? Over and over again, when he lay down for a few hours' rest on his hard bed in his miserable hut, his thoughts turned to her; and his passion and desire to obtain her grew so great that he felt he would even give up every chance of ever appearing straight with his fellow-men for her sake. He knew well that if by a few words—words which, in spite of himself, must give his position away—he did what she required, she would be true to her promise. She would become his wife, and neither reproach him nor bring up his ugly past to him. She would be, what he had always hoped, his faithful and true wife. He felt certain he could make her love him. He did not believe love so great as what he called his feeling for her could be unreturned. She would forget Keith, and give up her entire life to him. And yet again, when daylight broke and he moved amongst his brother officers, he felt that Mollie's conditions were beyond his strength. If he had hated Keith before, the bare mention of his name was enough to madden him now. He was torn between the desire to obtain Mollie and the terror of humiliating himself. He was weak, too, from many hardships, from sundry small wounds, and from insufficient food.

Kitty was confined altogether to her room. She was not ill enough to go to hospital, nor was there any hospital for her to go to, and Katharine was absorbed with her. Captain Keith avoided Strause, and went moodily about his duties. He was often seen wending his way to Observation Hill. He often consulted the heliograph. He would come gravely back, his face more sallow day by day, his step more languid. Major Strause learned to watch for him. Although he hated him, he could scarcely now endure himself except when Captain Keith was in sight. Mollie's absence from Ladysmith made it altogether a terrible spot to both the men who loved her. Yes, they both loved her, each after his own fashion; but Keith's love was unselfish, Strause's the reverse.

Keith now called daily to see Kitty. He went to her room when she was well enough, and sat by her bedside and talked to her cheerily. The little girl answered him in her gentlest fashion. She no longer showed the unworthy terrors which had possessed her on her arrival at Ladysmith. She expected very little, and did not talk as much as formerly about her future. It did not seem to Kitty now that anything mattered. She had to a great extent given up hope. With the absence of hope she became gentler and more bearable—less selfish too. She seemed to have got untold relief from the absence of Mollie. It was impossible for Captain Keith to go very often to Intombi. That he did go from time to time she knew, but now she could rest happily in the knowledge that he was not visiting Mollie daily. In his presence she was very patient, and no longer grumbled. Some of his old love for her returned. He liked to sit with her, to watch her slow-coming smiles, and to talk over matters with Katherine Hunt. He felt very much at home with Katherine, who showed herself a braver and finer woman each day.

Katherine managed to get the very best rations which the beleaguered town could afford for Kitty's use, and she often gave Captain Keith a nourishing meal. He accepted her ministrations without a word. He knew that for Kitty's sake, and perhaps for Mollie's also, he ought not to throw away his life. He was also fully confident that relief would come, sooner rather than later.

"We shall survive this," he said. "Buller is making way, not a doubt of it, and the Boers are only sitting down hoping to starve us out. As long as there is a horse left in Ladysmith we won't be starved."

He had taken quite kindly to his chevral, and tried to induce Kitty to take it. This she would not do. She burst into tears whenever it was offered to her, and in the end Katherine and Keith resolved that she should not be worried to take it. Keith spent almost all his available money in buying eggs and other dainties for the sick girl. Eggs rose to something like four shillings a piece, and even at that they were scarcely worth eating. But Kitty had what few there were to be obtained. Keith had another reason now for liking to be with

Kitty and Katherine Hunt. Katherine Hunt had heard nothing of those rumours which were making his life a hell on earth, neither had Kitty. In their presence he could still feel himself a gallant soldier of Her Majesty. He could still look squarely into the faces of these two women, and knew deep down in his inmost heart that they were not ashamed of him. But outside Kitty's sick-room things were otherwise. This was not a time when one brave soldier could be rude to another, but still marked preferences were shown, also marked aversions. Keith was more or less sent to Coventry. Even his own men heard the rumours which were rife about him, and were not quite as obliging and ready to obey his orders as formerly.

One day, about a month after Mollie had been ordered to Intombi, Captain Keith went up to Observation Hill. He wanted, if possible, to send off a heliograph. To his surprise he saw Major Strause coming slowly up the hill. The two met at the top. It was impossible for Keith to turn away. Before he could in any manner make his escape the major called him.

"I want to say a word to you," was his remark. "Don't go. I have something to communicate which will give you both pleasure and pain."

"You don't look very fit, Major Strause," answered Keith. "Is anything wrong?"

"I have been having a fresh touch of fever—a touch of the sun, I suppose. For the last few days I have been in the hospital down here—the Congregational Chapel: a beastly hole—no comforts of any sort; not a decent nurse in the place. I was looked after, if you can call it being looked after, by one or two orderlies. You may be sure I left as soon as I could. Oh what I suffered!"

"You look like it," said Keith.

"General White seems more hopeful," pursued Strause. "He is confident that relief will be ours before long. And have you noticed that the Boers are beginning to trek?"

"No, I have not. Is that the case?"

"Beyond doubt. If you look now, you will see something."

The two men went to the top of the hill, and noticed a long line, more than a mile in length, of wagons, slowly but surely going away from Ladysmith. Then they saw heavy dust clouds. The wagons were crowded with people. They went twining like snakes round the hillsides. They certainly looked like a beaten army in full retreat.

Keith's eyes sparkled. There came a streak of red into his sallow cheek.

"It can't be true!" he said. "We have waited so long for good news that now I can scarcely realize it!"

"It may or may not come," said Strause. "The general is confident. Another good sign is that there is no more horse-flesh ordered for the men, and we are put on full rations."

"Still I can scarcely believe it," answered Keith.

"The next few days will solve all our doubts," was Strause's answer. "But we are not out of the wood yet—by no means. For my part, I want a hand-to-hand fight. I would rather end the thing than go on as I have been doing. It is maddening. Everything has been maddening here lately," he added, with a sneer, and in a peculiar tone.

Keith looked at him. His face, which had assumed a kindly and interested expression while he and the major were watching the great trek from Ladysmith, now stiffened. It turned white.

"To what do you allude?" he said.

"I allude to the absence of the one woman who made Ladysmith bearable."

Keith made no answer. The major looked full at him.

"I did you a beastly wrong."

Keith stared.

"I am going to put it right. I cannot stand these things any longer. I dreaded for a time turning the opprobrium which has been your portion on myself, but I don't care *that* for a man's opinion any longer. Men live for the women they love, not for other men. I don't care what my colonel or my brother officers think. But I care all God's earth, the warmth of His sun, and the cheer of life for a woman's smile, and I mean to get it."

"Explain yourself," said Keith.

"I can do so in a few words. What was wrong shall be put right. I cannot tell you any more. What was wrong shall be put quite right. That is about all as far as you are concerned."

Keith turned his head away. His one desire was to get past Major Strause and go back to Ladysmith. Strause laid a detaining hand on his shoulder.

"I don't suppose you think well of me," he said, "although I am about to do the hardest thing a man like myself could ever do. I am going to bring myself down in order that you may show in your true colours. And I hate you, Captain Keith, as I hate no other man on earth. It would be a satisfaction to me to put a bullet through you! But there, I am going to put everything right for you; only I don't do it for your sake."

"Why do you detain me, Major Strause? I have urgent duties to perform. I will wish you good-morning."

"You must stay one minute. I am going to be square with you. I am going to do what I do, and you will be right, and I shall—"

He paused.

"Yes?" said Keith. His pulse beat rapidly. There had come a breeze something like health round his stagnant heart, his eyes had brightened, but now a cold and dreadful fear crept over him.

"Look," said the major—he pointed with his hand—"there lies the hospital."

"The Intombi hospital?" said Keith.

"There lies the hospital, and I gothere."

"You—you are not ill!"

"If I can go in no other way, I shall pose as a sick man. It can be done, and I go. You would like to know why?"

"Yes," said Keith.

"I will tell you." The major moistened his dry lips. "I am going there to see the one woman who is all God's earth to me. I am going to—*kiss her.*"

"You lie, you scoundrel!" said Keith.

"I may be a scoundrel, but on this occasion I do not lie. I go to kiss Nurse Mollie, and claim her as my promised wife."

"You lie!" said Keith again.

His face turned white as ashes. He trembled. It was with an effort he kept himself from falling. The major smiled at him—a strange smile of triumph. Then, without uttering another word, he strode past him, and was lost to view.

CHAPTER XXV.
STUNNED.

Captain Keith slowly returned to Ladysmith. He was stunned: there were a coldness and faintness round his heart; but he walked straight and stiff. Was he to get back his freedom at such a price as this? No; he would rather lie under the blackest cloud all his life. Was Mollie going to force the major's hand, and was his reward to be—herself? The thought was monstrous.

"She does not love him," thought Keith, "on the contrary, she hates him. And yet Major Strause would not have spoken as he did nor looked as he did if there had been no truth in the idea. Men like Major Strause do not suddenly turn into angels, nor humiliate themselves, for mere sentiment. Conscience is not the major's strong point. If he speaks the truth, he has a motive for his actions. Mollie gives herself to him that I may be cleared. It is like her, but I will not permit it."

Keith went straight to the hotel. He inquired for Katherine Hunt. She was in, and he went upstairs to the girls' sitting-room. He had resolved, in his extremity, to take Katherine into his confidence. When he entered the small room, he was relieved to find that Kitty was not there. There were folding doors between the sitting-room and the bedroom, and the folding doors were shut. After a moment they were opened, and Katherine Hunt came in. Kitty was lying on the bed in the other room. Katherine, without intending it, left the doors between the two rooms slightly ajar. Kitty noticed this. As soon as Katherine had disappeared, she raised herself on her elbow, slipped off the bed, and approached the door. She stood on the other side.

"I don't know why I am mean enough to listen," she thought, "but I will listen, come what may. Gavon has been very kind to me lately, but I am not sure of him."

Meanwhile Katherine had given her hand to Keith. She had looked full in his face, and said quietly,—

"Something is worrying you."

"Yes," answered Keith. "I am half maddened. I must confide in some one. No one can help me, unless you, Miss Hunt, will take pity on me."

"That I will," she replied, "and right gladly. Sit down, please."

He took no notice of this request.

"There is a rumour in the camp," he said, "that relief is not far off. There is also a rumour that the short rations are coming to an end. Both rumours may be wrong. You must know, however, Miss Hunt, that every one in Ladysmith holds his life in his hands. Our quietus may come to us at any moment."

"That, after a fashion, is true in all walks of life," she answered.

"Yes, but not to the same degree," he replied. "But at least, Miss Hunt," he continued, "while we live I hope we, who are soldiers of the Queen"—he bowed to Katherine as though to include her in the compliment—"will live with honour. Something happened to-day which affects my honour. I must tell you."

"Yes?" she said; "what is it?"

The door between the bedroom and the sitting-room creaked a tiny bit wider; but the two in the sitting-room were too absorbed with each other to notice it.

Katherine looked up into Keith's face. Her own was brave and strong. It had aged since she came to Ladysmith, but the lines of endurance seemed to bring out her true character. She had always in her the makings of a noble woman; now she *was* a noble woman. In this fact lay the difference between her old life and her present. She had been brought into a moral forcing-house, and the development of her courageous nature was enormous.

"Yes," she said again, "tell me."

Keith looked full at her.

"Things have happened," he said, "which in great measure have undermined my manhood. Things have been said for which I personally am not responsible. Rumours have been circulated with regard to me which make me in the eyes of my fellow-men not only a scoundrel wanting in honour, but a man on whom the hand of the law is heavily placed. According to my fellow-men in Ladysmith, I can be arrested at this instant for the blackest of all crimes. And yet, Miss Hunt, there is no man on God's earth more innocent of the crime to which I allude than I am."

"Then why do you fear?" said Katherine.

"Because circumstantial evidence is black against me, and because I am in the hands of one without honour and without conscience."

The little listener on the other side of the door gave a groan. It was a wonder Keith did not hear it.

"Miss Hunt, in connection with what I have just told you, I have heard a most terrible piece of news. This news is so terrible to me that my own unhappiness sinks quite out of sight by comparison. If it is true, before God steps must be taken. She shall not marry him in the dark."

"She! Whom do you talk of?" said Katherine.

Kitty clasped her hands together. The colour mounted in big spots on her cheeks; her dark eyes shone. Yes, Kitty knew to whom Gavon alluded. The next moment he had spoken the words she expected to hear.

"I have just seen Strause," said Keith. "He was on his way—that is, if he could get there—to Intombi. He tells me that he is all but engaged to Kitty's sister. He says she will marry him. And oh, he was going to kiss her! You can understand, I hope, Miss Hunt, that—"

Keith leaned suddenly against the wall; he raised his hand and wiped some drops from his forehead.

"You can understand," he continued, "that I—well, that I cannot permit this."

"I hope so," replied Katherine.

She felt glad that Kitty was not in the room.

"Even if I had never known Sister Mollie, I should be dismayed," he continued; "but as it is— I have no right to say anything more. She is Kitty's sister; let that be my excuse. Miss Hunt, it is hateful to speak against a brother officer; but the man is a scoundrel—he is worse!"

"It is hateful to speak against a brother officer; but the man is a scoundrel —he is worse!"

"What can you mean?" said Katherine.

"Things are so grave that I must speak. He has cast a shadow over me which in reality reflects on himself. Miss Hunt, the man is a—"

"What? I can't hear you," said Katherine.

The next words were spoken in the lowest whisper. Katherine gave a cry.

Her cry was echoed in the next room. A sharp note of terror fell on both speakers' ears.

"What is that?" said Katherine. "Kitty! Kitty!"

She rushed across the room, she burst open the door, and there was Kitty, lying half fainting on the floor.

Gavon Keith and Katherine laid her on the bed.

"I must speak to you, Gavon," said the girl. "No, I am not quite fainting. I must speak to you.—Stay if you like, Katheriue, stay if you like, but I must speak to him."

"I will go into the other room," said Katherine.

She went away at once, leaving the door between the two rooms slightly ajar.

"Sit there, Gavon," said Kitty. "Oh, you may be just as shocked as ever you like, but I *listened*. Is it true what you said in so low a whisper?"

"All I said is true, Kitty."

"And Major Strause is—"

Kitty could not form the next word. Keith was silent for a moment.

"I will tell you about Major Strause," he said then.

He bent towards her, and in a few words gave his own history—the history of himself and Aylmer. He unfolded to her the black plot, and the cruel shadow which was made to rest upon his own head.

"I met him just now, Kitty," he said in conclusion, "and he told me that he was about to put the thing right. I don't know how he could do it without implicating himself; but that part scarcely matters. He would not say anything, I know, to put my life in peril, but he does not mind killing my reputation. He said something else, though, which cannot be permitted. Kitty, he said he was going to marry Mollie. If Mollie marries him, she does it to save me; and, Kitty, she must not do it. I would rather go under for ever."

Keith had scarcely uttered these words before there was a commotion on the stairs and a knock at the room door. He went to open it.

An orderly stood without. Captain Keith was wanted at headquarters immediately.

The two girls were left alone. Kitty raised herself from her pillow with a perfectly blanched face. After a long time Katherine went up and spoke to her.

"You must be brave," said Katherine. "There is great excitement—strange news every where. I believe there is a great battle imminent; and yet here are you and I and two men in this small camp absorbed in our own personal affairs. It seems monstrous."

"Personal affairs must come first," said Kitty, in a gasping voice. "I won't stand this—I can't; I see myself as I am. Katherine, Mollie would not do this but for me."

"But for you, Kitty!"

"I urged her to do it—I implored her to do it. I told her it was the only thing. O Katherine, she must not marry Major Strause. What am I to do—what am I to do?"

"I will come to you presently," said Katheriue. "I must go downstairs now. There are things to be done, and I must find out what is the matter. Listen to the shells bursting. You have had no dinner; I must see what I can find for you."

Katherine went out of the room. She did not like Kitty's face. There was a wildness in her eyes which alarmed her.

The moment she was alone, Kitty slipped across the bedroom into the sitting-room. She went straight to the window. To her surprise, she saw Katherine walking down the street. She wondered where she was going. Shells were dropping all over the place, bursting as they fell. Katherine passed within a few feet of one which burst with a tremendous roar. Kitty looked calmly on. The time had come when the bursting of shells mattered nothing to her. She went back to her bedroom.

"I will do it," she said to herself. "I don't care. I am desperate. I see everything now. She shall not sacrifice herself."

Kitty hastily put on her shoes; she laced them on her little feet. She pinned on her hat, went to a drawer where she kept her purse—now, alas! very light —slipped it into her pocket, and, just as she was, ran downstairs. Some men were talking in little knots. A woman now and then appeared at the end of a passage, looked anxiously at the men, and disappeared again. No one looked at Kitty as she went downstairs. The time had come when the intense general interest was so profound that small minor interests were of no account whatever. It mattered nothing to any one in the Royal Hotel that the slender girl who had for a long time been an invalid was going out with shells falling around her. Kitty left the hotel. She walked down the street. Her steps were very feeble. She met a woman, one of the townspeople. She went up to her.

"Can you and will you help me?" she said. Her voice was very shaky.

"Who are you?" said the woman.

"I want to go to Intombi. Can I go?"

"The train with the sick and wounded has just left," said the woman. "No one will be taken to Intombi until this time to-morrow. You are in danger here," she continued: "a shell might burst any moment."

"I must not die," said Kitty; "I have something to do before I die."

"Is it anything of great importance?"

"It is of tremendous importance—tremendous—and must be done. Will you help me? I will pay you."

"Poor child!" said the woman. "I don't want the money. But you ought to get into shelter. Where are you staying?"

"At the hotel—the Royal Hotel."

"It is not safe there. They are always firing at the hotel. They think to kill Sir George White or some other important officer. But I could take you to a place of safety. I rushed home to get a toy and some food for a child. We spend the day in the caves by the river-side. Come with me; we are quite safe there."

"Oh, will you—will you really take me in?"

"I will truly take you in. Come; please God, we will get back to the caves in safety."

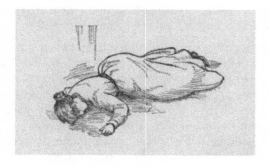

CHAPTER XXVI.
THE CAVES.

Kitty was just starting with the woman when an idea struck her.

"Wait one moment, only one moment," she said.

Before the woman could reply she rushed away from her. She ran wildly back to the hotel; she dashed up to her own room. There she opened a drawer, took certain things from it, folded them in a bit of paper, and came back again to the woman. She was panting and out of breath, but there was a new light in her eyes, and she did not look anything like so weak as she had done an hour ago, when she lay feeble and exhausted on her bed.

"You are a plucky one," said the woman.

That any one should call Kitty that caused her to smile very faintly, but it also sent a certain stimulus round her heart.

"I plucky! that is all you know," she said.

Then the woman gave the girl her hand. She herself had been an inhabitant of Ladysmith for years. She was an Englishwoman, and she wanted to see the old country again before she died. She was the mother of stalwart boys, and the wife of a good, sensible, matter-of-fact tradesman. She had no daughters, and this girl, slim and small and pretty, appealed to her.

"I will look after you, you poor little thing," she said. "Whether you were plucky or not in the past, you are plucky now. Come; you will be safe in the caves with me and my family."

A few moments later the woman and the girl had found shelter in one of the caves by the river-side. These caves had been excavated in order to afford bomb-proof shelter during the great siege. The woman had a little part of one of the caves portioned off for herself and her family. It was fairly comfortable; there was even a little furniture here. Kitty was offered the best chair the place afforded. They could hear the firing; but no shells burst anywhere near them. There was very little to eat; but Kitty was not hungry. The one thing which absorbed all her faculties and all her powers was how she was to get to Intombi. She, a poor, defenceless little girl, could not run the gauntlet of the enemy's firing. But she had an idea which might possibly be successful, and which she dared not tell to any one.

Presently the daylight passed, and the night came on. As usual, the firing ceased, and the cave dwellers prepared to return to their homes. The woman who had befriended Kitty packed up her things with right good will.

"You are our guest now, so you will come home with us to-night," she said to Kitty.

But the girl did not move.

"I am going to stay here," she said; "I am not going back. I want to stay here, please."

"Oh, that is nonsense," said the woman. "You cannot stay alone in these awful, lonesome caves. There will be no one with you. You can't do it, my dear. A pretty young thing like you! it's impossible."

"You may go or not, just as you like," said Kitty, "but I am going to stay."

The woman's husband, a man of the name of Burke, now came up and expostulated with the girl.

"We're right glad to give you shelter, miss," he said, "if only you can prove yourself an Englishwoman; but to stay here all night—it can't be done, miss. Come, march!"

He went up roughly to the girl, and raised her to her feet. But Kitty could be obstinate.

"I am not going," she said; "I shall stay here. No one will know I am here; and I promise to be very, very quiet. *Please* let me stay."

"Come, husband," said the woman. "If she chooses to make a fool of herself, I don't suppose any harm will come to her. No one wants to come near these caves during the night—horrid, damp, gloomy places. We have too much of them in the daytime.—I'll leave you a chunk of bread, miss, and a little water; that's the most I can do for you."

"Thank you," said Kitty.

Presently the Burke family went back to the town. Other families were seen wending their way in the same direction. The gloom swallowed them up. Just now in Ladysmith darkness was welcome as no light could ever be. The people disappeared one after the other, and the caves, which had rung with sound and movement, became absolutely still. Only the water-rats were heard, and the sigh of the wind as it rippled over the water. Distant sounds, however, floated over the breeze—the constant booming of guns, which were fired, even though it was night, in order to make sure that all was well. Distant lights in the enemy's camps were also seen, and now and then a searchlight made a vivid path of whiteness in the direction of the town. Kitty fancied she saw a silent party moving quietly like grey ghosts in the distance. They passed the caves. She wondered what they were doing, but she was not greatly interested in them. Her thought of thoughts was, how was she, a lonely, defenceless little girl, to find her way through the enemy's lines to Intombi? Nevertheless, whatever the danger, she had made up her mind to go.

"I have drawn Mollie into this dreadful thing, and I alone must save her," she thought.

Presently she unfastened the little parcel which she had all this time kept by her side. She took from it a nurse's apron and the cap which the nurses of the Red Cross wear. She pinned the badge of the Red Cross on her arm, crept away from the caves, and began to go slowly, and with many qualms in her heart, in the direction of the town. Each sound made her start. She had the greatest difficulty in keeping herself from screaming; nevertheless a new courage filled her heart.

Presently she saw a soldier standing as if at attention about twenty yards distant. She wondered if he were a sentry on duty. Beyond doubt he saw her, and was interested in her. She also stood still, and the man wheeled round and looked full in her direction. It was so dark that he could only see the shadow of a woman. Presently his voice rang out, "Who goes there?" Kitty knew she could not escape him; was he going to be friend or foe? She felt for her purse. Holding it in her hand, she approached the soldier.

"Who are you?" he said, gazing at her in astonishment. "Have you lost your way? Go straight on, and you will get back to Ladysmith, but you must be quick. What are you doing wandering outside the town?"

"I am a Red Cross nurse," said Kitty, "and I have lost my way. I wanted to return to Intombi to-night, but I lost my way. Has the ambulance train gone yet?"

203

"It went not long ago, but they are making up a second."

"Please take me to it, I am so afraid to be alone. Please take me to the train. I am due at Intombi; they want me very badly." Here she held the apron and cap out to him. "See," she said. She pointed to the Red Cross badge on her arm.

The soldier whistled, and looked at her significantly.

"I was in hospital," he said, "at Ladysmith, and a rough enough time it wor. If it weren't for Sister Mollie—"

"I know Sister Mollie," said Kitty. She hesitated as to whether or not she should say she was Mollie's sister. "I know her well, very well," she continued. "I have nursed under her. She is expecting me back. I lost my way."

"I don't know how you could," said the man.

"But I did. Oh, don't question me any further. Get me to the ambulance train, please. You are not a sentry, are you?"

"No, I am not a sentry."

"Then you can take me. And see, you shall have all the money I possess."

As she spoke, she opened her little purse and emptied it into the soldier's palm. It contained three or four shillings and a couple of pence. He looked at the money as it lay in his hand. It would buy a dainty for his supper; and even with full rations, dainties in Ladysmith were not to be despised. Nevertheless he was an honest British soldier, and nothing would induce him to take her last shillings from a Red Cross nurse.

"Take back your money," he said; "I don't want it. If you come with me quick, you may catch the train, but you were a great fool to lose it."

In a very few moments they found themselves at the station. A moment or two longer and Kitty had taken her place in the train—no questions asked, her uniform and the badge on her arm being sufficient. She could scarcely believe in her own luck.

"Safe so far; success so far," thought the girl.

In process of time the train, with its sad load of wounded and dying, reached the great hospital at the base. Kitty got out with the others. Her excitement now knew no bounds. She did not wait to assist any of the wounded men. The nurses—there were none too many of them—came out, the orderlies did what they could, and the sick and wounded were brought one by one into the tents. The damp of the place was fearful. The flies were a torture. The red dust lay in patches everywhere. There were few comforts of any sort. How different from the Town Hall hospital, which, poor as it was, was at least the soul of order!

But Kitty noticed none of these things. She wanted Mollie. If she could save Mollie, the wounded and dying mattered nothing at all. Presently she saw her. She was in the forefront, as usual. She held a lamp in her hand. She was giving directions. Kitty ran up and touched her.

"I have come," she said, "to help you."

Mollie turned and glanced at her. She saw a light in the wild brown eyes, a smile round the lips, and she noticed a queer, new, and very foreign expression on the small face. But all she did was to clasp Kitty's hand for one instant.

"Nothing personal now," said Sister Mollie—"presently, presently."

Kitty fell back, stunned and ashamed. After a few minutes, however, Mollie showed that she had not forgotten her sister. She turned and said,—

"All hands are wanted. If you are useful, I am glad you have come. Go and help the other nurses. I will speak to you presently."

With something between a sob and a cry of joy Kitty turned and went. With the little cap and the big white apron, and the red cross on her arm, she felt herself truly a sister of the Red Cross. The thought ennobled and raised her. There was a sense of rest all over her. Her wild expedient had succeeded.

Kitty, to the longest day she lived, never forgot that night—that night when she was completely and absolutely carried out of herself; when weakness and hunger were forgotten, and when, until the dawn broke, she ministered to the sick, the wounded, and the dying. There was no time at the Intombi camp to wait for trained nurses. Any woman's hand was sustaining; any woman could at least give a glance of sympathy and a word of comfort.

While Sister Mollie and the surgeons attended to the more serious cases, Kitty fulfilled her full quota of work. It was not until the morning broke that she had an instant alone with her sister. The dreadful firing had recommenced. It sounded far louder at Intombi than it did at Ladysmith. In the pause between the firing of one shell and another, Kitty, who was leaning up against the post of one of the tents, having just ministered to the dying needs of a gallant young dragoon officer, felt a light hand on her shoulder. She turned her white face, and encountered the eyes of her sister. Mollie's clear, steadfast brown eyes looked full into hers.

"Well, little brave girl," said Mollie, "and now why have you come? You

205

were of great use last night. But what is it, Kitty, what is it?"

Kitty put her hand to her forehead.

"I forget," she said.

"You must come and have something. I can give you a cup of tea—such an inestimable boon! You shall have it; you deserve it. Come with me now."

She took the girl's hand and led her across to one of the marquees in the centre of the hospital. Here she gave her some tea, and made her sit down while she drank it. Kitty swallowed the tea, and then looked full at her sister with big, frightened eyes.

"I know now," she said. "Have you done it?"

"Done what, dear?"

"Then you haven't done it! I am in time, and you haven't done it!"

"Done what, Kitty, what?"

Kitty again looked wildly round her.

"I have come," she said. "I told a lie to come. I said I was a Red Cross sister. I was not."

"In one sense you were. You have been plucky of the plucky last night. But why have you come, Kitty? and where is Katherine?"

"I know nothing about her. I had to come to—save you. Is Major Strause here?"

"Major Strause!" said Molly. A faint colour came into her tired face. "No," she said; "he would not be here unless he were wounded."

"Thank God! thank God! Then you are not engaged to him."

Kitty burst into tears. Mollie knelt by her.

"What do you mean, child?" she said. "Not engaged to him! But I thought you wished it."

"Not now. I have repented. I have heard something. Mollie, you must never, under any circumstances, marry him—never, never!"

"Thank God," was Mollie's answer.

She took the little slight figure in her arms. Presently she lifted the girl up and carried her into the hospital. There was an empty bed, from which a dead soldier had been removed for burial. She put a clean sheet on it and laid Kitty down.

"Sleep, little heroine," she said. "And did you really come straight through the enemy's lines to tell me this?"

But Kitty was too tired to reply; already she was sound asleep.

CHAPTER XXVII.
THE GREAT EXCITEMENT.

Major Strause had meant to go straight to Mollie from Observation Hill. He trusted to his luck to bring him safely through the enemy's lines to Intombi; but that luck was altogether against him. He soon saw that it would have been at the sacrifice of his life had he attempted to reach the girl he hoped to make his bride on that day. Sulky and miserable, therefore, he was obliged to return to Ladysmith.

There he found the whole place in a turmoil of excitement. The news that full rations had been ordered, joined to the hope of possible relief, and the fact beyond all doubt that the Boers were already making treks for safer quarters, filled every mouth. The women of the town came out in their best dresses and made holiday. The men talked and laughed, and stood about in groups. The women did their shopping just as if no shells were bombarding the place. The soldiers shouted hearty congratulations the one to the other.

"Have you heard the news? Full rations to-day—no horse-flesh."

Cheers in each case followed this announcement. The soldiers would, many of them, have gladly given five years of their lives for a full meal. For the time being the thought of the full meals seemed even more important than the relief of Ladysmith. The major heard them talking, and more than one officer came up and expressed satisfaction at the new hope which was filling every breast. But the major scarcely replied. His whole soul was centred on one desire—he must win Mollie's consent to be his wife. More than ever was it necessary if the siege was likely to be raised. He must see Mollie, whatever happened. How was he to get to Intombi camp?

But, after all, he did get there easily enough. He went there in the ordinary course; for when Kitty, in her shelter in one of the caves, had seen lines of shadowy figures stealing past in the darkness, although she knew it not, one of these figures belonged to Major Strause. He, with a contingent of Light Infantry and three companies of the Devon Regiment, had marched out in the hope of making a last sortie against the enemy. The immediate results, so far as this story is concerned, were as follows:—

Early the next day Major Strause was sent to Intombi, a dangerously-wounded man. Both legs were hopelessly shattered, and there was nothing for it but amputation. He was taken into one of the tents, which, as it happened, contained no other occupant at the time. The surgeons immediately put him under chloroform, and quickly performed their work. When the operation was over he was relieved from pain. He was given champagne, and even laughed as he drank it. He said he was free from all suffering.

There was a peculiar expression on his face, a sort of change—a lightness as well as a brightness. The surgeons looked at one another, and then they went out of the tent and whispered in the passage outside. They did not like the soldier's manner. Very few people survived double amputation. He must remain very quiet. What nurse could be spared to look after him?

Just as they were talking in this way, the small new sister of the Red Cross appeared in sight. She was refreshed by her sleep, and although she was very much dazed and puzzled, there was a new strength about her face. One of the surgeons called her at once.

"I do not know you," he said. "What is your name?"

The girl thought for a minute; then she said boldly,—

"Sister Kitty."

"Sister Kitty?" said the doctor.

"Yes, sister of Nurse Mollie."

"Ah," he said, "if you are anything like her, you are indeed welcome to Intombi! Can you undertake a case now—at once?"

Kitty longed to say, "No," but it was useless. She could not be at Intombi without taking up her appointed work.

"I will do anything you like," she said.

"It is a serious case," said the surgeon, dropping his voice. "There is a man in there who in all probability won't live long. There is also, of course, a vague hope that he may recover. Everything practically depends on his nurse. He must be kept cheerful but very quiet. He will want some one to be with him all the time, in case of hemorrhage setting in."

"What sort of case is it?" said Kitty.

"The man's legs were shattered. We have been obliged to perform double amputation. Come this way, nurse; there is no time to lose."

The doctor drew aside a curtain, and ushered Kitty into the tent where Major Strause was lying. He saw her, and uttered a quick exclamation. Kitty saw him, and every vestige of colour left her face.

"Why, you know each other!" said the surgeon, in some astonishment.

"Yes," said Major Strause swiftly. "Of all the nurses in the camp this young lady you have brought to me can be most useful. I want to say something to her. For mercy's sake, leave us for a little time, Dr. Watson."

The doctor gave one or two very brief directions to Kitty, and left the tent. As soon as he had done so, Major Strause called her to his side.

"Stoop down, little girl," he said.

Kitty bent over him. Then she remembered the words she had heard the day before, and started back.

"I can't nurse you," she said.

"Why not?"

"Because—I did not know what you were; but I know now."

"What do you know, little girl?"

"I cannot tell you."

The major looked full at her.

"Never mind what you know," he said, after a pause. "Do you see that champagne bottle? Fill me out half a glass. I have a sinking sensation; I am not accustomed to it. Hold the wine to my lips."

Kitty was forced to obey. The major sipped the stimulant slowly. Then he said with a sigh,—

"That has done me good. But what were the doctors saying? I heard them whispering outside."

"They said you were very ill," replied Kitty.

"I should rather think I am—both legs gone at a crash! Nothing but the stump of the old major for the future. Hoped I could retrieve my position. Felt nearly mad last night—thought that nothing mattered—wanted to get to Intombi, and could not. Have *reached* Intombi. Well, the curtain closes here, and perhaps it is best. I say, little girl, how did you run the gauntlet of the enemy?"

"I came in the ambulance train," said Kitty.

"A good thought. Very plucky. Why did you come?"

"To save Mollie. And I think," added Kitty, and a wild light filled her eyes, and she looked full at the major's flushed and yet paling face—"I think God is saving her."

"From me?"

"Yes."

"You are right. It was a plucky thing of you to do. Tell me something else."

"What?"

"Do the doctors think I will recover?" "I—

don't—know."

"Speak, child; do you think I am afraid? Speak out."

"They—"

"Speak out."

"They think that you are in—"

"Danger?"

"Yes."

"I believe them," reiterated the major. "A man rarely gets over this sort of operation. I have seen enough of it since I came to Ladysmith. Well, we must all join the great majority some time, and I suppose my turn has come."

Kitty was silent. She did not like the major enough even to give him false hope. She stood by the bedside, and the grey look crept up and up the dying soldier's face. He lay very still, his eyes staring straight before him.

"Sit down," he said at last.

The little figure dropped into a seat near the foot of the bed.

"You dislike me very much?" he said then.

"I—hate you," answered the girl.

There was another silence.

"It seems wrong to hate a poor chap who is dying, and who, after all, has given his life for his country," said the major then.

Kitty was silent.

"I would rather die without a woman in my presence who hates me," he said, after a pause.

"Shall I go?" said Kitty, rising.

"No. Bad as you are, you are better than no one; and I must have stimulants. I say, a little more champagne."

Kitty filled up the glass again. He sipped it.

"It doesn't seem to pull me round," he said then. "I want brandy; champagne is not strong enough. Do you know what it is, little girl, to sink?"

"No," said Kitty.

"Don't you?—to sink right through the tent, and through the ground beneath? That's what I feel. I am slipping, slipping over the brink. That is it—slipping over the brink, little girl. How dark it is getting! Why don't you come near me? Can you hate a dying soldier who has given his life for his country?"

"No," said Kitty, and she suddenly burst into tears. When her tears came she fell forward against the soldier's bed, and took hold of one of his hands and laid her cheek against it.

"No; forgive me," she said. "I—don't—hate you any longer."

Her words troubled the major; a new look came into his face.

"If you forgive me, little Kitty," he said, "I wonder if God Almighty will?"

"Let's ask Him," said Kitty.

She began there and then to pray.

"Dear Lord God in heaven, forgive Major Strause. He is a very bad man, and he is going to die."

"That's it, Kitty," said the major, "put it strong."

"A very bad man," repeated Kitty, "and he is about to die, but he is—sorry."

"That's it, Kitty," said the major again. "Put it stronger."

"He is *very* sorry," repeated Kitty.

There was a silence. Kitty's head dropped against the bed. The major breathed quick and hard.

"Where's your sister?" he said suddenly.

"You can't see her," cried Kitty.

"I must."

The girl sprang to her feet.

"You can't."

"One minute, little Kitty. If you will help me, we will both do something. I think we have done wrong in the past—you in your way, I in mine. But while your sins are comparatively venial, mine—O mercy! I seem to see his dying face, and he is reproaching me. It is poor Aylmer. Tell him to get away. He scares me. I did not think that I could be scared; but he looks at me, and he scares me.—I'll put it right, Aylmer; yes, I'll put it right.—Kitty, you must help me. You and I together, little girl, can put everything right."

"What do you mean?" said Kitty.

She trembled all over, but still she kept herself in check.

"Listen, child. There are two people whom you and I have done all that man and woman could to part. Suppose, now, I give them back to one another; suppose you give them back. I restore them with my death, and you with your life. How does that sound? Do you think you can do your part if I do mine?"

"I don't know."

"You have no time to think. Be quick. If you will do it, I will do it."

The major's eyes began to shine with fever.

"Be quick," he said. "I believe you will do it. Fetch Sister Mollie." And Kitty went.

Sister Mollie was indeed busy, for every tent in the hospital was full. If Major Strause survived another hour, soldiers would be brought to share his tent with him; but the surgeons had implored for an hour or two of perfect quiet in a case of so much danger. Kitty, with her white face and her startled eyes, rushed to her sister's side.

"Let them all go, let them all go!" she said. "It is life or death. Come at once—at once!"

"Yes, go, Sister Mollie; I will look after the cases," said another capable-looking nurse who stood near.

Mollie glanced at Kitty, read she knew not what in her eyes, and went with her.

"What are they firing about? what is the excitement?" said Mollie suddenly.

She stopped; then she ran to the door. Kitty ran with her.

"Why, what is it?" she said. "Who are those soldiers? Not Boers. No, our men, and galloping! No horses in Ladysmith have galloped for many days. O Kitty, Kitty, what *does* it mean?"

"I don't know," said Kitty. "But come; it is a case of life or death."

A wild, tremendous, all-inspiring cheer burst at this moment on the air, and the galloping horses came nearer, and the sick men who were able to move in the hospital raised their languid heads, and the orderlies and doctors shouted, and even the nurses came out, as Lord Dundonald, with a small body of mounted troops, made a dash across the hills, and passed Intombi on his way to Ladysmith.

"'Lift up your heads; for your redemption draweth nigh,'" said Mollie.

She looked at Kitty, but Kitty had scarcely heard the words.

"Quick! quick!" she cried; "there is something to be done—something for you and something for him." And she led Mollie to the tent where Major Strause lay dying.

"What is that noise?" said the major; "a fresh battle, eh?"

"Relief! relief!" cried Mollie.

"The relief of—death?"

"The relief of life," said Mollie. "Lord Dundonald has just ridden past on his way to Ladysmith."

The major looked dimly round him.

"It is quite dark," he said. "I do—not seem—to—understand. I can scarcely see—your face. Are you really Mollie Hepworth?"

"Yes," she answered.

"Stoop down—come very close; I should like to look at you once again. You promised, on certain conditions, to marry me?"

"I did."

"Come still closer. Now I can see your face; yes, thank God, in my dying moments I can see it. It is good and strong, and like that of an angel—an archangel. Did you mean your words, archangel?"

"Yes."

"Thank God for that too. You, of all women on God's earth, could have made a good man of me, and for you alone on my death-bed I repent. Listen. The story I told you about Keith was false as hell. I wanted money, and I thought I could blackmail him, and I seemed to see my way when Aylmer was reported to be in danger. It was I who changed the medicines. I put a wrong label on each bottle. Little Kitty here is witness, and you are witness. I was at the bottom of that dastardly plot. It was I who caused the death of Aylmer. Keith is one of the best fellows living—yes, Mollie, one of the best; and take him, take him as your husband, for little Kitty and I give him to you."

"Yes, Major Strause and I give him to you," said Kitty, and she fell forward against the bed.

The major looked at her, and then he looked at Mollie, and he smiled and tried to put out his hand through the darkness to clasp Mollie's.

"The only good woman—I ever knew," he whispered once.

His hand relaxed its hold. He was dead.

CHAPTER XXVIII.
"HE THAT LOSETH HIS LIFE SHALL FIND IT."

Three months afterwards, in a London church there was a brief ceremony. A man and woman stood before the altar, and were united in the bonds of matrimony. The man had the proud carriage of a soldier, and bore the gallant distinction of V.C., won for valour in the fight, after his name. The woman owned that greatest badge that any woman could wear, the Red Cross, bestowed upon her by the sovereign of the land.

The words which were to make them one for all time were spoken, and they turned away, husband and wife at last. Standing a little way off, a bright colour in her cheeks, an intense light in her eyes, was a girl who resembled the bride, and yet did not resemble her. Another girl was also present; she was watching this slight and delicate girl's face with a mixture of admiration and pain. The bride and bridegroom, in many ways the most unselfish pair in the world, were for the time so absorbed in each other that they did not notice Kitty as Katherine Hunt noticed her.

They started on their wedding journey straight from the church, and those few guests who were invited to drink their healths at Mrs. Keith's house returned there. Last in the group came Kitty and Katherine Hunt.

"And now, Kitty, you will do it?" said Katherine Hunt, and she took both Kitty's hands in one of her own.

"Yes," said Kitty, "if you wish it."

"My father has bequeathed to me a large fortune, which I may spend during his lifetime as I think fit. My present intention is to start convalescent homes here and there over England—convalescent homes where brave soldiers, commissioned and non-commissioned, can get comforts, and healing, and rest. I want you to take the management of one, and I will take the management of another. You can do it, and you will be happy in doing it, and many soldiers from the Transvaal will soon fill the comfortable rooms, and enjoy themselves in the fresh air. Those who can pay shall pay a trifle, but those who cannot pay shall come without money, and all shall be honoured guests. And you, little Kitty, will be the sunbeam in the house which you will rule."

"But I am unfit to rule," said Kitty.

"I don't think that," replied Katherine. "Things will be made smooth for you. You have conquered so bravely in another instance—"

"Don't speak of it," said Kitty. She coloured, and clasped her hands very tightly. "I have not really conquered," she said in a low voice. "I feel—"

"We won't talk of feelings to-day," said Katherine. "I think you have conquered. And surely 'he that ruleth himself is better than he that taketh a city.' Mrs. Keith must let you come back with me to-night; there is much to discuss."

So Kitty and Katherine went back to Katherine's beautiful home in Bayswater together, and long into the night they talked and made their plans, and when Kitty laid her head on her pillow she was too tired to keep awake. The next day the first thought that came to her was the life-work which she had undertaken: for Katherine Hunt was a very rich woman, and when she undertook things, she did them on a princely scale; and Katherine in her own heart had decided that if Kitty had denied herself, she would be the means of placing her in a fuller and richer life than she had ever dreamt of when she selfishly tried to absorb the life of the man who did not love her.

Thus all things came well, and Kitty, although the convalescent homes are only just started, is once again a happy woman.

THE END.

CPSIA information can be obtained
at www.ICGtesting.com
Printed in the USA
LVHW110041010920
664725LV00011B/519